Perilous

Tamara Hart Heiner

WiDō Publishing
Salt Lake City, Utah
Copyright © 2010 by Tamara Hart Heiner

Cover photograph by L.A. DeVaul
Cover and book design by Don Gee

ISBN: 978-0-9796070-8-0

Manufactured in the United States of America

www.widopublishing.com

Chapter 1

September 20
Havre, Montana

Detective Carl Hamilton shielded his eyes against the blaring blue lights and flashed his badge at the police officer. The man moved aside. Hamilton stepped off the two-lane highway just outside of Havre, Montana. Orange tape blocked off the crime scene, hidden by the darkness of early morning. He ducked under the tape and pushed his way into the dry shrubbery.

A sergeant shone a flashlight on his face and asked, "Are you Detective Hamilton?"

He gave a short nod.

"I'm Shirley White." Pressing her hand to her nose, she turned her attention back to the ground.

The stench of rotting flesh was strong. "Ma'am. What have we found?"

"It's a girl. We think it's one of the four you've been looking for."

Carl's stomach knotted. "Cause of death?"

"We'll have to perform an autopsy, of course, but it appears to be a gunshot wound. Is it one of them?"

"Where is she?"

"Under the bushes."

He crouched down and moved the bushes aside, breathing through his mouth. This never got any easier. The branches parted to reveal a young girl, features distorted by death but still recognizable. The open eyes stared blankly up at him. He released the branches and stood up, giving a nod. "Yes. It's one of them."

The case had just gone from a kidnapping to a homicide. And there were still three girls missing.

One week earlier
Shelley, Idaho

"Jaci!"

Callie Nichol's voice snapped Jaci Rivera out of her daydream. Jaci blinked once and focused on her best friend. "Yeah?"

Squinting her eyes, Callie stretched out across the sun-bleached wooden raft. "Where's that worm?"

Jaci picked up one of the slender pink worms she had dug up from the soil. It writhed between her fingers. "Coming." She waded out to the raft, dark brown hair spilling over her tanned shoulders.

Late afternoon sunlight glinted off the murky green water beneath their raft, and small dark shadows darted around the cattails. Callie took the worm. "Now what?"

Jaci laughed. "You put it on that hook in your hand, silly."

Callie wrinkled her nose and handed it to Jaci. "You do it."

The worm flinched as Jaci threaded it onto the rusty hook. She dropped the line into the water. "Not exactly fly-fishing."

Callie waved her hand. "Whatever." She narrowed her blue eyes. "Hey, Amanda said there's more news about The Hand."

"Oh, please. Save it for someone who cares." Callie's friend Amanda Murphy was obsessed with the criminal the media had named 'The Hand.' Jaci could care less. She shivered as a breeze blew by. "It's too cold to be swimming." Early September, and autumn was on its way to the northern half of Idaho.

"The Hand was in Utah. That's just south of us."

Jaci groaned. "I so don't want to talk about him."

"Fine," Callie sniffed. "We'll talk about him later at my birthday party."

"You think just because it's your birthday I'll want to talk about The Hand?"

Callie arched an eyebrow, shooting Jaci a mock glare. "You might not care, but everyone else will. By the way, did Amanda give you her new phone number? I tried her phone yesterday, and it was disconnected."

"No." Jaci never called Amanda. She was Callie's friend, not hers.

"What time do you think you'll be by tonight? Come anytime after six."

Jaci jerked, gripping the raft to keep from falling into the chilly water. The fishing line slipped from her fingers and disappeared in a swirl of greenish-gray.

"What time is it? I gotta go." Without waiting for a response, she jumped from the raft. The cold water snuck up her thighs and over her hips. She shuddered when it touched her stomach.

"Why the rush?"

"I've got to babysit. Dad left on another emergency business trip. Call me after eight." She winced as she hurried over the gravelly shore. Finding her bag, she wrapped her fluffy blue towel around her shoulders.

"Hey, wait." Callie dipped a foot into the water. "I'm not staying here alone."

"Sorry, Cal." Jaci ran the towel over her shoulder-length brown hair. "I'll see ya later. I need to get in shape for track season anyway, or Sara's gonna whoop me."

The wind would dry her off. She pulled her jeans on over her skin-tight swimsuit, grimacing at the way they stuck to her wet legs. She yanked her t-shirt over her head and slid her wet hair into a ponytail. "Bye."

"Bye," Callie echoed, almost to the shore.

Jaci started out in a hard jog, then slowed to a comfortable pace. Sara Yadle, her best friend after Callie, might outrun Jaci in a sprinting race, but Jaci could beat her at endurance anytime.

Jaci ran up the gravel drive to her red-brick, multi-level house, jumping the porch steps. The screen door bounced back once before it slammed shut behind her.

Upstairs, something fell with a loud clang. She rounded the corner in the upstairs hallway and came to a halt.

Her older brother, Seth, stood with one hand casually leaning on the doorframe to her room. The other was tucked behind his back. He looked at her, his long black lashes framing his wide brown eyes.

"What's behind your back?"

"Huh?" He glanced over his shoulder. "Oh, nothing."

"Seth…" she said in her best warning voice.

"Hey, calm down, *hermanita*. I was just looking for one of my CDs. See?"

"In *my* room?" She dropped her swimming gear in an effort to retrieve the Tim McGraw CD. "I know where you got that."

He frowned. "Hey, stop yelling, Mom'll hear you."

"I told you not to go in my room."

"No, Jaci," he corrected. Seth pronounced her name as 'Hah-SEE,' although everyone else said 'JC.' "You said not to touch your CDs. I didn't. This one's mine."

Jaci felt her temper flare. "I said not to go into my room. You're such an *arrogante*—"

"Kids!"

Their mother's voice reverberated up the stairs as she came around the banister to peer up at them. "Are you yelling at each other?"

"No, *Mamá*," Seth said in a calm voice, turning his angry brown eyes on Jaci. "We're fine."

Their mother watched them, waiting.

"Give me back my CD, Seth," said Jaci, extending a hand. *"Ahorita."*

Seth turned his back on her, disappearing into his room.

"Jaci?" Mrs. Rivera called up. "César is downstairs playing a video game. Thanks for watching him, *querida*."

"No problem," Jaci answered, hiding her exasperation. She hurried to her drawer and yanked it open. Her diary lay on top, and underneath it, untouched, was her Tim McGraw CD. She drew in a deep breath. Seth had been telling the truth.

She could hear him laughing in his room. He must be on the phone with his latest girlfriend. Jaci slipped out of her room and knocked on the door. He opened it and stood there, his back partially to her as his foot played with the doorjamb.

"Yeah. See ya in ten minutes. Bye." He turned off the cordless phone and looked at her with an air of annoyance. "What?"

Jaci felt herself losing steam under his reception. "I just wanted to apologize."

"Forget it." He handed her the phone. "Hang this up for me. I'm going out." Without another glance, he trotted down the stairs.

Jaci slinked after him, her eyes stinging a little. Seth was three and a half years older than her, and they used to be close. She heard the roar of his jeep's engine and the crunch of tires on gravel as he backed out of the driveway.

Chapter 2

Jaci's mom entered the kitchen just after eight o'clock and kissed her cheek. Opening the pantry door, she hung her purse on a hook inside. "How was everything?"

Jaci shrugged in response. Leaning against the bar, she propped her chin up with the palm of her hand.

Her mother eyed her. "Where's César?"

She pointed out the bay window behind her mom. "Jumping on the tramp."

"Did you have dinner?"

"Yeah. Some guy called, but I couldn't understand him. I think he was speaking Dutch. He didn't sound happy. Is Dad in Holland?"

"I don't think so, *querida*. I think he's ironing out accounts in Switzerland."

Her father's travel plans changed so often that his family couldn't keep track of them.

Somewhere in the living room, a jazz medley rang out.

Jaci hopped off the stool, fishing around in the couch cushions until she retrieved the flip-phone. She didn't recognize the number. "Hello?"

"Jaci? Hey, it's me." The noise in the background almost drowned out Callie's voice.

"Where are you? Weren't you going to have the party at your house?" Jaci pressed her ear into the phone.

"Amanda wanted to go to the mall. Have your mom bring you to the mall and then ride home with us. Your pajamas and tooth-brush are at my house because you left them there last week."

"Well." Jaci hesitated. Callie lived two minutes away, but the mall was twenty. "I don't know if my mom will want to drive me that far."

Mrs. Rivera interrupted. "It's fine with me, *mi hija*. I owe it to you, anyway. I'll take you."

Jaci grinned. "Really? Alright, Callie, I'm coming. See ya."

As soon as Jaci stepped through the double doors at the food court, the mixed aroma of sweet chocolate cookies and fresh bread dough wafted through the air.

"There you are." Sara, a small girl with blond hair and freckles all over her pale skin, grabbed her arm.

Jaci allowed herself to be dragged inside. She took one look at the pizza on their table and pulled out a chair. "What have you guys done so far?" She grabbed a slice, lifting it high to break the gooey strands of mozzarella cheese.

"Not much," Callie said. "Amanda wanted to look at engagement rings, so we went to Sears."

"Engagement rings?" Jaci raised an eyebrow, glancing up at Amanda. "Something you want to share with us?"

"Wait," Sara giggled, her hazel eyes sparkling. "We didn't tell you the best part."

Amanda tossed her mane of curly red hair and glared at Sara. "It wasn't that funny."

Callie laughed, pushing her glasses back up her nose. "Amanda opened the emergency exit and set off the alarm. The mall security detained us for fifteen minutes."

Jaci laughed. "Oh man, I'm sorry I missed that."

Amanda pulled a compact powder case out of her pink handbag. She focused on her reflection and smoothed her bangs. "It's not that big a deal."

"Hey." Callie waved at Amanda. "Tell her what you told me about The Hand. Even Jaci might like this."

"Fine." Amanda exhaled and leaned back, snapping her case shut. Her green eyes lit up. "You know Princess Di's necklace that was stolen two days ago? Well, The Hand's one of the suspects."

Jaci raised an eyebrow. "And that's important because?"

Amanda snorted and slapped the table. "She doesn't get it! It couldn't be him, Jaci. This guy shot down two security guards. Not his style. Not to mention, that necklace was worth about a million dollars. He usually goes for the petty cash—thousand dollar rings and bracelets, that sort of thing."

"Yeah." Jaci stood up. "What else were we planning on doing tonight?"

Sara took a sip of her soda, a strand of her dark blond hair falling between her eyes. "They're having a dress sale at Charlotte Russe."

"That sounds great." Jaci reached for her purse. Where was it? She bent over, examining the red and white tile floor littered with napkins and french fries.

"What did you lose?" Sara asked, looking at her under the table.

Jaci sat back up and shook her head. "My purse. I must've left it in my mom's car. Oh, well. Let's go look at dresses."

Window shopping with no money got old fast. They took their time exiting the mall, even when the stores began to pull down the metal grates. Only after they picked up a couple of stray admirers did the girls sneak out a side exit.

"Why can't we ever get *cute* boys trailing us?" Amanda sighed and looked at her watch. The exit they had taken was situated in an alley, and she had to step closer to the street to see the time.

"Stay here," Callie said, grabbing her arm and pulling her back. "Those weird boys might still be following us." She sat on the sidewalk next to Jaci and yanked Amanda down next to them.

Jaci liked boys, only not the non-talking kind who studied her through hooded eyes. Creepy. "If you hadn't smiled at him, Amanda, they wouldn't have followed us."

"I can't help it," said Amanda. "He smiled at me. What was I supposed to do, ignore him?"

The door behind them clicked as the automatic lock engaged.

Callie fidgeted. "Time, Amanda?"

Amanda tossed her hair over her shoulder and picked up a cigarette butt. "Nine-thirty at last check. Where's your mom?"

"Mom's only slightly late. Half an hour is her norm. Give her another ten minutes."

Amanda began writing on the sidewalk with the cigarette butt.

"That's gross," Callie said. "Besides, knowing my brother, he put up a fuss about how I'm at the mall and he's not. My mom probably had a hard time getting him to bed."

Cars vacated the mall parking lot. Jaci could count what was left on one hand. "I don't feel good about being out here."

Callie raised an eyebrow, the motion barely perceptible behind the wire frame of her glasses. "What is this? Is Jaci afraid?"

"I just don't like being out here in the dark."

"There's still plenty of light." Callie waved an arm at the parking lot lights. "And it'll be awhile before everyone's gone."

Even as she spoke, two of the remaining five cars roared to life, their headlights washing over the girls as they drove away. She turned to Sara. "Did you bring your phone?"

Sara shook her head. In the dim light from the exit sign, her freckles stood out against her pale skin. "Sorry. It died at your house, and I left the charger at home."

Callie shrugged. "Don't worry about it. I bet she'll be here in ten minutes." She looked at Jaci. "What about you?"

Jaci shook her head also. "In my purse. Mom's car. I thought you were getting a phone for your birthday?"

Callie beamed at her. "I am. My mom gave me the gift certificate. We'll go pick it out tomorrow."

"I'm getting a new one, too," Amanda said. "We had to change my number after we moved here because some kid from my old school was stalking me." She exhaled loudly and turned back to the cigarette butt.

Ten minutes rolled by. The lights inside the food court turned off, plunging the sidewalk around them into darkness. Only the red exit signs and neon lights glowed from the mall.

Amanda tapped her foot as the last car in the parking lot turned its headlights on and drove off. "There it goes. It's only us now. No one even offered us a ride."

"That's because we're hiding in the shadows and no one can see us," Jaci said, fighting the urge to bite her fingernails. She was really spooked. "Should we walk to a bus stop?"

Callie pulled on a strand of light brown hair, wrapping it around her index finger. "The last bus left an hour ago. If my mom's not here in ten more minutes, we can flag down one of the mall security guys and have him call her."

Jaci's unease deepened. "I haven't seen any of them tonight," she said. "They usually drive by a lot." She craned her head forward, hoping to catch a glimpse of the white car with flashing yellow lights.

Callie shifted her weight again. "You're right, Jaci, something about this isn't right. Let's find—"

"I hear a car," Sara interrupted. "I bet it's your mom."

Jaci shook her head as she listened. "Too big. Sounds like a—"

Amanda's voice cut her off. "Hey, look," she said, pointing.

The loud motor entered the parking lot, revealing a black van with the headlights off. It backed up to the Sears store three hundred feet in front of them. The dull mall lights glinted off the windshield. The engine stalled and went silent. Three masked men dressed in black slipped out and moved to the emergency exit door.

Callie's brow furrowed. "What are they doing?"

Amanda sucked in her breath. "That's the exit by the jewelry department. The same one I opened, remember? They're going to rob the store!"

Jaci stood up, fear warming her body.

"That's it," Callie said, her voice breaking. "We have to call someone and get out of here. Where's the nearest payphone?"

Jaci's heart raced. The payphone stood fifty feet from the store entrance. *We'll never get there without being spotted.*

An electronic grinding noise assaulted her ears, then a bright flash. The streetlights and warm red glows from the mall went out, followed by all the lights on the block. Sudden darkness engulfed them.

"How did that happen?" Jaci said. She could barely make out her friends around her.

"Ha!" Amanda's voice was too loud. "Someone knocked out the transformer for this block. There's a conspiracy."

"Shh." Callie waved a hand to quiet her. One of the men turned on a flashlight. "They haven't noticed us. That door will trigger an alarm. The police will be here soon."

Jaci's eyes were adjusting to the dark, and she remained riveted to the spot, staring at the flashlight's distant orb.

One of the men aimed the beam on the door while another one lay on his back on some sort of gurney, reaching upward to fiddle with the knob. A third shone a laser device through the crack between the door and the wall.

The door sprang open. The men glanced around them before stepping into the store.

"They broke in," said Sara.

Jaci's heart pounded so hard that she couldn't hear her own thoughts. She had the insane urge to scream at the top of her lungs. Thank heavens the lack of light and shadow of the alley kept them hidden. She forced herself to focus. *Think. What's the best thing to do?*

"Here's the plan," Callie said, chewing on her lip. "Somebody sneak over to the payphone and call 911. Everybody else stand close by and cover."

"I'll call," Jaci said.

"I'll keep an eye on the store," said Amanda. "Make sure no one comes out." She turned and started toward the door.

"Amanda!" Callie said, gesturing with one hand as if to pull her back. Amanda didn't even slow down. "Forget her. We don't have time to lose. Let's go."

They hurried to the payphone. Jaci glanced at the store. No one was outside except Amanda, back against the wall as she peered into the darkened opening.

"Sara, watch Amanda," Callie instructed. "Tell us if anything changes."

"All's clear," Sara said.

Jaci reached up and grabbed the phone. Next to her, Callie gave a shriek, and Jaci jumped, dropping the receiver. "What?" she said, blood rushing to her head. She blinked as a flashlight shone on them.

"Run!" cried Callie.

Jaci whirled around to chase after her friends, suddenly aware of the sound of running footsteps behind her. Her shoe caught on the uneven sidewalk, and she fell forward, hitting her face on the concrete. She heard a muffled yell a few feet away.

Behind her an engine sputtered and roared to life. Two boots stepped into her line of vision. She could see a figure fumbling with a flask and a small cloth. The man knelt next to her, dousing the rag with the flask and holding it to her face. She gasped, struggling against him. He pressed the rag over her nose and mouth, and an acrid burning filled her nostrils.

She panicked, struggling for breath. *He's going to kill me.* Her eyes rolled into the back of her head, and everything went dark.

September 13
Idaho Falls, Idaho

The phone under Kristin's pillow was ringing.

Carl Hamilton sat up in bed and turned on the lamp. "Kristin." He nudged her with his shoulder. "Kristin, it's one in the morning. Who would be calling you?"

Kristin pulled the pillow off her head, blinking in the lamplight.

"Hmm?" Her short blond hair stuck out in all directions. "Oh." She lifted her elbow. "It's your phone, not mine." She handed it back and buried herself under the pillow again.

Carl frowned and looked at the call log. Two missed calls, both from work.

He swore under his breath and rolled out of bed. He'd forgotten he was on call. He was supposed to be off, but he had agreed to switch shifts with another detective at the department. He better watch it, or Chief would follow through with the threat to make him get a landline.

Kristin was already asleep. How could she sleep like that? Flipping on the light in the kitchen, he held down the speed dial for the station.

"Idaho Falls police dispatch."

"Monica, it's Carl." His voice was groggy with sleep. "Who's working tonight?"

"Carl, there's a missing persons report for four teenage girls. Boss wants you on it right away."

"Lieutenant Stokes?" Stokes was over the detectives.

"No. Chief Miller."

Carl straightened. If someone had woken the chief, this was expected to be hot. "How long they been missing?"

"Four hours."

He ran a hand through his buzzed hair. "No answer on their cell phones?"

"No cell phones on them, Carl."

He grunted. "Did someone check their boyfriends' houses?"

"No known boyfriends, either."

Carl frowned. "Is there a parent present?"

"Yes."

"All right. I'm coming to the station." He flipped his phone shut and changed into a suit.

Before walking out the door, he opened the fridge and scanned the contents. He needed brain food. His jar of bread and butter pickles was almost gone. He grabbed the baby dills instead and headed out.

Seven parents waited for him at the station. He spotted them through the glass windows in the lobby before he entered the building. Carl opened the door, nodded at Monica, who was answering the 911 calls, and approached the parents.

"I'm Detective Hamilton. Give me a moment to get briefed on the situation, and then I'll sit with you and ask a few questions."

He motioned to a corner of the room. "We have a coffee pot and sugar. Help yourselves."

"Monica." Carl leaned his head toward the opening in the plastic window. "Who took the call?"

She took a sip from her white Styrofoam cup, leaving red lipstick on the rim. "I did."

"Okay. Tell me what happened."

She hit a switch on the computer, pulling up a black screen with green letters. "The 911 call came in at ten thirty-two. Woman hysterical. She had left her daughter and three friends at the mall. There was an accident on Yellowstone Highway outside of Shelley around ten to nine, and both lanes of traffic were closed for thirty minutes. By the time she reached the mall, it was nine forty and the girls were nowhere. I asked her if they were sitting in the shadows. She said she'd checked. I asked her to check the local gas station. She said she had. I asked her to call their friends. She said she'd called her husband and had him call everyone. At this point she was ballistic. I sent a patrol to the mall to scout the area and bring her back to the station."

Ten thirty. That was two and a half hours ago. "Did they find anything?"

"No. Everything appeared normal. But the mother said the street lamps were off. She said they turned back on around ten o'clock."

"And the mall security guard? What did he say? Did he see them?"

Monica raised a thin, penciled eyebrow. "The patrol couldn't find him."

Carl nodded, making a list in his mind. Suspect number one. "I'll go speak to the parents."

Stepping back into the lobby, he pulled up a chair to the shaking mass of parents in front of him. "Please sit down. I know this is very hard on you." He used his most sensitive tone.

The parents sat in pairs, except one woman. Carl pulled out his notepad. "I'm going to ask a couple of questions. Please don't be offended, and I'd appreciate it if you answer as truthfully as possible."

One man stood up, his face twisting. Stubble the color of red

16

clay dotted his face. "We don't have time for questions. You need to be out there, looking for them." He pointed his hand out the door.

Carl met the man's eyes and spoke calmly. "We've got officers out looking. The more information you give me, the easier it will be for me to do my job."

"Jacob, sit," his wife said, turning tired eyes up at him. Her curly blond hair fell in disorganized ringlets around her neck.

Carl eyed his notepad. "I know you already told this to dispatch, but tell me what your daughters' names are and who goes to which set of parents."

The single woman cleared her throat. Her thick black hair lay in uneven waves. "Jacinta Rivera is mine."

"Sara Yadle is ours." A man with dark brown hair and bloodshot eyes clung to his wife, a heavy woman with shoulder-length blond hair.

"Amanda Murphy." The hostile man, Jacob, deflated when he said the name. He pinched the bridge of his nose.

"Callie Nichols." The petite brunette said the name with a sob and buried her head in her husband's chest.

"And which is the parent who drove them to the mall?" Carl kept his voice neutral. He wasn't accusing anyone here, but they might perceive it that way.

"Me." Mrs. Nichols lifted her head, tears rolling down her cheeks.

"You were the one who went to pick them up also?"

She nodded, biting her lower lip.

"Do the girls have any other place they might hang out?"

"Yes," Mrs. Nichols said. "My brother's lake. They were there earlier today. But it's in Shelley."

Carl nodded and wrote it down. "What do they do for fun? Social life?" He included all the parents in this question.

"Jaci runs track," said Mrs. Rivera.

Carl focused on her. "Where's Jaci's father?"

"He's out of town on a business trip. I've tried to call him, but the hotel number he left me doesn't pick up."

"Any boys?" Carl threw the question out and held his breath.

"Oh, no," said Mrs. Nichols. "They're too young."

Mr. Yadle nodded. "Sara's not even shown an interest yet."

Interesting. He would check their ages later. He stood up, closing his notepad. "Thank you for your help. I'm going to authorize an *all points bulletin*. It'll be all over the news within the hour. We have people searching. Please go home and rest. We'll find your girls." He shook each of their hands as they said goodbye. As soon as they left, he strode back to Monica.

"Well?" she asked. "What do you think?"

"I'm not sure yet." He wrote down the name of the mall on a slip of paper. "We're going to issue an APB. If they don't show up by tomorrow morning, I'll interview mall employees. Keep the patrols out. Have them be on the lookout for parked cars, drunk driving, the usual."

"You think they're out causing trouble?"

Carl grimaced. "I hope they are. It's a lot easier to reprimand a kid than to pull 'em out of thin air."

Chapter 3

Someone was shaking her. Jaci opened her eyes to darkness. A cold metal surface pressed hard against her cheek. They were moving, a steady rocking and jolting, like a stroller going over a dirt path. She coughed in the stifling air.

"Jaci? Are you okay?" Callie's soft voice penetrated the darkness.

Jaci tried to sit up, but a wave of pain and dizziness kept her on the floor. She closed her eyes for a moment. When she opened them she made out Amanda, draped across some crates in front of her, auburn hair fanned out around her.

They'd been kidnapped.

Jaci fought a rising panic. She took several deep breaths like she did before a race. The throbbing in her head faded to a dull ache. The right side of her face hurt. She put her hand on Callie's shoulder and hauled herself to her feet, being careful not to hit the ceiling. A sliver of light snuck through the cracks in the back doors, but that was it. There were no windows; they were in the cargo hold of a vehicle. "Where's Sara?"

"Unconscious. By Amanda. She got hit over the head."

Jaci looked at the light coming in the back doors. They had slept through the night. "Have you tried to get out?"

"Yes." Callie's voice was a whisper. "It's got a latch on the outside."

Jaci stepped over to the doors and peeked out. The blacktop road flew by underneath the van. She lifted her eyes and squinted against the light, unable to see anything except a few clouds. Wiggling her fingertips against the cracks, she tried to pry the doors open. No luck. She couldn't even get her pinkie through.

Amanda let out a low moan. She rolled her head to the side, then opened her eyes. "Where are we?"

Someone banged on the wall between them and the cab. "Be quiet back there!"

The van made a sharp turn and began to bump around, as if going from blacktop to loose gravel. Sara sat up behind one of the boxes. Jaci flew forward, hitting her face on a crate. The van stopped. Jaci stared at the wooden box in front of her, her heart pounding in her throat.

The back door opened, displaying a broad-shouldered man with a small mustache. He wore baggy black pants and a dark green t-shirt. The sun reflected off his white arms.

"Bathroom break," he said in a gravelly, deep voice. "Take care of business and get back in." He looked like an escaped war criminal, with buzzed dirty-blond hair and bulging arms strong enough to break each of their necks.

Jaci followed Sara out of the van, keeping her eyes on the ground. They had driven off the road, into a cluster of bushes about twenty feet from the highway.

The road curved slightly to the right up ahead, and a large red-sand rock formation shaded them from view. Wind whipped up pieces of dust and dirt into her eyes. She moved closer to Callie.

"We've got to get out of here," Callie said.

Jaci nodded. "I know."

"If we make a run for it together, they won't have a target. We can get away."

Jaci looked at her. How could she be so calm?

"Will you come with me if I run?"

Jaci nodded. "Of course. But make sure it's the right time."

A shorter man with brown hair joined the big one at the back of the van, and they talked while looking over a map. The sound of another motorized vehicle echoed down the road, and both men turned toward the girls.

"Steady," the big guy growled at them, a warning in his voice. "Just act normal."

"A car's coming. Now's our chance," said Callie. "They can't shoot us if we're running toward a witness."

Jaci froze, hardly understanding Callie. She wanted to try to escape now? With those guys between them and the road? She shook her head. "We can't."

"Now, Jaci," Callie said, standing up. "I need you. Come on."

Jaci felt her whole body tremble. She couldn't. She was too scared. "Callie."

"Run!" Callie shouted. She turned and ran toward the road, waving her arms. "Help! Help us."

Jaci couldn't tear her eyes away. She saw it as if in slow motion: the blue Jeep quickly approaching from the right, Callie running for the road. The big man pulling his gun from its holster and leveling it at Callie.

"No!" Jaci screamed. The word echoed through her mind, ringing in her ears, and then Callie went down.

The blue Jeep roared by, oblivious to the scene.

Someone grabbed Jaci's forearm and yanked her up. She sobbed, not bothering to lift her feet as she was dragged over branches and rocks. The man with the bulging muscles, the one who had shot Callie, tossed Jaci into the back of the van.

"I warned you," he snarled, spittle flying from his mouth, features twisted with rage. "This isn't a game."

"Callie…Callie," Sara cried.

"Shut up. Shut up, shut up, shut up. Or I'll shoot you all and leave you here to rot."

Jaci forced back her own sobs and turned around to stare at Sara. "Don't cry," she mouthed. "Look at me."

Sara gulped and stared at Jaci, her hazel eyes filled with unshed tears.

The door slammed shut, and they were in darkness again.

"Callie?" Sara moaned softly.

"She can't be dead," Amanda said. "Maybe someone will find her. Maybe she'll be okay."

Jaci pressed her sleeve into her mouth and let the sobs spill out, wracking her frame. *Dear Lord, why Callie?*

It was her fault. If only she'd had the courage to run with her friend, they might have reached the blue Jeep in time.

Chapter 4

Jaci guessed they had been traveling two days when the van ground to a stop for the fourth time. She didn't open her eyes. It was cold now. She wrapped her arms around her knees, trying to keep warm. A constant pitter-patter on the roof almost lulled her to sleep before the vehicle stopped. Her stomach grumbled, but she didn't feel hungry.

The door swung open, and the man with the thick, muscular neck appeared. It was raining, and the street looked slick and dangerous in the black of night. He hadn't pulled off the road this time.

"Come on." He waved a flashlight at them. "Take care of your business."

Another man joined him. Jaci hadn't seen him before. He had shoulder-length black hair and was younger and shorter than the leader, but his wiry body was just as muscular. He moved his dull black eyes over the girls' bodies and licked his lips.

So there were at least three men in the van.

Amanda moved out first, crawling on her hands and knees and then dropping out of the van.

Jaci didn't want to leave. It looked so wet and damp outside, but she knew the men wouldn't wait. She pushed herself away from the wall, noticing that Sara hadn't budged.

"Sara," she said, tugging the younger girl's arm.

Sara shook herself and crawled after her.

The rain fell in Jaci's hair and soaked into her clothing. The men stood along the side of the road and shone flashlights on them as they squatted in the grass. Jaci felt nothing, no shame or fear. Only the desire to get back inside the van, where she could close her eyes and the world would disappear.

The two-lane road didn't appear to be well traveled. There were no street lamps. The humidity and ample vegetation made her think they were very far from home. She saw none of the familiar junipers and sagebrush that littered the terrain in Shelley.

The tall muscled man spun back around. "All right, time's up."

No hesitation on Jaci's part. She slipped and hit her shin on the van doorway. Amanda grabbed her hand and helped her up. The van began its sluggish forward movement.

Jaci settled herself back among the crates, the throbbing of her shin competing with her aching head. "What should we do?"

Sara lifted her head, eyes unfocused. "Do? What is there to do?"

The expression on her face made Jaci's heart lurch. She looked like she had given up already. Jaci sighed and pushed her hands through her hair, feeling it clump between her fingers. She pulled it in front of her face, staring at the dark strands. Her throat and eyes burned.

The van jolted as it went over a bump in the road. She listened to the wheels churn up the gravel. Sara put her head in her hands, her body rocking with the van's motion.

Jaci looked at her. "Sara. We're going to get out of here." She turned to Amanda. "What now? Tell us what to do."

Amanda lifted a shoulder. "Look for food, I guess. Let's go through these crates."

It gave them a place to start. The girls started opening the unlabeled boxes, most of them empty. They didn't find any food, but they did find a few jewels in one of the larger crates.

Amanda's green eyes lit up, and she slipped a necklace down her shirt. "Oo, this one's really pretty!" She opened a smaller box and pulled out a large and ornate pearl necklace. She lifted her shirt up and snapped it around her slender waist.

It didn't quite close, so she found a bracelet to join them together. Then she dropped her shirt again. Not even a bulge showed under the clothes.

"Are you crazy?" Jaci said. "What do you think this is—a shopping spree? Our lives are in danger here."

Amanda lifted her chin. "Why shouldn't I take it? We might need it later."

"They're going to look for that," said Sara.

"Ha." Amanda put a few other necklaces in the small box and closed it, then shoved it back under the other boxes. "Like he'll notice a few missing. I doubt he knows what they grabbed. They were in a hurry."

They rode in stillness for several more hours. Jaci leaned her head against the metal wall of the van, trying to guess the time of day by the exterior temperature. One of the tires seemed slightly flat. She could hear it bumping along the road.

The drive leveled out, and the van stopped. The engine shut off.

"Are we getting gas again?" asked Sara. The skin around her eyes tightened, and she pressed her lips together.

The two gas stops had been the only times the engine shut off. But they had already gotten gas twice that day, and Jaci doubted they needed it again. She reached out and squeezed Sara's hand. "It's okay. Whatever it is, let's just stick together."

The doors banged open. The early morning sunshine assaulted their eyes, bringing with it the crisp, late-summer air. Jaci blinked and glanced back at her friends. Their faces were pale, dark shadows under their tired eyes.

A large outline blocked her view, and they looked up to see the muscular man with the buzz cut standing in the doorway. He stood with his feet apart and patted a baseball bat into the palm of his hand. "Out. Follow me."

The fat-lipped man and the one with dark eyes joined him, all dressed in baggy black pants and green t-shirts.

Jaci remembered the gun tucked away in his pants. She gazed at the mountain looming over them. There was nothing to see except a dense forest, the undergrowth thick and stifling. No roads or houses were in sight except for the four-story brick mansion at the end of the long paved driveway.

The trees encircled the large plantation house and descended a steep hillside in front of it. A large, open garage, which contained two other identical black vans and a yellow Camaro, was attached to the side of the house. White marble pillars ran from top to bottom, and symmetrical windows covered the entire surface.

The colors seemed muted, lacking the usual luster and brilliance of nature. A dismal pallor covered everything. As her gaze slid over a ring of steps on the porch, she spotted a thin, small man standing in the entryway of the house. He watched the girls with sharp, piercing eyes, scrutinizing them as their captor led them closer.

He must be the boss. Jaci tried not to stare at him.

They walked past him into the house. Jaci felt his steely glare on her back, and she suppressed a shudder. She lifted her chin and tried to ignore him, focusing instead on the interior of the house.

It was sparsely furnished, only a few tables and chairs in the entry. A long red carpet covered the tile floor, leading down the hall. An end table with the granite bust of a woman on top sat under a coat rack.

Stolen, Jaci thought, studying it. Probably worth thousands of dollars.

Armed men surrounded them as their kidnapper pushed the girls up several flights of stairs. They came to a stop under a trap door in the ceiling of the fourth floor. A deadbolt sealed the door into the framing around it.

The thick-necked man undid the bolt and pulled the trapdoor down. A ladder appeared.

"Been a long time since we've had guests," he drawled. He pulled out his gun and gestured for them to climb.

Jaci flinched and drew back at the sight of the weapon. He nudged Sara in the back with his gun. "Up. Go."

Sara gripped the ladder, her face chalky. She started upward, and Jaci saw the streaks of tears on her cheeks.

"Claber."

An authoritative voice behind them made all of them turn, except for Sara, who hurried up the ladder and disappeared into the attic.

"Yes, Boss?" the big-necked man grunted.

"I'll take it from here."

It was the man Jaci had noticed outside. The smaller man with the penetrating gaze. He eyed them with a strange curiosity.

The big man, Claber, nodded, casting one last glance at the girls. His mustache twitched, and he grinned. "Take a rest, ladies. Maybe tonight you'll have company." His heavy footsteps clunked down the hall.

"No company today, girls," the boss man said, turning his hard, cold eyes on Jaci and Amanda. "This is my house, and I'm in charge. Do exactly what I tell you, and I won't hurt you."

A ghost of a smile crossed his face. "I don't know about Claber, though. He'll be in charge of you most of the time. Up, now. Go on."

Jaci and Amanda climbed up the squeaky wooden ladder after Sara.

The boss man folded it up and slammed the door shut, leaving them in the dark, musty attic. Jaci heard him slide the bolt into place.

A small amount of light drifted in from a round window, catching dust particles in its beams. A few muslin sacks lay on the wooden floor.

Amanda shuddered, one hand under her shirt, toying with the necklace again. "I know what that creep has in mind, and if he dares come near me, I'll poke his eyes out."

Jaci clenched her fists together, feeling tense and ready to snap. "Amanda, you're just as scared as the rest of us."

Amanda looked at her. "No, I'm not."

Sara wandered over to the window, no bigger than her face, and dusted it off with her sleeve.

"This is not good," Jaci whimpered. A hard lump formed in her stomach. Thoughts of her family, Seth, Callie, flashed through her mind. She forced them away. "I knew something bad was going to happen."

"What?" Amanda turned on her. "What do you mean, you knew? And you didn't do anything? Then I guess that makes this all your fault."

"Shut up, Amanda," Sara snapped. "If it weren't for you, we'd have called the police and been fine."

Again the anger rose inside Jaci. It was so easy to feel anger. It gave her something else to focus on. "Sara's right. It's your fault we're here." There. She'd said it.

"My fault?" Amanda said, her eyes widening. "It was Callie who shrieked and attracted their attention!"

"Don't you even try to put this on Callie," said Jaci.

"Callie screamed because they dragged *you* into the store, Amanda," Sara said. "Did you want us to just walk away and leave you?"

"You're the runner," Amanda retorted. "Why didn't you run for help? You could've saved us all."

"Oh, so it's everyone's fault except yours, huh?" Jaci jumped to Sara's defense.

"Did you call 911?" Amanda demanded. "That's what you were supposed to do at the phone. I was keeping watch for you guys. Did you even call?"

"I—" The blood drained from Jaci's face. Stupid, stupid, stupid. She remembered now how she had dropped the phone without dialing anything.

The brief moment of silence was enough to cool the atmosphere. "Fighting won't help anything," Sara said, her voice empty again. She turned back to the window and drew in a shuddering breath.

Jaci turned to Sara, her anger fading in a rush of guilt. "You're right. Sorry." *I'm sorry, Callie. So sorry.* Tears formed in her eyes, and she didn't brush them away.

Sara sank to the floor beneath the window. "If we're lucky, we'll make it out alive."

"Let's get some sleep," Jaci said. "We'll think better when we wake up."

"No way," said Amanda. "We've got to figure out how to get out, *now*. There's no time to sleep. What if he comes back?"

"We're stuck in this attic, and we don't fit through that window." Sara's words slurred with exhaustion. "Let's sleep."

Jaci spread out one of the muslin sacks and lay down. The hard floor bit into her shoulder blades and tail bone. She swallowed, trying to moisten her dry throat. The blood pounded in every limb of her body. She closed her eyes.

Amanda coughed, waking Jaci. Judging from the darkness outside the window, it was late evening. Jaci sat up. "Well, at least we didn't get any *company*."

"Thank goodness," Amanda agreed. "Though some water would be nice."

"There is water." Sara's quiet voice came from the corner of the attic. She rolled a large bottle of water at them. "Someone put this up here while we slept. I saved some for you guys."

Amanda grabbed the bottle, barely waiting to get the lid off before she started chugging.

Jaci rolled up the edge of her sack. It slowly unrolled itself. Her long fingers found the edge and rolled it up again. "I wonder when we'll get home."

"If we get home," said Amanda.

"We will." Jaci took the water bottle from Amanda and tried not to gulp it down. It was stale, but it ran down her throat like a river in a desert.

"But what if—"

Jaci forced the bottle from her mouth. "No 'ifs.' We'll get home."

A bang against the floor made them jump.

"Have excess energy?" a voice roared. "Then I've got plenty of work for you to do. Keep it quiet."

"Like you haven't hurt us enough already?" Amanda said loudly. "What?"

Amanda gasped. "Nothing."

Jaci clenched the bottle of water, white-fisted. "Amanda, you're going to get us all killed."

"I'm scared," Sara said, curling her knees up to her chest and holding them to her.

"Me, too. I want to go home." Jaci's throat ached, and hot tears started down her face. Sara scooted closer to her and touched her arm. Jaci couldn't look at her. She put her head down and sobbed.

Sara began to cry, too. Jaci wrapped her arms around her for a long moment, then lay down on her sack, rolling over with her back to the other girls.

The tears continued down her face, spilling over her nose and lips. She stared at the wooden rafters and tried to pray, but no words came.

The night lasted forever. The darkness in the room closed in around Jaci until it felt like a thick blanket, suffocating. Her eyes shot open, her heart pounding, but the attic remained bathed in the mellow moonlight that glided through the window.

She closed her eyes and tried to ignore the pressure building around her head. It pressed against her face, making her ears ring. Burying her face in her hands, she prayed until it faded into the background.

She thought of her mom, probably crying herself to sleep. Did her dad know yet? Was Seth sorry they had argued? The tears sprang to her eyes again, and she prayed harder, trying to force all other thoughts from her head. She prayed until sleep finally claimed her.

September 15
Shelley, Idaho

Carl waited outside the three-story brick house. He glanced at his watch. Nearly a minute had passed since he had rung the doorbell.

The door opened, revealing a pale, disheveled woman. Her short blond hair sat in unkempt layers on her head. "I'm sorry," she said. "I was—resting."

Sara's mom. She had been crying. Just like Callie's mother. "I understand, Mrs. Yadle. May I come in?"

She nodded and opened the door further. "Please do."

Her bare feet didn't make any noise as she led him across the tile. Carl took in the white carpet and white couches in the sitting room. A white banister led to the upper stories. It didn't look like a teenager lived here. "Can you show me Sara's room?"

"Of course."

Carl followed her up the staircase, flipping through his pictures of the four girls. His examinations of the mall employees had turned up empty. The security guard was found in the morning, gagged and knocked out with chloroform. He hadn't seen a thing.

And someone had robbed the jewelry store.

Thieves and kidnappers had two very different profiles, but maybe this one saw profit in stealing teenage girls. The jewelry store thief remained the number one suspect.

He entered Sara's room. Track medals dangled from the bedposts, stuffed animals lounged on the floor. "She's a runner, huh?" Always careful to use present tense.

Mrs. Yadle nodded. "Yes. She's very good."

Carl picked up the pink Motorola camera phone on the bed. Expensive. "Is this Sara's?"

"Mm-hm."

"Can I take it?"

She nodded, clasping her hands together.

He put it in his pocket. Lots of contacts in there, maybe some text messages. Cell phones were gold mines of information. "Does that computer have internet access?"

"Oh—yes. But Sara hardly ever uses it. She's always outside."

Right. That's what all the parents thought. "Are there any passwords on it?"

"I don't think so."

"I'd like to have a look at it before I go."

"Okay."

He braced himself. No parent liked the next question. "Did Sara have any boyfriends that you know of?"

She shook her head as quickly as Callie's mom had. "No."

The phone and computer would tell the truth. "How would you describe Sara's personality?"

"Cheerful. Always smiling. A little shy sometimes."

He pulled her picture out, examining the spread of freckles over Sara's nose, the sandy-blond hair and the slender frame. Her smile revealed perfectly aligned teeth. Only braces could make teeth that straight. She looked nothing like her parents. "How was her relationship with you and your husband? Is he her father?"

She frowned. "We're her parents. But actually, Sara's adopted. And… she just found that out three months ago."

Carl flipped open his notebook, pen and paper out before he realized it. "Tell me the story."

"We adopted her when she was a baby. We opted for a closed adoption. Her parents were dead, but there were some other family members who wanted to be a part of her life. Well, we didn't think that would be good for her. Too confusing. We wanted her to think of us as her real parents. We didn't ever want her to wonder if we loved her as much as we would a biological child. After the adoption was finalized, we never heard from her relatives again.

"Honestly, Mike and I didn't think about her adoption. She was our baby, our Sara. Well, then she found the adoption certificate in her baby book behind her birth certificate. She went nuts. We tried to calm her. But she was so angry with us."

The woman bit her lower lip. "I've never seen her so angry. She demanded to know more about her family. But we didn't have any information."

Interesting. "Who does have that information? Where would she have to go?"

"The courthouse, where the final documents were signed. I believe those are the only records of her previous family members."

"Does she know where that is?"

"I don't know."

Carl nodded. "I'd like to see that adoption certificate, if I may." He didn't think it likely that the four girls had decided to go on a quest to find Sara's family, but he wasn't going to rule it out.

"I'll get it for you."

She left the room, and Carl seated himself at the computer. Time to get to know Sara.

Chapter 5

Jaci opened her eyes. Had she slept at all?

Claber slammed the attic door down with a thud that vibrated the wooden floor. "Come on, get up." He stood over Jaci and kicked her in the side. She pushed herself up, blinking to clear her head.

"Ow!" Amanda folded her arms across her face and received another kick. She jumped up, glancing at him once and then quickly lowering her eyes.

Claber grabbed Jaci's forearm, forcing her to look at him. "The basement needs cleaning." He narrowed his eyes. "You better keep your friends in line. Or you know what can happen."

Her mind felt fuzzy and her knees trembled. She stared at her toes, trying to stay on her feet.

"Got that?"

Jaci nodded.

"Good. Then follow me. Keep up." With a grunt, he heaved himself down the ladder.

"What now?" Sara asked in a small voice.

Jaci looked up and swallowed hard. Apparently she was supposed to be the leader here. "Well, I guess we follow him to the basement, and then we clean."

Taking a few strides to the door, she started down the ladder, hoping her outward demonstration of bravery inspired the others.

Amanda spoke under her breath, following Jaci. "Maybe now we can escape. Watch for the weaknesses of the house."

"There are none." The baritone voice came from right next to them. Amanda squealed and nearly fell off the ladder.

Clutching the rungs, Jaci saw the boss man, his arms folded across his chest. He looked at Amanda with his jaw tight, high, protruding cheekbones making his eyes look deep-set. "Where would you go? To the police?"

A sneer graced his chiseled features. "Enough. For now, you're my prisoners." His eyes flicked up as Sara started down the ladder next. He lifted an arm and pointed down the hall, where Claber waited. "Go."

Jaci started down the hallway, Sara and Amanda falling into step with her. She said, her mouth barely moving, "Keep your eyes open. Anything, anything that might be useful, take note."

Neither of them responded. She hoped they had heard her.

Claber led them down three, four flights of stairs, past closed doors and entry ways. The house was far from empty. Several men wandered in and out of rooms, marching down hallways with purposeful strides. One man, the dark-eyed one who had helped kidnap them, followed Claber.

"Clean the basement," Claber growled. He opened a closet and let a pile of brooms and mops fall onto the floor. "There's a sink with water and soap. Rags are under it."

Turning his attention to the dark-eyed man, he said something and then stomped upstairs. The other man remained standing at the foot of the stairs.

Sara poked her shoe at a spider, its legs curled up, dead in an old cobweb. The large basement was damp and not well lit.

Jaci wandered over to the sink and picked up a rag. A dirty white door across the room caught her attention. She opened the door and stared into a bathroom, consisting of a toilet on yellowed, peeling linoleum and a rust-stained sink. The stench of old urine burned her nose. "A bathroom!"

Amanda dropped her broom with a clatter and ran forward. "Let me use it," she demanded, shoving Jaci aside.

"Hey," Jaci protested. There were footsteps on the stairs. Jaci turned to a lamp and started dusting it furiously.

The third member of their kidnapping party, the white man with fat lips, joined the dark-skinned man. They exchanged words before the man with black eyes started up the stairs, leaving the fat-lipped guy behind.

Movement out of the corner of her eye made Jaci turn. Amanda had left the bathroom. Jaci clutched her rag and hurried in. She locked the door and dropped to her knees, feeling an instant sense of gratitude for the isolation. Putting the rag on the floor, she put her head in her hands and cried.

"Dear God," she prayed, rocking backward and forward on her knees, "how do we get out of this mess?"

A whisper made her draw in her breath. She scanned the tiny bathroom.

The voice came again, from the upper corner by the toilet. Crawling forward, Jaci spotted a vent. She climbed onto the toilet and stood on her tip-toes, getting as close as she could. The words drifted down to her, muffled but audible.

"...said no stops. Get the necklace and come straight home. What happened?"

"We stopped in Idaho Falls to get a bite—"

"What were you doing in Idaho?"

"Got a call from our contact in Idaho Falls. Said he needed a new cover, the police were suspicious. So we drove up to take care of business." It was the voice of their captor, Claber. Was he talking to the boss man?

"Why wasn't I notified?"

"I assumed he called you first. Idaho's not far from our Montana entry. I figured we'd kill two birds with one stone."

"Go on. What did the contact say?"

"We relocated him and gave him a new cover. Since he knew we were coming, he had already bribed the mall security guard for us. It should've been quick and easy."

"Where'd the girls come from?" the boss man snapped. "I'm a jewel thief, not a kidnapper. I'm wanted for burglary, not murder."

"They were spying on us. It was either kill them or bring them along. They'd seen too much."

"They saw a black van." The boss man's voice rose to a shout. "You should've drugged them and dumped them in a ditch. And the girl that's dead. What happened there?"

"She was running to flag down a Jeep."

"What, are we going to leave a trail of dead bodies from Idaho to Canada? Lead them right to us?" Abruptly his voice lowered. "You know what's on my head. No false moves. We can't afford it. Everything we pull in this year goes to pay that debt, understand? At least we've still got the Swan Lake necklace. Claber, get me Sid. He'll buy those girls for half a million, maybe more. We're still in the game."

"Hold on, Truman." Claber spoke softer, as if farther away. "I'll call Sid, but didn't you recognize the little Latina girl? That's Gregorio Rivera's daughter."

Jaci gasped and put a hand to her mouth. How did they know her father?

"Who's Gregorio Rivera?"

"The Carcinero."

Jaci jerked and lost her footing on the toilet. She slipped, hitting the wall with a clunk, and froze. Had they heard her?

The doorknob to the bathroom rattled. "Hey! Open this door."

She jumped up and hurried to unlock the door. "Sorry," she said with a meek smile. "Habit."

The man eyed her and peered inside. "Leave the door open next time."

"Yes, s-sir," Jaci said, her mind buzzing. They knew her father's name. And they had called him the *Carcinero*—the Butcher.

Chapter 6

It took hours to finish the basement. When they were done, their fat-lipped blond guard moved them to a large suite on the first floor. It was devoid of furniture, and the floor and chair molding had almost grown together with cobwebs.

Jaci's stomach growled. She wasn't sure which was stronger, her hunger or her thirst. At least she had taken a drink of water in the bathroom.

They dusted until the molding shone, spraying down the walls with a chemical that smelled of bleach. Each time Jaci thought they were done, the guard would point out invisible spots to clean.

Her thighs hurt from squatting, and her hands were chapped. She put down her rag and studied her fingers, white in the joints from the chemicals. A shadow loomed over her and she grabbed up her rag, wiping quickly at the wall.

It was Claber. "Time for dinner," he growled.

Jaci dropped her rag. The thought of food made her knees weak.

She expected Claber to send them back to the attic with… well, with dinner, whatever it was. Instead, he led them down the red-carpet hallway. Before they reached the entry way, he turned a corner and the house changed, looking like a historical museum instead of an old, unused mansion.

Paintings dotted the walls, each room full of priceless antiques and monuments. One of the paintings, as large as the wall, covered it like a mural. It was done in a renaissance style, with large bubbly people and muted reds and blues.

For a moment Jaci let her mind wander, imagining what it would be like if this weren't a scene from a horror movie—and then she smelled the food.

A huge dining table was set in the middle of a white room, with pillars in the corners and crown molding running along the tops of the walls. Paintings of fruits and gardens decorated the walls, but none looked as lovely as the arrangements that covered the table.

Jaci shook her head, coming to her senses. This wasn't a buffet, it was a prison. She focused on the man standing at the head of the table. It was the boss man. What had Claber called him? Truman?

Jaci examined him surreptitiously, keeping her eyes lowered. He wasn't old, maybe mid-thirties. He had high, square cheek bones and his brown hair was cut in precise, sharp angles. Although a slight man, his demeanor commanded respect.

He bowed and pulled out his own chair. "Please. Sit." He motioned to four chairs pulled out from the table. Serving bowls close to him held cuts of meat, vegetables, and slices of fruit.

In front of each place was a bowl full of a bright green soup. Jaci felt a stab of disappointment. She leaned over and sniffed. It didn't smell too bad.

Truman piled his plate high. Spearing his broccoli, he looked at them. "I don't particularly like the color of pea soup either. There's fresh bread." He indicated a cloth-covered basket in the middle of the table.

Jaci grabbed rolls from the basket, stuffing one into her mouth and dumping several others in her lap. The soft buttery texture melted in her mouth, and she relished it, closing her eyes.

She opened them and felt her face grow hot; the boss man was watching her with a smile. Ducking her head, she poked her spoon at her pea soup.

"So," he said, placing some golden, deep-fried shrimp on his plate, "why were you watching the robbery?"

No one answered. He turned to Amanda, seated on his left. "Well?"

She didn't look at him, and his eyes fell on Sara. "What do you think, girl?"

Sara's eyes lifted from her bowl. "Curiosity."

He raised an eyebrow. "Dangerous."

His gray eyes lightened a little. "Such beautiful girls. Do you have names? How about it? Red?" He nodded at Amanda. "By far the most beautiful of the group. Exquisite beauty."

He looked at Sara. "And you are nothing but a child. Yet your innocence is so captivating."

Turning to Jaci, a half-sneer spread across his face. "And you."

Chills ran down her spine. "What about you?" she asked, trying to act calm. "We don't know your name."

"Of course you do. Who else would I be, but The Hand?"

Amanda gasped, her eyes wide, staring at him.

"Never mind. I already know who you are. You're all over the news, though the police are hesitant to link your disappearance to the robbery. They haven't found your friend's body yet. That will throw them off track; I don't usually deal in homicides."

Callie. Jaci choked on her soup. She reached for her cup of water with a trembling hand.

"An unfortunate incident. I do regret it." He began to cut his steak. "Life is cruel. There's no way around it."

He proceeded to put some cuts of meat into each of their bowls. "Eat. I'm not trying to starve you. You're no good to me dead."

He watched as they fished out the meat and ate it. Standing, he pushed his chair away from the table. "Grey."

The second guard from the basement, the one with the fat lip, hurried into the room.

"I'm done. Get them back to the attic."

September 16
Shelley, Idaho

"Amanda's a bit boy-crazy. But she's a good girl. She would never run away with a boy." Mrs. Murphy's hands twitched in her lap, and she wrung her fingers together.

She might have been a beautiful woman once, but the puffy skin around her tired blue eyes and the lines around her mouth had aged her.

Carl nodded, taking a few notes. He believed her. He had double-checked Sara's emails and text messages. All had appeared innocent and frivolous—comments about homework, track practice, and where to meet up before and after school.

Besides that, their disappearance on the same night and from the same location as a robbery, coupled with the fact that nobody had seen or heard from them, pointed to a kidnapping.

Or homicides.

Carl preferred a kidnapping. "So Amanda didn't have a boyfriend?"

"No one special. She had lots of crushes. A few dates."

The front door opened, and Mr. Murphy walked in. Carl stood

and offered a hand. "Please join us. I was just asking a few questions about Amanda."

Mr. Murphy shook his hand. "Any new developments?"

Carl looked down. "No." He wished he had something, anything to offer these people.

Mr. Murphy sat on the couch. "Go ahead."

Reseating himself, Carl focused his thoughts. "Did you ever see signs of unrest or rebellion in Amanda."

"Absolutely not," Mr. Murphy said.

"Well, rebellion, no." Mrs. Murphy shook her head. "Sometimes she did get bored, but she wouldn't have run away."

"Would she go along if someone else wanted to?"

She frowned. "I don't think so."

Carl leaned forward, putting his elbows on his knees. "The girls have been gone for three days. Each day that passes lessens our chances of finding them. If you can think of anywhere she might have gone, anything she might do—it might help me."

Mrs. Murphy averted her eyes. "Well, she did have kind of a silly obsession with The Hand."

Carl leaned back on the couch, his heart skipping a beat. "What do you mean?"

"We'd go over the news together. It was kind of a fun activity, you know. Then she'd plot out his raids and try to guess where he might go next."

Carl wrote quickly. Could she have anticipated The Hand's next move? "Did her friends know about this obsession?"

"Yes, yes. They shared it with her."

Carl looked up, meeting Mrs. Murphy's eyes. "You know it's not normal for a teen to fantasize about a criminal. It's not healthy, either. There are a lot of psychological implications, starting with her wanting to change something in her life, or feeling like something is not under her control, but not knowing what to do about it."

The woman wilted under his gaze, her eyes dropping. She shriveled against the upholstery. "I didn't know it was bad."

Mr. Murphy crossed his arms over his chest, his jaw set. "I told you not to indulge her so much."

Tears rolled down Mrs. Murphy's face, and she shot a hostile glare at her husband. "You indulged her as much as I did. It's your fault we moved to this horrible town."

Carl put his pen down. Things were not well in the Murphy

house, and he didn't think it started with Amanda's disappearance. "How was Amanda at home?"

Mrs. Murphy wiped her eyes with her knuckle. "She didn't show much interest in things after we moved here. She wanted to go back to California. We were glad when she found something to divert her attention. Even if it was a silly obsession."

"When did you move here?"

"Six months ago."

"Did she like her friends?"

"They were different from her friends in California. More naïve and not willing to try new things. That bothered her."

Amanda was sounding less and less like the other girls. "So she wanted an adventure."

Neither parent responded.

Carl ran his hands over the pleats in his suit pants. "Any stress at home? Anything to make her want to escape?"

Mr. Murphy let out a sigh. "We moved when I lost my job. I had an offer here that didn't pan out. For two months I've worked at odd jobs."

"It's been stressful on Amanda," Mrs. Murphy said, grabbing a tissue from the end table and shredding it to pieces. "And on me."

Mr. Murphy added, "We're getting a divorce."

Carl looked back and forth between them, careful to keep his face neutral. "Do you think this has had an impact on Amanda's behavior?"

"Amanda doesn't know." The woman put the shredded tissue pieces back on the table. "We haven't told her yet."

Carl sat in silence for a moment, collecting his thoughts. He doubted Amanda was oblivious. He stood. "Thank you so much for your time. You have my card. Call if you think of anything or hear from her."

He let himself out of the house. Three down, one to go.

It was hard to get Mrs. Rivera's attention. "This is César, my baby," she said, kissing her eight-year-old on the forehead.

He made a face and pushed her away, then chased the cat around the room.

"César! *Deja el gato en paz.* You had some questions for me?" The shadows under her eyes gave away her stress.

Carl glanced around. "Will Mr. Rivera be here soon?"

"He's not back from his business trip."

Carl raised an eyebrow. "Does he know about his daughter?"

"Oh, well, of course." Her cheeks flushed and she glanced at César.

The boy hissed and started throwing couch pillows at the cat, which hovered under the computer desk.

"César! *Para ya!* His job is important." She shoved a lock of black hair out of her eyes. "It's unpredictable. But he should be home tomorrow."

"What does he do?"

She licked her lips. "César, if I tell you one more time to leave the cat alone, you will go to bed with no dinner."

The garage door slammed and a young man stepped into the room. "*Mamá, llegué.*"

Carl appraised the tall, dark-haired youth that entered. He had thick, wavy hair and deep brown eyes.

"Hi. I'm Seth." Seth stuck a hand out. "You must be Detective Hamilton. Mama's mentioned you're looking for Jaci. Any luck?"

Carl shook his head. "No breakthroughs yet. Do you have anything you could help us with?"

He took a deep breath. "No, but I am worried about her." He shoved his hands in his jeans pockets. "We fought, you see. I left angry at her."

"Seth," his mother said softly.

"I just want to help. If I can help you find her—tell me."

Carl nodded, touched by the boy's plea. "Did you know her friends, Seth?"

"Sure. They were here all the time."

Carl looked at Mrs. Rivera, aware that she hadn't answered his questions. "Would you show me Jaci's room, please?"

"Of course."

Carl searched her room, looking for names, clues, anything. "We were saying. What does your husband do?"

"He's a traveling consultant. He helps other companies with their accounts and auditing."

"Oh? What did he get his degree in?"

She clasped her hands together in front of her pink skirt. "Ah, accounting, I think."

"You're not sure?"

"Well, it was in Mexico. I can't remember if the university had an accounting program. But that's the equivalent in America."

"Ah." Carl nodded. Yet something didn't click right. Maybe it was her nervous manner. "What university was that?" He opened a drawer and pulled out a dried rose.

"The National University of Mexico?"

"Are you asking me?" Carl looked up, meeting her eyes. "Is there something you're not telling me?"

She put a hand to her forehead. "No—I just can't remember. It's been a long time. And I'm nervous. My husband is not home, my daughter is missing, and I'm scared. I don't know what to do. I'm not quite myself."

Carl tucked a hand-written note into his pocket.

"Why don't you come back tomorrow? My husband wants very much to talk with you."

"I will. Thank you for your help." He slipped down the stairs and out the door.

Chapter 7

Sara broke the silence in the small attic. "I know where we are."

Jaci stared at the flecks of dust floating in the shafts of light sneaking in through the roof.

"You do?"

"I found a postcard in the basement with an address on it. Rue Landry, Victoriaville, QC."

"QC?" Amanda echoed. "What state is that?"

"Canada," Jaci said. "They drove us all the way to Canada." She cleared her throat. "I've got news, too. I overheard a conversation today. The Hand is going to sell us."

"Sell us!" Sara gasped.

Jaci put a finger to her lips and nodded.

"Trafficking." Sara gripped the edge of her bedroll, knuckles white.

Should she tell them they knew her father? No, Jaci decided. She needed to figure out what that meant first.

They slept until the wiry, black-eyed man woke them up. He took them out on the balcony at the break of dawn.

Claber waited for them. "Thanks," he grunted, a tool belt strapped around his waist.

The man turned to leave, and Claber called out, "Eli."

Eli paused. "Yes?"

"Bring some toast. For the girls. They'll be working hard today." Claber's lip curled upward, disappearing behind his mustache.

"Got it." Eli disappeared into the house.

They spent the day on the roof, fixing potential leaks. By the time they came back inside and headed into the attic, Jaci felt too tired to climb. She gripped the ladder rungs in her hands, her head sagging.

Amanda had already made it up, and Sara lingered behind her. So many times Jaci had looked over the edge at that four-story drop and wondered what it would be like to fall. Would she be scared? Would it hurt when she hit the ground? Or would it happen so fast that all she would feel was a huge gust of wind, and then it would be over?

She sighed and crawled after Amanda, over the bumpy wooden floor. The trapdoor closed behind them, the deadbolt clicking as Claber latched it into place.

"Where's Sara?" Amanda asked.

The haze cleared from Jaci's mind. "I don't know. She was right behind me."

Amanda pounded on the trapdoor. "Hey! Sara! Where's Sara?"

A numbness closed over Jaci's chest as she backed up against the attic wall. A cobweb brushed her face. She stumbled forward, joining Amanda. Together they screamed and pounded on the trapdoor until they were hoarse.

First Callie, now Sara. Who would be next?

Someone touched her shoulder, and Jaci swung her hands up, blindly slapping before realizing it was Amanda.

Jaci grasped Amanda's arm, clinging to her. "This is it," she said, a sob building in her throat. "We're going to die. They're going to separate us."

"Jaci. We're going to find Sara, and we're going to get out of here. It's not the end."

Taking several deep breaths, Jaci forced herself to relax. "All right. We'll find Sara."

"Yes. Tomorrow. And then we run. No matter what."

"No matter what," Jaci echoed.

September 17
Shelley, Idaho

Mr. Rivera, a tall, broad-shouldered man with glittering black eyes and cropped black hair, opened the screen door. "I've been waiting for you, Detective."

Carl followed the man to the white porch-swing. "I'm terribly sorry about your daughter. What an awful thing to come home to."

"Yes." Mr. Rivera focused his dark eyes on Carl. "I had a few things to tie up. I came as soon as I could."

His accent was thicker than his wife's. Carl glanced down at his notes. His palms were sweating. "What company did you say you work for, Mr. Rivera?"

The man leaned back in the swing. "Call me Greg. I work for International Accounting Alliances, based out of Dallas. I spend a lot of time traveling."

"Your wife said you got your degree in accounting at the National Autonomous University in Mexico. But she wasn't sure she had the right university. Do you recall what it was?"

He was giving Mr. Rivera a chance to give him the right data. He had already checked with the university, and they had never had a Gregorio Rivera enrolled.

One corner of Mr. Rivera's lip rolled upward. "Are you interviewing me? I was going to interview you. No, it wasn't the National University of Mexico. I went to the University of Pedrita in Zacatecas, doing my studies in business negotiations."

"And where was your first job after college?"

Mr. Rivera stared at him. "Gatorland."

"Gatorland?" Carl raised an eyebrow. "Where's that?"

"Theme park in Orlando."

That was unexpected. Carl wrote it down. "When did you move your family here?"

"I met my wife in Orlando. Almost twenty years ago." He leaned forward. "I want to know about my daughter. What leads do you have?"

Carl flipped through his notes. "We don't have any leads. At this point, we do believe it was a kidnapping."

Mr. Rivera narrowed his eyes. "You have no suspects on the robbery?"

Carl shook his head. "None. The only fingerprints we found were Amanda Murphy's, in the door frame."

"Then it had to be The Hand."

The Hand. The robber was so-called because the first few burglaries, a decade ago now, each had a crayon-traced hand, minus the fingerprints, on the unbroken glass of the jewelry case. He had quit leaving the calling card years ago, but the name had stuck.

"I'm hesitant to blame every robbery on him."

"He was in the area. We know he was in Utah. Why not Idaho, too?"

"Kidnapping has never been a part of his game."

Mr. Rivera pressed his index fingers to his forehead. "And you don't know where his base is?"

The Hand always vanished. Sometimes for months, sometimes years, only to reappear again and disappear as quickly. "The Hand's a cat thief. High-tech burglar. He's not been a top priority because he's more of a nuisance than a danger. However, if he really took the Swan Lake Necklace in Houston, which included two homicides, and kidnapped the girls, he has managed to jump a little higher on the list."

Mr. Rivera shook his head and jumped off the swing. "Thank you for speaking with me, Detective. If I learn anything, I'll be in touch." He went inside.

Carl stood there a moment, a slight frown creasing his brow. That hadn't gone how he had expected. He looked over the notes he had taken. He would check these sources.

He needed a reward. The last of his Claussen pickles were calling him.

Chapter 8

The low murmur of voices in the hall under the attic woke Jaci. She felt sore from lying on the wooden floorboards all night.

A movement next to her distracted her. It was Sara, curled in a fetal position, arms around her head.

"Sara! You're back."

Sara lifted her face, her eyes blank.

Amanda sat up and let out a cry. She grabbed Sara into a hug. "Where were you?"

"Here," Sara answered. Her voice sounded empty and dull.

Something wasn't right. Not sure what to say, Jaci wandered to the small round window. She saw The Hand walk out the front door. The yellow Camaro sat in the circle drive, driver sitting at idle, passenger door open.

Jaci snapped her fingers. "You guys, come here. He's going somewhere."

Amanda joined her. The Hand was giving instructions to someone in the doorway. Three of his men were with him. Jaci recognized two of them. Grey, the guy with the fat lips, and the dark-eyed one with razor eyebrows—was his name Eli?

"Where is he going?" Amanda asked. Her shoulders touched Jaci's as they each tried to peer through the tiny opening, barely bigger than one of their heads.

The Hand glanced up at the window, his face implacable as he saluted in their direction. Then he slithered into the passenger seat and the car sped away.

Just as the vehicle pulled around the house, another car pulled up, one with a red and blue rack of lights on top and white-on-blue lettering on the side. Jaci gripped Amanda's hand. "It's the police."

"They found us!" Amanda cried.

The trap door swung open, and one of The Hand's musclemen poked his head up. "Come on down."

He was taking them down? They must not have noticed the police car. If they could just be seen—or get someone's attention.

The man's head popped out of view, and the girls followed him down the ladder. He waited for them below. She tried to remember his name, but came up empty. He looked kind of like Homer Simpson, so she dubbed him Homer.

"Someone's coming to see you." Homer smiled without mirth. "You need to use the bathroom and get cleaned up. Come on."

They followed him downstairs to the bathroom on the main floor. They turned a corner to see two officers, laughing and talking to Grey and another man.

Jaci and Amanda exchanged glances, and together they launched themselves at the policemen.

"Help us," cried Amanda.

Jaci threw herself at the feet of one of the men. "We've been kidnapped. Please, take us away!"

The officer looked down at her in total silence, and then all the men burst out laughing.

He hooked his boot on Jaci's shoulder and shoved her. "Get off me."

"Stupid girls," Homer snarled, reaching out and backhanding Jaci across the face. "These are The Hand's police. Didn't he tell you he has his own force? Wolves among the sheep?"

Understanding washed over her, and Jaci felt the blood drain from her face.

"Now get in the bathroom and get cleaned up. One at a time. And don't try any more stupid stunts." He shoved Jaci and Amanda back toward Sara.

Still chuckling, the fake officer placed his hat back on his head and Grey escorted them out of the room. Homer kept his eyes on Jaci and Sara.

Sara looked at Jaci and shook her head, her hazel eyes hooded.

Jaci leaned against the white wall and studied her dirty fingernails. It was hopeless. How to get away when they were shadowed every minute?

Amanda came out of the bathroom, and Sara went in. Poor Sara. She hadn't said more than a word since returning during the night.

From the other room, the phone rang.

"Claber, come watch them!" Homer hollered. "I've gotta get the phone. It might be Truman with Sid."

"Right," Claber yelled from the higher floor.

The guard turned to the girls. "Don't move." With that, he trotted away.

As soon as his back was turned, Amanda yanked open the bathroom door. Sara stood by the sink, washing her face, eyes wide. Amanda grabbed Jaci's forearm and thrust her inside, then closed the door and locked it.

"Quick," she said, "we have to hurry." Amanda rushed to a window over the toilet and pushed it open.

"There's no screen," Jaci said, stating the obvious.

"And it's not locked. Go, go, go, go." Amanda climbed through.

Jaci scrambled after her. There was a bump outside the bathroom door, and she paused with one leg out the window.

"Hey, Sanders?" came Claber's voice. "Was it this bathroom?"

Jaci dropped to the ground outside, then reached up to help Sara. They pulled her through the window, and Amanda closed it.

"Run!" said Jaci.

The forest was about ten yards in front of them. They made a mad dash for it.

"Hurry, hurry," Jaci gasped aloud as they ran. "Don't stop."

"They'll search the house first," Sara said. "They won't know we were all inside the bathroom."

"They'll know," Jaci panted, "when they check and it's locked."

"Don't talk," snapped Amanda. "Just run. And pray there's no dogs."

Chapter 9

Amanda came to a sudden halt, panting and holding her side. "Stop," she gasped. "I can't keep running."

Jaci and Sara pulled up and walked back the few feet to her. Jaci, out of breath, grabbed a tree trunk for support. She was an endurance runner, not a sprinter, and she welcomed the break. She had already tripped over a branch, fallen on a rock, and scratched her face going through thorns. "They'll be right behind us."

"Maybe we should split up?" Amanda suggested.

"No!" cried Sara.

Jaci reached out and squeezed her shoulder. "We'll stick together. Find a place to hide and lay low until nightfall. Then we can keep going."

"Are you sure?" asked Amanda. "Wouldn't it be better to get away as quickly as possible?"

"We can't just hurry down this mountain. We've got to think. They'll be waiting at the bottom for us."

Amanda nodded. "Okay. Let's find a place to hide—a tree, overhang, cave, something. Go."

In an instant they were off again. Jaci prayed as she stumbled over the undergrowth. "Please, Lord. Please, Lord. Please, Lord." She never formed a deeper thought.

As she ran around an uprooted tree, she tripped.

"Oh!" Her hands shot out as the world fell away. It took her a moment to realize she was in a hole left by the uprooted tree. The hole disappeared into the forest floor, hidden by the overhanging, broken roots. "Sara, Amanda. In here."

They hopped in next to her. Jaci pulled dead leaves and debris into the hole, covering themselves with the foliage.

Sara stopped her. "Shh. Listen."

They froze. The sound of feet crashed through underbrush nearby.

"Faster," Jaci said. They piled up leaves quickly, stopping when the footsteps got closer.

Jaci sunk into the leaves, huddling close to her friends. *If anyone looks inside the hole, they'll see us.* Jaci breathed her little prayer, her lips moving soundlessly. She could feel Amanda's heart pounding under her elbow. Sara's knees crushed against her ribcage.

Footsteps rustled the leaves near their hiding place. Jaci tensed, her muscles preparing to catapult her from the root-hole and fly down the mountainside. Amanda gripped her forearm, pinching. A spider crept across the leaves under nose. She stared at it.

Amanda spotted it too. Her eyes widened as she drew her head back. A soft gasp escaped her lips.

"Hey!" The man's voice came from right above them.

Jaci squeezed her eyes shut and lowered her shoulders, trying to slide further into the leaves.

"Find anything?" The second voice was further away, but coming closer.

Jaci's heart pounded. She knew they could not outrun these men.

"No." Dirt kicked into their hole as a large boot walked by. "Nothing over here."

Jaci didn't breathe. She listened to his footsteps jog away. The running feet turned into shouting voices that faded as they traveled down the hill. It took several minutes before Jaci found the courage to open her eyes.

They were safe. She felt Amanda's grip on her arm relax.

The girls didn't move for about an hour. Every time Amanda checked her watch, her tangled red hair brushed Jaci's cheek. Jaci's legs were starting to cramp and the adrenaline was wearing off, making her tired and irritated.

"What now?" Sara said.

"We wait," Jaci said back. "At least 'til nightfall. Maybe even 'til tomorrow. They'll be looking everywhere for us."

Amanda shook her head. "No, we can't wait that long. I say we wait until nightfall, then make a run for it. The forest is big; they can't be everywhere. We have to trust our luck or risk being trapped in here forever."

Jaci glanced at Sara, who watched her with brooding eyes. "All right. We wait until dark. We don't run. We watch each other. If one person stops, we all stop. And not one word. Got it?"

She met each girl's eyes in turn, and they nodded. Jaci opened and closed her fists uneasily, then leaned her head against the rotten wood.

It was the longest hour ever. Jaci memorized every leaf in front of her. She listened to the birds cooing. She watched an insect crawl around the debris. She wondered how many small, white termites crawled in her hair.

Someone's stomach gave a furious growl, and Jaci began to huddle tighter and rock a bit. "I never got to go to the bathroom," she said.

Amanda gave her a tight smile. "Just don't do it now, okay?"

"I need to go again, too," Sara said.

The sun began to set, and she could feel everyone tensing in anticipation. There had been no further sign of the men. The occasional squirrel scampering by had set Jaci's heart into a staccato break dance, but the men appeared to have moved on.

When it was too dark to clearly see the trees in front of them, they pushed away the leaf barrier and crawled out. Jaci crouched over the damp leaves, shaking and trembling as she tried to keep herself up. She exhaled, relieved to empty her bladder.

It was a dark night, with a sliver of moonlight poking through the branches. They could barely see each other as they moved through the forest.

It took several hours before they reached flat ground. The trees cleared a bit, and then they were in a grassy meadow. Without the tree foliage to block the moonlight, they had better visibility.

They continued their hunched walk until they reached a chain linked fence.

"Is it electrified?" asked Sara.

Jaci grabbed a stick and threw it at the fence. It bounced off. "I don't think so."

"I'll go through," said Amanda. She reached out a finger and poked at the fence. When nothing happened, she put her hands on it and climbed up. She winced as she dropped to the other side. "I'm over."

Jaci hurried after her, with Sara right behind. "Welcome to the road," she said.

In front of them was a black top road. A few yards ahead, the road split into a fork, the left side curving around the hill they had just descended, and the right side leading away.

"Get across the street and into the grass on the right side of that fork as quickly as possible," said Jaci. "Put distance between us and this mountain."

"Let's go," Amanda said. "Speed walk pace."

"The road should lead to a city. We find help and get home." Invigorating energy pumped through Jaci's limbs. *We did it. We got away!* "Walk in the tall grass. If you hear any cars, duck. And hope they don't see us."

Chapter 10

The early morning sunlight bathed the tall grass in an earthy orange glow. Jaci dragged her feet, eyes burning every time she blinked. She half slept as she stumbled through the grass.

Sara grabbed Jaci's arm, digging in her fingernails. "Car," she breathed.

The fog cleared from Jaci's mind. "Hit the grass. Fast!"

In an instant, the three girls flew forward, falling flat on their bellies. The red sports car came to a sudden, sputtering stop next to them.

"We've been spotted," said Amanda.

"Not yet." Jaci tensed, peering through the thin reeds and pulling her elbows and knees up under her. "Get ready to run."

The driver's side door opened, and someone got out. Jaci watched in breathless anxiety as the person came around the front of the car.

"*Super*," a woman said in angry exasperation. "*Au juste de ce que j'ai besoin. Un plat.*"

It was just a girl, in her early twenties, with short blond hair cut in a bob. She spoke French in a lilting and pleasant voice and was dressed in a stylish, tight red top and black, stretchy capris.

She knelt down to examine her tire, then went to the back of the car and opened the trunk.

"Anyone speak French?" Jaci mouthed at her friends. She received helpless looks and head shakings in response.

"*Juste ma chance—et naturellement Chris a mon téléphone portable.*" She tugged on the spare tire, talking to herself.

"*S'il juste—*" she grunted as she succeeded in removing the spare—"*achèterait une nouvelle batterie, il n'aurait pas besoin de mon telephone.*"

She dropped the tire on the road. *"Je ne sais pas changer un pneu."* She threw her arms up as she grumbled to herself, coming back around to stare at the tire.

Jaci might not understand the words, but she knew the meaning. On impulse, she stood up. "I can help you with that," she said very slowly, pointing from herself to the tire and back again.

With a gasp and a shriek, the woman jumped back, her hand going to her throat. "What on earth—were you hiding there?" she asked in clear, accented English.

"Oh, you speak English."

"Of course I do." She sounded insulted. "I am educated. Did you sleep there? There are leaves in your hair."

"Actually, there are three of us. And if you'll give us a ride into town, I'll change your tire for you."

The woman stepped closer to Jaci, cocking her head. "Wait a minute."

She peered behind Jaci at the other two still hiding in the bushes. "Something's going on here. You're in some sort of trouble, aren't you?"

"No, no trouble," Jaci said, shaking her head. "We haven't done anything wrong." That part was true, at least.

The woman shrugged. "Well, okay. Sure, if you'll change my tire, you three can get in. Just don't get it dirty, okay, it's my boyfriend's car. My phone for his car, you know. Good exchange."

"Not a problem," Jaci replied, eagerly removing the jack from the trunk and grabbing up the spare.

She was suddenly very grateful to Tio Oscar for insisting she know everything about cars. "At least you have a full spare and not a donut."

"What's your name?"

Jaci hesitated as she unscrewed the nuts to the tire and began to jack up the car. *Should I tell her?* She couldn't see any harm in it. But it wouldn't hurt to play it safe, either.

"Julie," she said as she pulled the flat tire off and put on the spare. "What's yours?"

"I'm Natalie."

"Hi, Natalie," Jaci said in a cheery tone, concentrating on replacing the nuts. "Okay, that's it. Good as new."

"Thank you." Natalie smiled. "Now I help you." She opened the door and pushed the seat forward. "Into the back, girls of the grass."

For the first time, Sara and Amanda stood up. Giving Natalie shy smiles, they climbed into her car.

A familiar black van screeched to a halt on the other side of the road.

Sara screamed. "Jaci, it's him, it's him, get in!"

"What is it?" Natalie cried in alarm.

"We've gotta go," yelled Jaci.

The door opened and several men got out. With a stab of fear, Jaci recognized Claber at the head of the group. "Help us, Natalie," she pleaded. "Those men will hurt us."

"Hey." Claber called in a friendly voice. "Where are you girls going?"

Natalie didn't wait for him to finish. She shoved Jaci into the passenger seat and slammed the door. Running to her side, she jumped in and started the car.

He turned his back on them and reached inside the van.

Natalie hit the gas. Jaci glimpsed a small black square that Claber held eye-level between both hands and aimed at them.

Forcing herself to look away, Jaci stared at the speedometer. In a moment they went from zero kilometers per hour to one hundred, leaving the black van behind.

"Please don't slow down," Sara sobbed from the back. "Don't let them catch us."

"No one's going to catch us," Natalie snapped.

Coming to a T in the road, she veered left. The tiny sports car took the sharp turns easily. They pulled onto a highway, and within moments blended in with every other car on the road.

"Thank you," Sara said.

Natalie slowed the car down to match the speed of traffic. "I hate reckless driving. It makes me nervous." She shot a glance at Jaci. "You're in trouble. Should I take you to the police?"

"No police," Amanda said. "Not here."

"You don't want to go to the police?" Natalie sounded a bit suspicious.

Jaci stared ahead, not offering an explanation.

Natalie turned off the highway into a suburban area, arriving at a small, brown stucco apartment complex.

A pretty girl with pale skin and dark brown hair met them at the door of an apartment. Her smile faded when she saw the girls. *"Natalie, ce quisur terre?"*

"English, Rachel. They don't speak French. I'll explain later. Go back inside."

Natalie ushered the girls in after Rachel. A wall separated the entry room from the kitchen. A staircase was visible through the kitchen doorway.

"How long has it been since you've eaten?" Natalie asked.

"About twenty-four hours, I think," said Amanda.

Natalie gestured to the couch. "You can sit down. That long? Rach, do you have any frozen pizzas or anything? I'll pay you back. Do you have any clothes you might give away?"

"Yes," Rachel replied, her expression stiff. "Are you being the good *samaritain* again?"

"Let us get some pizza going, and I'll see what I can find out from them."

Rachel got up from the couch, glancing again at the girls as she walked away. "There's something familiar about them."

Jaci felt edgy and suspicious. She shut her eyes and pressed the back of her head against the cushion behind her. She wanted to block out the memories of the past few days. The gunshot—Callie—

Natalie leaned across the couch, bending her head toward theirs. "Do you want to tell me what's going on? I want to help. Your accent is American, yes?"

"Do you mind if I use your phone?" Amanda asked.

"To call the States?"

She nodded. "Yes."

"I don't think Rachel's cellular phone will make an international call. Let me ask." Natalie walked into the kitchen and began to converse with Rachel in French.

The buzzer went off and Natalie came back. "She says she's misplaced the house phone, but you can use it as soon as she finds it. Why don't you call after we eat? Then you can shower and put on some nice clothes, and we'll talk."

Natalie had such a genuine smile. Jaci tried to relax. "Well, I guess that'd be okay."

Chapter 11

There was nothing, Jaci decided, as cleansing for the soul as a shower and clean clothes. She sank into the clothing, breathing in the freshness. The soft, long-sleeved T-shirt smelled like roses. The shampoo-scented steam from the bathroom floated out of the open door, billowing into the adjacent room.

Sara was dressed in a tight pink blouse and light blue jeans. She lay on the bed, staring at the ceiling. Amanda came in, wearing a baby blue T-shirt. Her hair was still damp, the auburn ringlets separating and framing her face.

"You look nice." Sara smiled at her.

"You too," Amanda said, smiling back. Then her face turned serious. "Sara, I just wanted to ask if you're okay. I mean after—"

Sara caught her breath, turning her face away.

"I mean, after not sleeping all night," Amanda backtracked. "How are you feeling?"

"Fine," she said. "I'm doing great."

Jaci winced. "So, what do you think of Natalie?" she asked, trying to change the subject.

"She's great." Amanda spoke a little too loudly. "Callie would have something to say about Rachel's eyebrows. Probably about them being too thin."

Jaci didn't want to talk about Callie. "I'm getting a glass of water. Be right back."

She stepped down the stairs, relishing the feel of plush carpet under her bare feet. The sound of someone speaking rapidly and urgently in French attracted her attention. Jaci paused outside the closed bedroom door, wishing she could understand the words.

She went into the kitchen and stared at the cupboards, no longer interested in a drink. They needed to leave. She fled the kitchen and hurried back up the stairs. "Amanda—"

Natalie came in behind her. "Okay, girls. You've eaten the pizza and used all the hot water. You ready to explain who you are?"

"Natalie, we need to go. Thanks. Bye." Jaci grabbed Sara and Amanda's hands and tried to pull them from the bed.

Amanda jerked her hand away. "Now? But we should call our parents first."

"Hey." Rachel came into the room, her face tight. She turned her back to the girls and spoke to Natalie in French, waving a small piece of paper at her. Natalie took it and read it while Rachel talked.

"Explain this to me," Natalie said, her lips drawn. She tossed the paper on the bed.

Amanda leaned forward and Jaci tried to peer over her shoulder. "What is it?"

"It is an insert included with the newspaper this morning." Natalie's demeanor was no longer friendly and helpful. "Well?"

Jaci read the flier.

Wanted for robbery
three housemaids, ages 16, 16, 17
Beth Thomas
Dana Adams
and
Gabby Athens
Reward: 500,000 CAD
Call (514)-555-1212
Officer Fayande, Montreal Police

And there was a picture of each of them.

"All right, girls," said Natalie. "You have to tell now. Is it true? Is that why you didn't want to involve the police?"

"Do you know how much money that is?" Rachel said, her face flushed. She reached up and pulled her dark brown hair off her neck. "We could buy a house."

"It's not true," Amanda interrupted, shaking her head and waving her hands. "He kidnapped us. We're just trying to get home."

"*Quoi?*" Natalie said.

"She's right," Jaci said. "In fact, I'm surprised you haven't already seen us on a missing person's report or something. It was The Hand. Have you heard of The Hand? We're from—where are we, anyway?"

"Canada," Natalie said. "Victoriaville. Close to Montreal."

"I was right," said Sara.

Natalie looked at Rachel. "Did you find the phone?"

Rachel trotted down the stairs and came back with a cordless phone, slapping it into Natalie's hand.

Natalie held the phone out to Amanda. "Not everyone pays attention to the American news, you know. Call your parents."

Jaci shook her head. "We don't have time. We have to go."

"Why?" Amanda frowned.

"Amanda, I don't feel safe. We have to go."

"You're safe here," said Natalie. "Nobody knows you're here. I won't call him."

"Do I have to dial anything special?" Amanda asked, staring at the phone.

Natalie shook her head. "No. It's a more expensive call, but you make it the same way."

She turned to Rachel. "Get the phone book. I want the phone number to the RCMP."

Jaci jumped up. "No. We have to go *now*."

Rachel came back into the room with the phone book. She tossed it to Natalie just as the cell phone attached to her belt rang. She silenced it, staring at the girls. "There's the number for the RCMP."

"Is that the police?" Sara asked, yanking a strand of hair around her finger.

Natalie shook her head. "*Non, ma cheri*. It's the Royal Canadian Mounted Police. It's like the FBI."

Jaci stared at Rachel, something tugging at the back of her mind. Rachel met her gaze, then blinked, turning her eyes away.

"You called them, didn't you?" She forced herself in front of Rachel. "You told them where we are. They are coming here now."

Natalie's eyes widened. "Rachel?"

Throwing her arms up, Rachel launched into a lengthy tirade in French.

"Forget it," said Natalie. "They must be on their way. We leave now. And you are coming, Rachel."

They all hurried down the stairs, back to the small red sports car parked in front of the building.

"Where are we going?" asked Amanda.

"My house," Natalie said. "Rachel's house has been compromised." Natalie backed down the driveway.

Rachel's cell phone rang, and she grabbed it with a gesture of annoyance.

"Bonjour? Oh oauis, salut, Chris. Ouais, elle se trouve ici. Nat." She handed the phone to Natalie. "Speak fast. The battery is running out."

She turned and stared out the window, her expression flat.

Natalie took the phone. "Chris, I cannot talk—what?" There was a pause, and her brows knit together. "Oh, no, Chris, these men are bad." She hesitated. "You gave my address? No, don't call them. I—no. We have to go now. Meet me at Den Lou's in ten minutes."

She closed the phone and glared at Rachel.

"What is it?" Rachel asked. "Are we going to eat at Den Lou's?"

"They have my address." She pulled back into the driveway, slamming the car into park. "They know this car. Rachel, get the key to your roommate's car."

Rachel jumped out of the car and ran back into the apartment.

A small gray SUV was parked in the driveway. Dirt caked the hubcaps, and paint flaked from the doors. When Rachel returned with the key, they clambered inside.

"What's going on?" Jaci asked as Natalie squealed out of the driveway.

"We're going to Den Lou's," Natalie said. "About twenty minutes ago, two men showed up at Chris's door. They told him I was in danger and they needed to secure my house. He said they were looking for my car, and he gave them my address. So we'll meet Chris at Den Lou's, and we'll figure out what to do from there."

"The diner isn't open," Rachel said.

"We are not eating, we just need to plan." Natalie glanced at the girls in the back. "You'll be fine. You'll see."

"If they're even telling the truth," muttered Rachel.

"Rachel, where's the number for the RCMP? Let's call them right now."

Rachel arched a penciled eyebrow. "It's in the phonebook you left on the bed."

Natalie hit the steering wheel and said something in French. "Does anyone happen to know their number?"

"I don't even know who they are," Amanda grumbled.

"Natalie," said Jaci. "We didn't mean to get you involved in this. I'm so sorry. They know who you are now. Your names, your addresses."

Natalie's hands gripped the steering wheel tighter. "We'll tell the RCMP everything once we're far away from here. I trust them to protect us."

"It's a lot of money," Rachel said.

Natalie glanced at her but said nothing.

Traffic was sparse, and it didn't take long to reach the diner. They pulled into the empty parking lot.

"Chris isn't here yet." Natalie tapped the steering wheel uneasily.

A sleek silver car with darkly tinted windows pulled up and stopped right next to them.

"Is that Chris?" asked Rachel.

Natalie frowned and locked the doors. "I don't think so. He'd have to borrow his brother's car, and that's definitely not it." She put her hand on the gear shifter.

They watched as the passenger side door opened. In one fluid motion, a man in a black suit got out and grabbed the door handle.

The sunglasses might hide his eyes, but nothing could hide those fat lips. Grey.

Sara screamed and ducked her head, wrapping her arms around her skull.

"That's them," Amanda cried while Natalie shifted the car back into gear and jammed her foot on the gas.

The sudden acceleration forced Grey to let go of the car. He jumped back into the silver car, spun in a circle and followed in pursuit.

Chapter 12

"Come on, come on," Natalie grunted, pumping the gas pedal of the old car. "Two car chases in one day—this is too much for me."

"I know how to lose them," said Rachel. "I know this city better than they do."

"Lead me."

"Go toward the train tracks, but take the route past the elementary school. They'll have to slow down."

"Maybe they'll get stuck behind a cross walk."

Rachel pulled out her cell phone and looked at the time. "The three-thirty train will pass in three minutes. Jump across as the bars are lowering, and they won't be able to follow. It will buy us at least twenty minutes."

"Wonderful," said Natalie, swerving right and heading for the school. She managed to put several cars between them as she slowed down to forty kilometers per hour in the school zone. The silver car slid into place three cars back.

"Hurry," Rachel urged. "The arms are lowering."

The train rapidly approached from the left, riding on the middle of the three tracks. Natalie sped up.

"Too late," Jaci groaned. "We're going to be stopped on this side, with them behind us."

The arms were almost lowered, and the train's horn was blowing. Natalie veered into the other side of the road and drove across the track, putting themselves right into the path of the train.

"What are you doing?" Amanda screeched, gripping the door handle.

Jaci could see the engineer's face. His mouth was open, his expression twisted as he pulled down on the horn. She locked eyes with his and screamed. "We're going to collide!"

She ducked her head and squeezed her eyes shut. The car cleared the track, swerving back into its own lane. Behind them the train blared past, the force shaking the vehicle like a strong wind.

"Putting distance between us and them," Natalie replied. "That went well."

Rachel clutched the armrests. "Yeah," she said.

Amanda released the door handle. "Ha," she gloated. "I'm sure they're cursing that train now."

"Okay." Natalie glanced in the rearview mirror. "We're safe for a few minutes. Rachel, call my cell phone and find out what happened to Chris."

Rachel dialed the number. "Busy."

"Wait a second," said Natalie, tapping a finger in the air. "How did they know where we'd be? My phone! They must've tapped my phone when they were at Chris's house!"

"Wow," Rachel said. "These guys are good."

"What about 911?" Amanda asked.

"That takes us back to the police," said Jaci.

Natalie nodded. "I don't know if they will help. Rachel, give your phone to the girls."

Rachel stared at Natalie. "Why?"

"Because I want them to call their families."

Rachel pressed her lips together. "I don't have international calling." She tossed the phone to Jaci.

Jaci's fingers flew over the dial pad. She pressed the phone against her ear, listening to it ring. And then the phone gave three quick beeps and turned off.

"What?" she said. "It turned off."

She pulled it away from her ear and stared at it. "It died."

Rachel stuck her hand out. "Sorry."

Jaci slapped the phone into her hand.

"Never mind. Do you girls have identification on you?" Natalie asked.

"No," Jaci answered. "They took our purses."

"I've got some jewelry," Amanda offered, reaching under her shirt and lifting up several necklaces.

Jaci took a second look at the necklaces. The thick diamond cord with five large pearls dangling from it caught her attention. That necklace alone must be worth a fortune.

"Pretty," said Rachel, leaning backwards, "but gaudy. Not my style."

Still focused on the road, Natalie said, "The easiest thing would be to take you to the United States border and let you get across. But the closest port of entry is hours from here."

Sara shook her head. "They're watching us. They'll intercept us."

Natalie tapped her fingers on the steering wheel. "Why do they want you so bad?"

"We walked in on a robbery," said Amanda.

"They want that necklace, Amanda," Jaci said.

Amanda pulled her shirt back down. Not even the large pearls showed under the clothing. "It's our only bargaining chip."

"What about the American Embassy?" Jaci asked Natalie.

"It's in the capital. Only a few hours away. Want to head that way?"

Jaci nodded, icy fingers of fear gripping her heart. "Yes. There has to be someone who can help us."

"Can you describe The Hand to me?" Natalie asked.

"Perfectly," Sara said, an edge to her voice.

"Rachel, write it on a piece of paper. We'll give them a reason to hunt us. The RCMP wants to get a picture identification of this man."

"Okay." Rachel opened the glove compartment. She pulled out paper and pen and wrote down Sara's description.

"Average height. Short, dark brown hair. Deep-set blue eyes. High cheek bones, square jaw."

Natalie turned onto a quiet road, slowing down to match the speed limit. They drove in silence. Jaci kept her face glued to the window, watching the houses and cars roll past them.

"*Vous êtes près de carburante.*" Rachel pointed at the fuel gauge.

Natalie groaned. "Not now."

There was a gas station on the left. "We can't stop," Jaci said, panic creeping into her voice as Natalie pulled up to the station.

"Stay here," Natalie instructed, jumping out of the car.

"Jaci," Sara said. "That man—with the blond hair, in the pick-up truck?"

Jaci looked around and saw the man. His shoulder-length hair was stringy and dirty, and the red truck had a dent above the back wheel. "Yeah?"

"He's looking at us."

He was cleaning his windshield with a squeegee. "Are you sure?"

"No," Amanda answered for her, her eyes closed as she rested her head against the window. "She's just paranoid. Not that I blame her."

"Look!" Sara said.

Jaci squinted. It did appear as though he were staring at them. But why?

He reached into the cab of his truck and pulled out a piece of paper. Pulling out a cell phone, he began to punch in numbers while studying the paper.

Alarm shot through Jaci as she suddenly understood. "He's calling about the reward." She threw open the car door. "We've got to go now. Natalie."

"What?"

Jaci pointed. "We've got to go. He's calling The Hand!"

Natalie hesitated a split second. Then she screwed the cap back on and jumped into the car. "Here we go again."

They sped out of the gas station down the winding road. Jaci kept her eyes trained on the red pick-up. "He's following us."

"Do you hear that?" Amanda asked. "Sirens."

Natalie clenched her teeth and veered left down a residential street. "Girls, I am sorry, but I think the sooner we part ways, the safer you'll be."

"Safe?" Amanda cried. "How will we be safe without you?"

"You won't be safe with me," she retorted. "By now this car and license plate are all over the police radios. They'll chase us down."

"What about the RCMP?" Jaci asked, trying one last time.

"I'm sorry." Natalie jumped a curb, drove through a backyard, and bumped down into another street. "I can't keep you safe. There is no time."

Jaci felt her last shred of hope dissipate. "Are you just going to abandon us?"

"Listen, here's what I'm going to do. I know a place where there is no border control, hundreds of miles of wooded areas with no patrol. I take you to the head of the trail and drop you off. Get across and get home. You will pass over some roads, but very few, it's mostly forest. Don't speak to anyone."

She gestured toward the back of the SUV. "There's a soccer bag of snacks from our last campout. Take it. It's a three-day walk."

Jaci reached behind her and pulled out the bag. She did a quick inspection. Snacks, energy bars, tampons.

An hour later, Natalie pulled the car off the road. The forest dropped away from the roadside, leaving a ravine about six feet deep.

"Come on," she said, putting the car into park and getting out. She led them to the edge of the ravine.

"There." She pointed to a path cutting its way through the large oak and maple trees. "There used to be a cabin about two days into it. We never went there, but maybe you could sleep for a night. It's rumored that the American government has put cameras in all the woods around here. Maybe a patrol will find you."

"Cameras?" Sara lifted her head and examined the trees above them.

Jaci nodded. "All right, you guys, let's go." She paused, and turned to Natalie.

"And Natalie… thank you. I don't know if we'll even be able to contact you again."

"Good luck," Natalie said with a half smile. "I never did find out your real names."

September 19
Idaho Falls, Idaho

"Carl? Are you out here?"

"Yes." The crickets chirped in the trimmed bushes next to the house, and somewhere in the tree line an owl hooted.

Kristin sat down next to him on the steps, pulling her robe closer. He put down his beer can and wrapped his arms around her.

"It's late," she said. "Come inside."

"I just keep going over this in my head. I don't know where to look now. I keep thinking, something's going to fall into place, and I'll know where to go."

Kristin pulled away and picked up his beer, then put it down and began shifting through the pile of pictures on the concrete. "You're drinking."

"Yeah." He tried not to sound defensive.

"You only do that when you're troubled."

Carl shook his head. "Sometimes the dullness can actually bring something into focus, something I'm missing."

"You want a jar of pickles?"

"Not right now."

"Well, what are your leads?"

He spread his hands out on his knees, palms up. "Nothing. The searchers don't know where to look. Nobody else is missing from the girls' school, neighborhoods or churches. Unlikely they ran away with anyone. It's possible that Sara's biological family found her and kidnapped her, though not likely, and they certainly wouldn't take her friends, too. The biggest link seems to be the robbery that happened the same night, at the same place. They have to be connected. The Hand is our first suspect in the robbery, and for the kidnapping as well."

Carl grimaced. "I hate it when the FBI gets involved. The chief bows to them. He'll pull me from the case, or give it to Stokes."

"Hmm." Kristin placed a picture of the four girls, grinning over a lunch table, on the top of the pile. "You called the FBI yesterday?"

"Uh-huh." It had felt like a failure on his part—his way of admitting that he didn't know what to do next. "They haven't been keeping up with The Hand. They've plotted his raids but that's it. Until recently, he wasn't causing enough trouble."

"So what changed?"

"I have no idea, little lady." He brushed Kristin's nose with his. "I can tell you this. The answer is here. I know it is. And I'm going to find it."

"No leads on the hotline?"

"All kinds, most of them bogus." People thought they saw the missing teens everywhere. He had gotten calls from California to Mississippi to Maine. Even a few from random places like Portugal.

"Are you following through?"

"Of course. First thing we do is call the police department of the city in question and send out a squad. Everyone's looking for these kids." The girls should've been found by now. If they were still alive.

"Maybe he separated them."

He grunted, staring out into the night. "Not a good thought. Young girls are worth a lot of money. If he separated them, it means he sold them."

"Oh." Kristin's brown eyebrows lifted, and her eyes pooled with moisture. "I hope that hasn't happened."

Carl stood. "Me, too. I'm going to grab another beer."

She faked a smile and poked his belly. "That's why this is growing."

"Better me than you, hey?"

Her smile disappeared, and Carl winced. He had meant it to

be a compliment on how fit she was, forgetting that recently she mentioned it might be nice to have a baby.

They had agreed not to have kids, but sometimes Kristin seemed unsure. "Hey, forget about that beer," he said. "I'm coming to bed."

She hooked her hand in his. "I'm glad."

Chapter 13

Drizzling rain woke them in the morning. Jaci didn't even remember lying down. Damp leaves and mud clung to her face, dead branches poking her hair and clothes.

Nobody said much as Jaci elbowed her way through a briar patch, making a path for her friends to follow.

The sun drifted higher into the sky. Massive trees grew closer together, and the air felt chillier as the sunlight fought its way through the branches.

Jaci paused to pull her sock up yet again as it kept falling beneath her foot. She switched the duffel bag from one shoulder to the other. The woven strap rubbed her shoulder.

The day wore on. Gnats swarmed around Jaci's face, buzzing in her ears, getting into her nose. She picked several out of her eyes. Talking took too much energy. The three wandered in silence.

Jaci felt her stomach twist angrily within her and thought of the pizza they had eaten at Natalie's the day before. Her mind wandered. She thought of the last time she'd gone bowling with Callie and Seth. Seth had given them a ride and Jaci had not expected him to stay, but he had. After Callie beat them all, Seth took them to buy Slurpees. What she wouldn't give for one of those Slurpees now.

Jaci pulled out of her memory when she bumped into Sara, who had stopped walking. "What's wrong?"

"We've been walking for ages," Sara said. "Can we stop and eat something?"

Amanda looked at her watch. "Wow. It's almost five."

"Okay," Jaci said. "Let's rest."

Ten minutes later they had devoured their rationed amount of food. Still they sat, tired and not eager to begin the journey again.

Sara drew in the dirt with a stick. "Do you think our parents are freaking out yet?"

Amanda looked surprised by the question. "Of course. It's been… how many days has it been?"

Jaci tried to calculate the time in her head.

"How many nights were we at his house?" Amanda asked.

Sara shook her head. "Three or four. Then another in the woods—"

"And last night," Jaci finished. "It's not even been a week, then."

"I'm sure it's all over the news," Amanda said. "When we get across the border, we'll say, 'here we are!' and people will rush us home."

"Let's go." Jaci pushed herself to her feet. "Let's cross the border and test Amanda's theory."

"I'm so thirsty." Amanda hauled herself up. "I need water."

Jaci didn't comment. They all needed water. No point in talking about it.

"I think I hear water." Amanda lifted her head, eyes brightening. "This way."

Jaci and Sara hurried after her, hearing it now, too. Jaci's throat clenched in anticipation until a sick, rotting smell reached her nostrils. She ground to a halt.

"It stinks," said Sara.

Amanda examined the stream trickling past their feet. "It looks fine."

Jaci shook her head, disappointment heavy in her chest. "The water's bad. Don't drink it. Something died around here."

"I really don't think there's anything wrong with it." Amanda knelt down and took a sip. "Tastes fine."

"I won't drink it," declared Sara.

"You guys are dumb." Amanda cupped her hand to her mouth. "Dying of thirst and won't touch water."

A flash of lightning made them look up. Jaci glanced around. The foliage wasn't dry here like in Idaho. The lightning couldn't start a forest fire—could it?

"It's going to rain. You should've waited for *that* water, Amanda," Sara said, and they huddled closer together.

The gathering clouds eroded what daylight was left.

The rain started, but not the same light drizzle from that morning. Thunder clapped overhead, and the water came down in sheets.

Jaci shivered. The rain soaked through her clothing, and a piercing wind cut into her skin. Their body temperatures would soon drop.

"I'm hot," Amanda said.

Jaci looked at her. "How can you be hot?"

Amanda sank into the wet ground. "I don't feel so good." She wrapped her arms around her stomach and rocked back and forth.

Jaci knelt in front of Amanda and touched her face. She felt feverish. "This isn't good."

Amanda pressed her hand to her mouth. "I'm going to puke."

Jaci jumped up and pulled Amanda's hair back, just as she leaned forward and vomited forcefully. She leaned back against Jaci, groaning. Rain ran down her face.

Sara began to cry. "What do we do, Jaci? It had to be that water."

Jaci wiped Amanda's face. "We need to find shelter. We can't stay here like this."

"What about that cabin Natalie mentioned?"

"Let's look for the cabin," said Jaci. "We have to find it."

Amanda jerked forward and threw up again. "I don't think I can walk."

"We'll help you." Jaci beckoned to Sara, and together they helped her up.

Water ran down Jaci's nose, and she stuck out her tongue, welcoming the cool liquid. She and Sara dragged Amanda between them, Jaci's arms burning from the effort.

The ridiculous duffel bag kept banging against her calf. She wanted to leave it behind but knew they'd need it.

The moving was slow. There was nothing in the darkness except rain. Trees came into view only seconds before they reached them.

At last they saw the lights of a house in the distance. They twinkled between the trees, beckoning them forward.

"There it is," Sara cried, pointing. "And there's light. There *must* be people."

Amanda stopped moving her feet. "I can't. I can't. I need a bathroom."

Jaci reached out and clasped one of Sara's hands. "Sara, run to that house and get someone to come back here. We'll wait for you."

She hated to send her by herself, but Sara was the better sprinter.

Holding her stomach, Amanda sank into the dirt and shook with the dry heaves.

They waited. Raindrops dripped onto Jaci's eyelashes, and she brushed them away with the back of her hand. *I shouldn't have sent her. What if something happens to her?*

Worry and guilt gnawed at her stomach as she debated her options. Keep hauling Amanda over the rocks and ground till she reached the cabin? Or leave Amanda behind and rescue Sara? She checked Amanda's watch again. It had only been eight minutes.

Time ticked by. A sudden light shone on them, temporarily blinding her.

"Jaci, Amanda!" Sara stumbled over a fallen tree and collided with Jaci.

A tall, thin man with graying hair and short stubble on his sunken cheeks followed behind Sara

"Sara!" Jaci smothered her in a hug. She turned towards the grim, specter-like figure at her side. "Is this our help?"

Sara nodded. "He and his wife don't speak English, but he could tell I was in trouble. I think they were getting ready for bed. They'll help us."

"How can we be sure?"

Sara looked at her, hazel eyes wide and solemn. "I just know."

Jaci nodded as the old man picked up Amanda. "I hope you're right."

September 20
Havre, Montana

Carl collapsed face-down on the cheap motel bed, barely able to keep his eyes open. Dust particles floated in the sunlight. The digital clock flashed the time: six in the morning. He needed to sleep, even if just for a few hours.

It was a seven-hour drive from Idaho Falls to Havre, Montana, but he had done it in less than six. He'd left Idaho as soon as the Havre police department called him, telling him they had found a body. They thought he might want to take a look. That was enough for him.

Carl leaned sideways and dug into his vest pocket. He pulled out the familiar pictures, worn around the edges and smudged with fingerprints. Callie Nichols, a pretty, blue-eyed brunette with wire-framed glasses.

He picked up the motel phone and dialed Kristin's cell.

"Hello?" Her voice was groggy but awake. She would be getting ready for work.

"It's me." He cleared his throat, trying to shake away the heaviness.

"I know." Sounded like she had bobby pins in her mouth; the words came out unclear. "What news?"

"It was one of the girls."

"Oh, Carl." The bobby pins came out. "Are you sure?"

"Yes."

"What happened?"

"Gunshot."

"I'm so sorry." Kristin paused. "What now?"

Carl shrugged. Chances were small that the call would be intercepted, but on his cell phone he always had to be careful. "I've got a new lead."

"Are you staying there?"

"No. I'm coming home. I'm sure her parents have been informed, and I want to pay my respects. Plus I need to get ready for another trip."

"Okay. When will you be home?"

"Tonight." Sleepiness descended upon him like a blanket, and he rubbed his eyes. "Gotta go, Babe. Drove all night."

"I know. See you tonight, then."

"Yeah." He hung up the phone, then sat there staring at it for a moment. Grabbing a pillow, he pulled it over his head the way Kristin always did.

He needed to sleep, and afterwards he would arrange for the body to be transported back to Idaho. There'd be an autopsy, but it was a formality. The girl had died of a gunshot wound to the back of the head.

At least he had a lead. The highway continued north into Canada, and Havre was less than an hour from the border. He was certain that was where they were going.

It wasn't over yet. If The Hand's lair was in Canada, it would explain why they hadn't found any trace of him in the States.

As soon as he got back to Idaho, he would make sure his passport was in order.

Chapter 14

Jaci rolled over on the soft couch, gradually coming out of a sleepy haze. Reality descended upon her with a cold somberness and she sat up, plunging her feet onto the wooden floor. A hand touched her arm, and she turned to see Sara lying on the floor next to her.

"It's okay. We're safe here," Sara said.

Where was here? Jaci took in the large sitting room, the wood-paneled walls, and the old piano. The house creaked from footsteps on the floor above them.

"We're in the cabin," said Sara.

"Where's Amanda?"

"Shh." Sara pressed a finger to her lips and pointed at Amanda, who slept on a pink quilt in front of a cast-iron wood stove. "She quit throwing up a few hours ago."

"Are we safe?"

"I've been exploring. There's no electricity here, no phone lines, no cars, and they don't speak English."

Jaci smiled and lay back on the couch, pulling the blankets up to her chin. Nobody knew they were here. "How long have you been awake?"

Sara shrugged. "An hour. Want to see the house?"

Jaci kicked off the blankets. "Sure." She glanced around the single room, taking in the carpet rug and the single-pane windows.

She tried to remember the night before. The old man and the old woman helping them inside, the man taking Amanda into another room, and the woman getting blankets for them.

"Where are the old people?"

Sara pointed up a narrow staircase. "I think their room is upstairs."

She led Jaci into the front room. A table and piano decorated it. The wooden piano sat against the wall, three candles on top of closed keys.

"The parlor." Sara waved her hand around. A lantern hung unlit on the wall. "No lights anywhere."

She pulled Jaci over to a window. "Look out there." She pointed at a wooden shack in the trees. "An outhouse."

A gasping groan carried from the other room, and the two girls hurried back.

Amanda sat up, head in her hands, wavy auburn hair falling over her face. Her head shot up when Sara's foot creaked a floorboard. Relief flooded her bloodshot eyes. "There you are."

Footsteps sounded on the ceiling above them, and then heavy steps descended. The three girls watched the stairwell.

The man appeared first, tall and thin, eyes sunken in his head, lips formed into a grim line. Without looking at them, he clomped across the room in his big black boots and out the front door.

The woman came next. She wore a large pink dress. Tying an apron around her waist, she stopped, touched Amanda's forehead, gave a nod, and padded into another room.

"How do you feel, Amanda?" asked Sara.

The girl shook her head, her skin pasty white. "Not great. But better. At least the dry heaves have stopped."

"I'll see if I can get you some water," Jaci said.

She wandered into the kitchen, where cool air drifted in from an open window. She stepped up to the woman who tossed oil and flour together in a bowl.

She cleared her throat and touched the woman's hand.

The woman stopped making dough and looked at her.

"Hi." Jaci licked her lips and patted her chest. "I'm Jaci. Jaci."

The woman nodded and pushed a strand of gray hair back into her bun, leaving a streak of flour on her forehead. "Silvet."

"Can I have water?" Jaci mimed drinking from a cup. "Water?"

Silvet opened a cupboard door and pulled out a wooden cup, putting it down on the counter with a clunk.

Jaci hesitated. Was she supposed to just take it?

Silvet went back to her dough.

Jaci picked up the cup and looked for the fridge. None, of course. No faucet either. Now what?

The woman noticed. With a sigh, she took Jaci's hand and led her outside. She pointed to a stone structure several yards from the house, then went back inside.

Jaci stared at the rafter with a rope and a bucket hanging from it. A well. She should have known.

After two days, Amanda was better but still nauseous and unable to eat. She did, however, keep water down.

Jaci helped Silvet drape a sheet over the clothesline. Sara stood at another line, hanging dresses and long johns.

Sara hadn't spoken much since the first day they had arrived. And Silvet responded in grunts, if anything.

Silvet left the wooden bucket of wet clothes between the two lines and marched back into the house.

Jaci paused, hand poised to secure another sheet.

Sara blinked, pushing a strand of hair out of her face. The wind blew it back again. "Is she done out here?"

Jaci watched the back door, but the woman didn't reappear. She gave a shrug and finished pinning up the sheet. "Looks like it."

"Humph." Lately, Sara seemed like a taut rubber band, ready to snap at any moment.

The wind picked up and Jaci shivered. "Maybe it'll rain again."

It had rained every night since they arrived. The cabin rattled with the thick drops, wind blowing hard enough to shake the rafters.

A movement near the pumpkin patch flashed through Jaci's peripheral vision. She stiffened.

"What?" Sara said, eyes on her.

"I thought I saw something." Jaci dropped to the ground, using the clothes bucket as a shield. Sara followed her lead, her face ashen.

Jaci crept forward, heart pounding. Was she imagining it? Or had someone come out of the woods and hidden in the pumpkin patch? She crouched, clinging to the brown grape vines and peering through the posts.

The dirt crunched behind her and Sara screamed. Jaci grabbed a rock and whirled around, ready to pummel someone to death.

Sara sat with her hands clamped over her mouth, her face red. Next to her stood the old man, stooping to pick up the bucket of wet clothes. He frowned at Sara.

Jaci let out a short laugh and dropped her rock. The old man.

Why did he sneak up like that on them?

He took the bucket to another clothesline and began hanging up the clothes, ignoring the girls.

Sara pushed herself to her feet, tears pooling in her hazel eyes. "Stupid. Stupid, stupid, stupid." She turned around and ran for the house.

By the fifth day, Amanda was eating again.

Jaci brought water into the kitchen and lit a candle. If the water was hot enough and she scrubbed really hard, the food came off the dishes easily, and even faster than in a dishwasher. Almost therapeutic.

Sara came in with a sigh, putting a lantern on the counter and picking up a towel and a dish. "We've got to get out of here." She dried the dish and put it away.

Jaci handed her another one. "We'll leave soon. We haven't been here that long."

"He's going to find us, Jaci. We've got to go."

"But he doesn't know about this cabin."

Sara let the plate drop into the cabinet with a clink. "He'll find it."

"Maybe he doesn't care anymore." Jaci stared into her reflection in the bowl she washed. Her almond-shaped brown eyes stared back at her, unblinking.

Sara snorted. "Yeah, right. Silvet doesn't care if we stay or leave. We're helping out around the house. That's all that matters."

"At least we know her name," Jaci tried to joke, but it fell flat. They knew nothing about the old couple except for their names.

"They don't talk. Not even to each other. It's like they're tele-pathic or something."

The flame in the oil lamp flickered, and Jaci pulled her hands out of the hot water to extend the wick.

The man spent all day working his crops, the woman doing tasks around the house. Jaci wondered if the Canadian government knew these people existed, if anyone knew they existed.

"We leave tomorrow," said Sara. "We can't stay."

Jaci wasn't ready to go. She felt safe here. She needed more time to prepare for what was ahead. She racked her mind, trying to find a reason. One more day. Just one more day.

Sara threw the towel on the counter. "I'm going to bed. Tomorrow will be busy." She walked away.

Sara was right. They had to keep moving. They couldn't stay here forever. But the uncertainty of being out in the world again frightened Jaci.

September 24
Shelley, Idaho

Carl squinted against the bright sunlight coming from the eastern side of the graveyard. A few colorful leaves drifted around the hole in the ground, indicating that fall was close behind.

It looked like the whole town of Shelley had shown up for the funeral. Carl swallowed and worked hard to keep his face straight.

The preacher finished up his words and closed his Bible. Someone said a prayer. Carl watched them lower the white casket into the ground. A young, beautiful girl lay in there, cut off before her time was done.

Beside him Kristin wiped her eyes. Mrs. Nichols gathered her younger children around her and sobbed.

A line formed to pay their respects to the Nichols family. Carl waited his turn. He had news from his trip to Canada that he hoped would be some sort of condolence.

Kristin touched his arm. "I'll wait at the car."

He nodded. "Okay."

The line dwindled down. He put on his best business face and approached the Nichols family.

Mr. Nichols saw him first. "Detective Hamilton." He reached out and clasped Carl's arm. "Thank you for coming."

"Yes," Mrs. Nichols said, her blue eyes shining like sapphires.

"I'm sorry we couldn't find her before this happened." Carl took it personally every time they lost someone. Especially a kid.

Mr. Nichols inclined his head. "So are we."

"I'll be leaving for Canada in the afternoon. The Alberta flier had a Montreal phone number."

"Do you think the other girls are still alive?"

"If they are, we'll find them. The flier was printed less than a week ago. Obviously they have escaped. At this point they could be running, or someone may have turned them in. Hopefully Montreal will have some answers for me." He looked toward the car, where Kristin waited for him.

Mr. Nichols nodded. "Please let us know. Good luck."

"I'll be in touch." Carl shook his hand and strode away. He hoped that would be the only funeral he attended.

Chapter 15

The day they left, Silvet came into the room and handed an armload of clothing to Jaci.

"Thank you," Jaci said. Silvet walked back out.

Jaci turned the clothes over in her hands, examining them. They were well worn, hand-knitted sweaters. Jaci divided them among the shoulder bags Silvet had given them in exchange for the duffel bag. "I guess it's time to say goodbye."

Amanda shook her head. "I've been saying goodbye all morning. The old man got so sick of me, he locked himself in his room."

Jaci tossed a bag to each of them. "Silvet's already put some homemade jerky and bread into each bag. Should last us a few days, at least. One bag has a flashlight and a compass and another one has matches and candles."

"That was nice of her," Sara said. "Where did they find a flashlight and compass?"

"Beats me. Probably some camper left it behind. The flashlight works, but the batteries won't last long." Jaci took a deep breath. "All right. Let's go."

The girls filed out the front door. The old woman stood waiting on the deck. She turned her cheek to receive a kiss from each girl, then watched them walk down the porch.

Her hand raised in a wave, her mouth moving inaudibly. She went back into the house. The old man didn't even come out.

The girls followed a rough, two-lane road for most of the day. They watched for cars, but few passed. When the road turned west, they left it to continue their southward journey.

As much as they tried to ration the food, that first day they ate all the bread and jerky from two of the bags.

The next day they reached what Jaci assumed was the boundary between Canada and the States—a fence overgrown with trees and bushes.

"Any cameras?" Amanda asked.

They glanced around but didn't see any guards or cameras. Jaci half expected to be stopped as they slid between two old fence posts.

They made it across without being detained. Anxious to get past the fence, they took off into a run, racing several hundred yards before coming to a stop.

"We made it. We're in America now!" They laughed and hugged each other.

The forest continued to draw on in front of them, with no end in sight, and finally they trudged silently onward. Nightfall came, and they were still in the forest.

All of their food was gone. Jaci's stomach twisted in hunger, so violently that she thought she would gag. And it was cold. She pulled Silvet's pink sweater out of her bag and yanked it over her head.

"I saw a movie once where a homeless man put newspapers and leaves in his clothes," Amanda said. "At night. For insulation."

"Worth a try." Sara scooped up dried leaves and stuffed them down her shirt.

Jaci grabbed her own handful. "I guess we're stopping, huh?"

No one answered. Jaci took that for a yes. She lay down and wrapped her arms around herself, burying her head under arms.

September 26
Montreal, Canada

"Can't you at least tell me who printed this ad?" Carl tried hard to keep the frustration from his voice. He had visited five police stations in the past two days, all proving as unhelpful as this one.

He had a horrible craving for one of those giant, arm-sized whole dill pickles. His mouth puckered in anticipation.

The officer peered at him from under the rim of his red cap. "We don't keep a record of ads printed in the newspaper." His thick French accent dripped with sarcasm. "Did you try the newspaper office?"

Carl bit back a retort. Nobody at the Toronto Sun had been able to give him any information. The address they had on file was bogus; the name equally so.

Carl was reluctant to call the phone number on the ad and risk tipping his presence to The Hand.

"What about Officer Fayande? Is he here? He was listed on the ad, and the online directory said he works in this department."

The man stiffened ever so slightly. "I don't know the name."

Red flag. "Let me speak with your superior." Carl pulled himself up to his full height, trying to appear imposing. He didn't have any power or jurisdiction here, and the Montreal officer knew it.

The man stepped into a glass-enclosed office. Carl took the opportunity to lean over the desk. He didn't touch anything, but his eyes flicked over the papers.

There had to be something. If the phone number was from Montreal, The Hand lived close by. Or at least had a hide-out close by.

Not that he expected The Hand to be making waves here. No, of course not. This was home. He would want a safe haven. And privacy.

Carl straightened. Maybe he was in the wrong place. Maybe he should be checking with the department of land and agriculture instead of the police station.

A noise behind him made him turn. The officer stood by the door to the glass office. "The chief will see you now."

Carl stepped away from the desk, giving his best innocent expression. "Thank you." He entered the chief's office, pulling the door closed behind him.

The man behind the desk leaned back in his chair, putting his fingers together and raising an eyebrow. One corner of his mouth curled upward. "I am Chief Pierre. How can I help you?"

Carl pulled out his badge and slapped it down in front of the man. "I'm Detective Hamilton, from the Idaho Falls police department. Two weeks ago, these four girls went missing."

He slapped down the picture of all four girls. "Last week, the Toronto Sun printed this flier." He slapped down the flier with pictures of the three surviving girls.

"I have reason to believe that their kidnapper lives here in Montreal. Why can't I get any information?"

The man kept his steely gray eyes on Carl, not even looking at the pictures. "I don't know what you expect us to do. I haven't seen the girls. We didn't print the flier."

"But you saw the flier!" Carl slammed his fist down. "You knew those were the girls. Did you start a search for them to counteract this ransom?"

Pierre's lips pulled down in a sneer. "I do not follow the U.S. news enough to know that those were the girls. Nor did I pay much attention to the flier. I hadn't seen any girls, after all."

"What about this man?" Carl pointed to the name under the flier. "Officer Fayande is the contact on the flier. May I speak to him?"

If Carl hadn't been watching for it, he might not have noticed the brief conflict in the chief's eyes. "He is away on business."

So Fayande *did* work here. "Is this number on the flier his phone number?"

"I will have him call you as soon as he returns." The words came out hostile.

Carl straightened up slowly. Pierre's attitude wasn't making sense. He should be apologetic, sympathetic, helpful. Instead he was—condescending and defensive. *He's covering something.*

Carl kept his face neutral. If the man knew that he suspected, any chances of finding answers would slip away.

"Thank you for your time." Carl pulled back the pictures and his badge.

Pierre's face relaxed. "Good luck on your search."

"Same to you." Carl ducked out of the office. The pieces were here. He just had to put them together.

He stepped outside into the busy sidewalk, moving out of the way of pedestrians. He walked to a bus stop and waited.

The girls had been here one week ago. Had someone called and turned them in? Or had they made it out of town? And if so, where would they go?

To the States, of course. They would make a beeline for the U.S.

He could call the number listed on the flier, but not from his cell phone. He didn't know if he would be calling Officer Fayande or The Hand. Even though it was restricted, the number could be traced.

What were the police hiding? What did they know?

The bus arrived, and he climbed on. He hoped he would have better luck with the RCMP.

Chapter 16

The girls slept longer than expected.

Jaci was hungry. Her body felt sluggish, unable to function. She lifted her head from her arms and noticed pools of water on the curled brown leaves in front of her. She picked a leaf up and licked it. "There has to be water around here. For the wildlife."

Amanda slung a shoulder bag across her body. "Let's find it then."

They picked the leaves out of each other's hair before starting off again.

We're so quiet, Jaci thought. Her legs ached, her shoulders were raw from the bag, and her stomach cramped.

It was spooky out there. They jumped at squirrels rushing, and birds rustling through branches sent them whirling around, trying to identify the source.

The forest continued in front of them, exactly the same as behind them. If it weren't for the compass, they would have no idea where to go.

"I'm so thirsty," said Sara.

"We can go up to three days without water," Jaci said, trying to be encouraging. "We had water yesterday when it rained."

Sara paused. "Wait. Listen."

There was a whispering. Definitely a creek of some kind. The girls quickened their pace.

Jaci was so intent on reaching the water that at first she didn't notice the other sounds. She grabbed Sara's arm, pulling her to a stop.

"People."

Amanda moved past them. "People aren't a bad thing."

"But we have to know what we're going in to."

Voices reached Jaci's ears. Children's voices.

"It's a park." She hurried forward, arriving at the small stream. Only a foot deep but six feet across, the fast-moving water bubbled over rocks and branches as it hurried downstream.

Jaci knelt down and scooped the water up to her mouth.

Amanda stopped beside her. "How do you know that water's good?"

"It smells good."

Sara joined Jaci. "Good enough for me."

Amanda looked out over the water. "I'll pass. Let's just get across. There's people. We can get real water." She stuck her foot in the stream and gasped. "It's cold."

Jaci stood, having quenched her thirst. "Just go."

The water was freezing. Jaci winced as it slipped into the gaps in her shoes and stung her ankles.

Children laughed and played several yards away from them, squealing as their fathers pushed their swings.

The playground was in the middle of a glade, forest on one side and landscaped flower gardens on the others.

Across the street, houses lined the park, clustered close together. A parking lot cut across the glade. It was full of cars, from mid-size sedans to full-size vans.

And every single one of them read 'Vermont' on the license plate, with the words "Green Mountain State" beneath.

Across from the park, suburban houses offered plenty of sidewalks and shade. A walking trail wound around the park and through the flower garden.

Sara stepped onto the cobbled pathway. "We need to get back into hiding." She glanced back at the children playing, now too far away to hear clearly, and quickened her pace.

"Into hiding?" Jaci frowned at her. "Now's when we need to get help."

"Look, a payphone!" said Amanda. She rushed toward it, tripping on a broken piece of the sidewalk.

"No." Sara blocked the phone. "Not the phone. They've tapped the lines."

"What?" Amanda furrowed her brow.

"She might be right," Jaci said, trying to remember what she'd heard from The Hand. "He said he knows who our families are. Let's play it safe."

They were too close to Canada. The Hand would know the

quickest route from Victoriaville to the United States. They needed to put distance between themselves and the border.

Amanda shrugged. "Fine. Let's find the police department."

"The police?" Sara shook her head. "I don't think that's safe either."

Amanda poked her. "We're in America now. Nobody owns the police here."

"Do you girls need help with something?"

Startled, Jaci turned. She hadn't heard the black car pull up next to them.

A man leaned across the passenger side, one hand on the steering wheel as he rolled down the window. He squinted against the sunlight and smiled at them. His dirty-blond hair and tanned skin gave him a handsome, rugged appearance.

"Why would we need help?" Jaci asked, her guard up.

Sara slid closer, nearly disappearing behind Jaci.

He shrugged. "You look a little lost."

"Who are you?" Amanda asked.

He stuck his hand out the window. "Kyle. How can I help?"

"You can't. We're fine." Jaci grabbed Amanda by the elbow and started to pull her back.

"Wait." Amanda yanked her arm back and stood her ground. "Can you tell us how to get to the police station?"

He nodded. "I sure can. It's about six blocks from here. Go straight two blocks and turn left at the stop sign. You'll see it by the fire station."

He paused and added, "Or I can just give you a ride. It'll be faster."

Sara, still cowering behind Jaci, cried, "No!"

Amanda shook her head, taking a step back from the car. "No, thanks. We'll walk."

"Are you sure? It'll take five minutes. Here, come on, get in."

Red flags went up in Jaci's mind. "No. We'll be going now." Her leg muscles tensed, ready to run.

His smile disappeared. The back door opened and another man got out. Dressed in a black suit with sunglasses, his short black hair matching his ebony skin, he looked strong and threatening. He stood against the car and pulled a small gun from inside his jacket.

"I'm not inviting," Kyle said. "I'm ordering. I haven't wasted two weeks of my time watching the border for nothing. You took some-thing from The Hand, and he's not stopping till he gets it back. Cost my buddy his life. No fussing and no one gets hurt."

"We don't know what you're talking about," Amanda said, her eyes wide.

"We'll give it to you." Jaci grabbed at Amanda. "Just leave us alone!"

The black man wrapped a hand around Jaci's wrist and spoke in a deep voice. "Is this the one we want?"

"One of them. Get her in the car."

Sara made a strangled noise. With a scream, she bolted across the street.

The man hugged Jaci to his chest and aimed his gun at Sara.

"Not her," Kyle yelled. He jumped out of the car and pushed the man's arm to the left.

Sara disappeared into a yard with no fence.

"Hey!" A man from the park called out. "Is everything okay?"

"Fine." The black man yelled back, his voice deep and throaty. He tried to hide the gun behind his body.

The man started to jog forward, a few other people following him.

The black man was distracted, and that was all Jaci needed.

She pushed up the sleeve of his suit and bit his arm. She felt the skin break, tasted blood, but clung like a mad dog.

The man jerked his arm away with a grunt, and she scrambled backwards, stumbling over broken pieces of sidewalk. Stooping, she picked up a chunk of concrete and threw it at his gun hand, hitting him.

He dropped the gun, and Amanda snatched it up. She pointed the gun at the two men, waving it back and forth.

They froze, watching her warily, and keeping an eye on the people approaching from the park. Kyle's hand started to slip into the car, and Amanda aimed right at him. "Hands on the hood!"

Kyle smirked as he slid his hands onto the car. "You don't even know how to shoot that thing, Missy."

Amanda pointed the gun toward the sky and pulled the trigger. The smirk disappeared.

Kyle jumped back into the car. "I know where you're going. You have nowhere to hide."

The other man barely had a chance to jump in before Kyle hit the gas and sped away.

Amanda stared after them, her hands shaking. She opened her hand and the gun hit the sidewalk with a clunk.

Someone grabbed Jaci's shoulder, and she whirled around with a gasp. It was the man from the park.

"Did he hurt you?" the man said.

"N-no." Jaci shook her head. "We're okay."

Another man hurried toward them from a house across the street. "Are you okay?" he shouted. "I just called 911. The police will be here in a second."

They had to get out of there before the police showed up. Kyle might be bluffing, but they couldn't take the chance.

"We have to go." She pulled away from the first man. "Thank you."

She took Amanda's arm and pulled her across the street. "We have to find Sara."

A woman ran out onto the sidewalk in front of them, her brown hair pulling loose from its clip. "Girls, you can't leave. You have to tell the police what happened."

"No, we don't. We need to go." Jaci tried to move past her, but the woman danced in front of them.

"You're witnesses, and he's still out there!"

Jaci jerked Amanda to her side and pulled her around the corner, away from the crowd.

They headed in the direction Sara had gone, running past several houses before coming to one with no fence.

A puking noise from the backyard attracted Jaci's attention. Sara knelt next to the house.

She looked at Amanda, accusing. "Natalie said don't talk to anyone. Don't trust anyone. Why can't you listen, Amanda?"

Amanda shook as she sank into the leaves. "I'm sorry," she said. "It won't happen again."

Sara pressed her forehead into the wall. "We can't trust anyone. We can't go to the police."

"Maybe he's bluffing," Jaci said.

"Nowhere," cried Sara. "He'll find us. We can't go anywhere."

Thunder rumbled overhead and dark clouds covered the sky.

Jaci pulled on Sara. "We've got to go. We need to find a place to lie low and hide for tonight."

They wandered through backyards, staying out of sight. They heard the sirens of police cars. Jaci wanted to talk to an officer, but she didn't know who was good and who was bad. It was foolish to take the chance.

Finally the police sirens faded away. They stuck to hedges and shadows for several blocks, until the rain started to fall.

They found a large house with a deck for cover. It was an older house, with a light pink stone exterior. There were no cars in the driveway and all the lights were off.

They huddled on the concrete porch under the deck, trying to keep dry. Rivulets of water ran through the dirt around the porch, and the tree branches shivered with the force of the rain.

"What time is it?" Jaci asked.

Amanda glanced at her watch. "Three p.m." She turned to a white deck chair and sank into it.

"Maybe we should start traveling at night," suggested Jaci, pulling another plastic chair up next to Amanda. "We have a flashlight."

Amanda shook her head. "Bad idea. Nights are dangerous. Bad things happen. And with a flashlight, anyone can see us." She opened her backpack and dug around. "Looks like I'm out of food, ladies."

"You're not the only one," Jaci said. "Let's just stay here the rest of the evening. Even if anyone comes home, they won't be lounging outside in this weather."

"One thing I'm wondering," Amanda said, her eyes on the water spilling from the roof, "why did they want you, Jaci?"

She could feel both sets of eyes on her. So they had noticed that. "I don't know."

"No idea?" Sara asked, suspicion in her voice.

She wonders if something happened to me like what happened to her. "I don't know," she repeated. "But I did hear them say something once, back at the house in Canada."

"What?" Amanda asked.

"I heard The Hand say that I was Gregorio Rivera's daughter."

They sat in silence, watching the rain pour off the roof.

"How do they know your dad?" Sara asked.

"I don't know."

Amanda turned cold green eyes on her. "Exactly what does your dad do when he goes out of town?"

"He—helps businesses. With their auditing, their accounting."

"Then how would The Hand know him?" Sara asked, her brow furrowed in a slight frown.

"Maybe that's not really what he does." Amanda's voice was dark.

Jaci had nothing to say to that. Her own questions plagued her. She hugged her knees to her chest and rocked her body. She wouldn't tell them the nickname they had for her father.

After awhile she got used to the cold, and the constant patter of the rain became almost melodic. "It's peaceful here."

Amanda nodded, purple rings under her eyes making her look sickly. "Yeah. It makes me feel calm."

Tears welled up in the corners of Sara's eyes. "It feels so clean."

Amanda said, "Hey Sara, didn't your adoption certificate say you were born somewhere out here?"

She shrugged. "Yeah. Some small town in New York."

"New York's just west of us. We could try to find some of your relatives."

"I don't have any relatives."

Amanda waved her off. "Sure you do."

"I don't want to. If they wanted to see me, they could have found me. End of story."

"Well," said Amanda, "we have to go west anyway. We'll cross through New York."

"We need a map," Jaci said. "We can stop at a gas station and get one. And food. We need food to make a trip like that."

September 28
Westmount, Quebec

Carl poured over the huge wall map of Quebec in the Westmount RCMP office. The city of Montreal and its surrounding suburbs took up most of the state.

Inspector Ancelin had been assigned to the case. He studied the flier in his hand, his brow creased. The red jacket he wore suggested the British history behind the RCMP. "We should've been notified of this flier."

Carl tried to hide his annoyance. "Well, doesn't anyone in your office get the Toronto Sun?"

"We get the national paper, The Globe and Mail. Only if we're looking for something particular will we buy our own individual papers."

"Ah." Carl turned back to the map, his mind racing.

Had The Hand known that? Had he placed the ad in the paper he knew the RCMP wouldn't read? More and more, it looked like The Hand had an important connection somewhere.

Ancelin stepped up to the map. "The girls could take any of these roads out. However, they would've been stopped at the border. To avoid detection, they might have traveled through the uninhabited forestland," he pointed on the map, "and come out somewhere in Vermont."

Carl held his breath. They had left Canada, all right. He was certain of it. "The day this flier printed—were there any calls into your office?"

"About the girls?" Ancelin shook his head. "None that I recall. The police may have received a few. I can pull up the logs and see."

"I'd like to leave the police out of this. If we can." Carl chose his words carefully. He doubted the RCMP would take kindly to an American being suspicious of the Canadian police force.

"Well, let me pull up the logs for all the calls we got here for the past several days."

It was a tedious process, reading the brief call descriptions.

After several hours Carl's eyes began to burn. He didn't even know what he was looking for, but his instincts told him there was something here.

A quarter after five in the evening, Ancelin yawned and stretched. "Coffee?"

Carl nodded, not looking up from the computer screen. "Please."

His eyes were swimming. Everything was listed in French and English. He was getting too tired to focus on the words when the word "kidnapped" leapt out at him.

He pushed the back button and the screen popped up again.

"September 22. 0900 hours. Rachel Brosseau reports missing friend, Natalie Denis. Missing two days. Natalie's boyfriend not answering phone calls. Believes they've been kidnapped.

"Action taken: recorded phone number and all addresses involved. Contacted Montreal police. Police agreed to send out a patrol. Report from police: Natalie with boyfriend. Wanted privacy. Returned call to Rachel, left message. Case closed."

On the surface it looked perfectly normal, easy to see why the case was closed. But it didn't feel right. Why hadn't Rachel answered the return call? Could be any reason. No big deal, just leave a message.

A quick conversation with Rachel would rule this out. He pulled his phone out and dialed the number listed in the record.

It rang once and then went to voicemail. A female voice launched into a chirpy recording, followed by a beep.

Carl hung up, a knot of dread building in his stomach. "Inspector."

Ancelin walked in, carrying two cups of coffee. "What did you find?"

Carl was busy jotting down addresses. "I need to get to these addresses and talk to this girl. Her friend saw something. Maybe Rachel knows about it."

Ancelin peered over his shoulder and grunted. "Victoriaville. Small city. About two hours from here."

Carl jumped up. "Then we better get going."

Carl tried not to get his hopes up as he and Inspector Ancelin approached the last address on the list. Natalie's boyfriend, Chris, was their final hope.

The other houses had held no answers. The apartment still had two girls living in it, but they hadn't seen or heard from Rachel for almost a week. They weren't worried because she often took trips without telling anyone.

Natalie's house had a family living in it. Her sister and her sister's husband, or something like that. Natalie hadn't been home in days. But when they had called the police, the police had told them that they had already investigated her disappearance. She and her boyfriend had gone on a secret rendezvous.

Same story the police had told the RCMP. But Carl didn't buy it. Where was Rachel now?

Ancelin had been on his cell phone ever since leaving Rachel's apartment. His voice was snappy and urgent while he spoke with different men in his department. He parked the car at the last address and hung up.

Carl looked at him. "What do you think?"

"It's too convenient that they all went on vacation at the same time."

Carl nodded. "Let's see what we find here."

Carl rang the doorbell to the slender townhouse and waited. No answer. Frustrated, he reached out and tried the door. It opened.

Ancelin shook his head. "We can't go in."

"Maybe you can't," Carl grunted. "But nothing's stopping me."

He stepped into the apartment, taking in the hospital smocks on the sofa and the shoes in the corner.

The bedroom had an unmade twin bed in it. A bag of chips lay open on the dresser. Socks and pants littered the floor.

Pulling open dresser drawers, Carl ran his fingers under clothing, looking for anything out of the ordinary.

He went into the bathroom. The toiletries were gone. First clue. Gone out of town.

He wandered into the kitchen, spotting Ancelin hovering in the doorway. Carl opened the fridge. Old food. He stepped around the table and stopped short. A slick, new Blackberry sat by a dirty plate. Carl frowned and picked it up. Now that was odd.

"Anything?"

"A phone." He waved the Blackberry. Nobody would go out of town without bringing this along. "Something's going on. I want to ask the neighbors if they saw anything."

"I'll ask." Ancelin straightened his jacket. "They'll answer me."

Carl followed him out the door, his fingers counting the missing people: Natalie, Rachel, Natalie's boyfriend. Three. Where were they?

Ancelin rapped loudly on the door of the next townhouse.

The door opened, revealing an old woman with crystal blue eyes and wispy gray hair. "*Oui?*"

Carl followed their gestures as they conversed in French, illuminated by the lit street lamp over head—Ancelin indicating the house, the old woman pointing to the road.

More questions. Ancelin handed her a card and moved to his car.

Carl followed him. "Well?"

"It's late. I'll take you to your hotel. But tomorrow we're going to the police station."

"What's going on?" asked Carl.

"Chris stopped by her house. Asked her to keep his cat. He had on a backpack and said he was going on a trip for a few days. She agreed to take the cat. He was walking away when a police car pulled up. He turned and ran. They gave chase and forced him into the car. Caused quite a commotion."

Ancelin squealed out of the parallel parking space. "The police are lying to us."

Carl slipped his fingers into the handhold and looked out his window, glad that he hadn't been the one to suggest the idea.

Chapter 17

Jaci curled up tighter, shivering and feeling cramped. Uncurling her arms, she tried to stretch, but tumbled off the porch into the dirt. "Ow!"

She heard Sara laugh.

"Sorry," the fair-haired girl said, extending a hand. "Watching someone roll off a porch first thing in the morning is pretty funny."

Jaci rubbed her sore back as Sara helped her onto the porch. No sign of the rain today. It was a clear, beautiful morning.

Amanda stood and stretched. "My whole body aches. Maybe we could sneak to the police station one by one?"

Panic crossed Sara's face. "They'll be watching."

Amanda's lip twisted up. "They can't be watching everyone, everywhere. There must be someone—"

Sara lifted a hand. "Shh."

From inside the house came voices and what sounded like chairs being scraped across a wooden floor. In an instant the girls scrambled off the porch, shoving together against the wall, out of sight from the windows.

"I thought they were out of town," Amanda said.

"Hush," said Jaci, jabbing her in the ribs with her elbow.

Sara's fingers clasped together tightly, her knuckles white, hands shaking. Her eyes were wide, her face pale.

"Sara," Jaci said. "Are you okay?"

Sara focused on her and nodded her head.

Jaci leaned in to Amanda and breathed, "Post-traumatic stress syndrome."

Jaci reached out and put a hand on Sara's arm. "No one's going to hurt us." She glanced behind her at the house, ignoring the sound of laughter and the buzz of voices.

"Let's sneak away. We'll stick to the houses and nobody will dare to harm us in a neighborhood," Amanda said.

"I'll lead the way. We'll go around to the front and walk like normal people." Jaci started to creep forward, the other girls crawling after her. She went around the house and pulled up short.

Amanda came up behind her. "Look at all the cars."

The driveway, lawn, and street seemed to have become a parking lot. Even as they watched, other cars pulled up and stopped next to the house.

"Is it a party?" Amanda questioned.

Jaci frowned and shook her head. "Doesn't make sense. At nine in the morning?"

A young couple got out of their car and opened the back door to get out a baby. The man wore a white shirt and tie, and the woman was wearing a skirt and black heels.

"They look like they're going to church," said Jaci.

"Church?" Sara said.

The three of them looked up at the brick house. Almost on cue, an electric organ began to play the familiar notes of a hymn.

Jaci smiled. "We'll be able to get help here. Come on, let's go inside."

"Okay," said Sara. "If we sneak in the back."

Jaci opened the door and stepped in, followed by Amanda and Sara. The sound of a hymn being sung in broken harmony wafted down the hall.

The girls hurried down the hall, following the singing. They entered a large living room just as the opening prayer finished.

As choruses of 'amen' filled the room, they filed into a row of empty chairs set up in the back. An old man glanced at them, turned away, then turned back to stare.

Jaci felt her face flush pink, but she sat down, avoiding anyone's eyes. She sat on something hard, and she stood up again to pick up the hymn book on her plastic folding chair. There were maybe sixty people in the room, including children.

"That old man keeps staring at us," Sara said. "We aren't safe here."

Jaci wished she could reassure her, but she suddenly felt anxious. "Let's go. We shouldn't be here."

"Agreed," Amanda breathed. "Let's slip out."

Sara put her hymnal down, and the three of them tiptoed from the room, stepping out into the bright sunshine.

A teenage boy ran past Jaci, nearly tripping her.

"Hey, wait," he said, touching Amanda's elbow. He looked about eighteen, athletic build, with reddish-brown hair. His triangular face was very pleasant.

"Yeah, what?" Amanda asked, pulling her arm back.

"You left in a hurry," he said, eyeing them. He stepped closer. "Anyway, my mother sent me after you guys. She said you looked like you needed help. Come and meet her—she's real nice, and she'll help out. Where are your parents? What are you doing for dinner?"

He took Amanda's forearm, already starting to haul her back.

"No." Sara launched herself at him and yanked Amanda out of his grip. "We don't need any help. We're fine."

Both the boy and Amanda gave her startled looks.

"Sara, what's wrong with you?" asked Amanda.

Jaci slipped to Sara's side. "She's right. We can't." She turned to the boy. "Tell your mother thanks for the offer, but no. We really prefer to be left alone. It's kind of difficult to explain."

The boy nodded, looking confused. "You're on the run?" he guessed. "Are you runaways? Done something wrong?"

"Something like that," said Jaci.

"Wait here and I'll get some food from home. You can take it with you."

Amanda nodded. "That's very kind of you."

Jaci hesitated. "We'll wait inside for ten minutes."

"Please don't betray us," Sara said to the boy.

"I'm just gonna go tell my mom. I have to tell her."

They followed him back into the house while he hurried off to find his mom. The girls stood in a corner of the empty entryway.

A moment later he was back with his mother. He glanced at them once, waving slightly, as he and his mother left the building.

The girls watched through the window as they drove away in a big, tan pick-up truck.

Jaci wanted to get a message to him—somehow she had to do so without Sara noticing. Her eyes landed on a stack of pamphlets displayed on the hall table.

"Watch the clock, Amanda," reminded Sara.

"Why? What could possibly happen?" Amanda countered.

"What if we're being watched?" she responded. "What if someone follows them and delays them and they never come back? What if they call the police and tell them where we are?"

Sara bit her lip. "We should never have agreed to this."

"Stop worrying," Amanda said, rolling her eyes. "We need the food. We won't make it without it. We had to take the risk."

Sara didn't reply, but glanced at Jaci.

Jaci froze over the paper she was marking, feeling Sara's eyes on her. She blushed and covered it with her arm.

"What are you doing?"

"Nothing."

"Where'd you get pen and paper?"

She held up the pamphlet. "I tore the paper from here and found the pen on the floor."

Sara narrowed her eyes. "And what were you writing?"

"Nothing," Jaci insisted. "Just doodling." *Please, don't let her ask to see it.*

"Let me see," Sara said, holding out her hand.

The tan GMC pulled up, and the boy climbed out of the passenger seat. A woman came around the other side.

"They're here," Amanda interrupted, getting up and grabbing her bag.

Jaci pocketed the paper and stood, too. They hoisted their bags and hurried out the door.

"My name is Alice," the woman said, handing a loaf of sandwich bread to Sara as they joined her at the door of her truck. "This is my son, Aaron."

The boy nodded at them and handed Jaci a Tupperware of cut fruit. She shoved it into her bag.

"Here is my phone number," Alice continued, handing a slip of paper to Sara.

"Here's some cheese," Aaron said, holding out a package of processed cheese. Amanda took it and put it in her bag. "And sandwich meat." She grabbed that as well.

Aaron turned back to the truck, reaching inside. "And we've got some spaghettios, a can opener, and a small sack of flour. You'll be regular pioneers."

"I'll help," Jaci volunteered, climbing up into the cab.

"Here," Aaron said, handing her the flour. "And here's—"

"Take this," she interrupted, thrusting the paper into his hands. "Don't open it 'til we're gone. Just do what it says." She jumped down before he could say anything.

"And some bottles of water," Alice said, helping Sara load up the bags with water. "Are you sure you won't come over? You girls need help. You can use my phone. Let's call your parents, tell them to come get you. You can stay the night if you want. Come on, you'll fit in the car."

Get in the car. Come with me. Jaci wasn't frightened of this woman. But the words frightened her. She took a step backwards. "We have to go."

"Well—" Alice hesitated. "Well, you've got my phone number. Whatever you need, give me a call."

"Thanks," Jaci said, still trying to shake off the sudden, eerie feeling.

"Let's go," Amanda said, shouldering her bag, now laden with food.

They went around the block as quickly as they could, putting distance between them and the church.

"You know, Sara," Amanda said, running her hand along some bushes, "I think it's good to be cautious, but do we have to be so suspicious of everyone? I mean, we can't walk from here to Idaho with no help. At some point, we have to trust people."

"But not here, Amanda," Sara insisted. "They know we're here."

Amanda turned to Jaci. "What was on that piece of paper you gave him?"

Jaci gave Amanda a warning look, but it was too late.

Sara whirled around. "What? What did you do, Jaci?"

"Calm down, Sara." Jaci rubbed the palm of her hand on her jeans. Sara was making her jumpy. "I just gave him a piece of paper with my phone number on it. I asked him to call my parents and tell them we're okay."

"*Is that all?*" Sara retorted. "Because they probably have the phones tapped. They'll know exactly where we are."

"I'm counting on it," Jaci said. "I said to tell them another family in Vermont befriended us and we are catching a ride to Maryland. From there we'll try to contact them before we continue west."

Sara cocked her head, and then she smiled. "To put them off our trail, huh?"

"Trying. Of course, our parents will have a tizzy when we don't contact them again. And the good guys will be looking for us in Maryland, too. But at least they'll know we're still alive and trying to get home."

"The Hand will look for us in Maryland," Amanda said. "Good thinking."

"Okay." Sara relaxed. "What's the real plan?"

Amanda reached into her pocket and dug out the compass. "We're heading south for at least another day. Then we turn west and cross into New York."

"There's a huge national forest between New York and Vermont," Sara said.

Jaci brightened. "It's perfect. Nobody will find us there, especially if they're focusing on Maryland." She took a deep breath. "Okay. We've got food for several days. Let's make it last."

September 29
Victoriaville, Canada

Carl sat on his hands to keep from fidgeting as Ancelin drove them to the police station in Thetford Mines. Since it was the biggest city close to Victoriaville, Ancelin believed it would've been the Thetford Mines police who arrested Chris.

When they reached the station, Ancelin parked the car and hopped out. Carl hurried after, straightening his jacket and tie as a gust of wind flapped them into his face.

Ancelin burst through the door, brandishing his badge as if the red coat weren't enough to give away his identity. He yelled out orders in French.

A woman stepped out of the elevator and froze, files in hand, eyes wide behind her glasses.

Ancelin spun around. "Detective, wait here. Make sure no one leaves."

Carl crossed his arms over his chest and backed up against the double front doors.

A minute later, the phone rang at the front desk. The officer standing there picked it up and motioned to Carl, who stepped away from the door, a little suspicious.

Carl took the phone, keeping his eyes on the officer. "Hello?"

"Hamilton. Ancelin here. Come up. Take the elevator, second door on your left. We've got some answers."

Carl fought down the jubilant glee that rose in his chest. He crossed to the elevator.

Ancelin had cornered all of the officers into one section of the room upstairs. He closed the blinds and paced in front of them.

"This is Detective Hamilton. I'm going to ask you the same questions I just asked, this time in English. Where are Chris Coton, Rachel Brousseau, and Natalie Denis?"

Ancelin stared at a stout man with a blue police hat and a stubby red beard.

The man shifted. "They are at the courthouse on Rue Saint-Alphonso. They have been detained for questioning."

"On whose orders?"

The man licked his lips and looked away. "My supervisor's."

"For how long were you planning on keeping them?"

"Until told to let them go."

Ancelin leaned in closer. "Why did you lie to the RCMP?"

"A matter of state security. Sir."

Ancelin reared back on his heels. He glanced at Carl. "I've called the RCMP in Drummondville. We're taking the whole station into custody."

Carl nodded. He fingered his belt loop. If this really was The Hand, he was a bigger fish than anyone had imagined. How many people did he have networked up here?

The three young adults looked ill at ease in the RCMP waiting room. The tall girl with short blond hair clung to the boy. The brunette sat slumped forward in a padded red chair, head in her hands, hair covering her face.

Ancelin stood next to Carl, arms tight across his chest. His lips were white and he breathed heavily. Carl had the feeling he wasn't taking the knowledge of a police coup very well.

Carl handed out cups of coffee. "I'm Carl. I'm a detective from the States. I know your names, but I'm not sure who's who. Do you mind introducing yourselves?"

The brunette's head shot up. "We haven't done anything wrong. We shouldn't be here."

"Hey." Carl held up a hand. "It's okay. Calm down. We're here to protect you."

The blond asked, "Are we in danger?"

"I don't know," Carl returned, meeting her eyes. "Tell me who you are and what happened. Do you have any idea why the police might detain you?"

The brunette pointed to the blond. "Ask Natalie."

Carl looked at her. "So you're Natalie? And this is Chris?"

They both nodded. "I know why they wanted us," she said. "I picked up three girls on the road. Turns out they were runaways from The Hand."

"That's what they told us," the brunette put in, narrowing her eyes. "The cops say they are thieves and that is why they arrested us. Harboring criminals."

"Please continue, Natalie." Carl kept his gaze on her.

"I tried to help them. But The Hand found us and trailed us. I lost him and got the girls away. I called Chris and told him to leave town. Then I drove to my house to make sure my sister was okay. That's when they found me. The police, I mean. They arrested me and brought me here."

"Why would the police arrest you?" Carl frowned.

Natalie waved a hand. "Everyone knows The Hand can take what he wants around here. The police don't do anything. Maybe The Hand is the commissioner or something."

Carl raised an eyebrow, feeling his skin prickle a bit. "Chris, how did you get involved in this?"

"Natalie was driving my car. Two men showed up at my house, looking like RCMP, asking me about the car and Natalie. I thought she was in danger and gave them her home address. Sometime in there they took my phone and bugged it, but I didn't know it."

That explained why he had left the cell phone in the kitchen. Carl turned to the brunette. "You must be Rachel."

She nodded.

"How did you get involved in this?"

"Natalie brought the girls to my house. I recognized them from a flier. I thought they were criminals and I called the number to turn them in. When Natalie realized they had my address, we left. I waited two days for Natalie to come home from her sister's house, and she didn't. The only people I trusted were the RCMP, and I called them to report Natalie as missing. Within a few hours I was arrested."

Carl intertwined his fingers and pressed his lips together. "Natalie, where did you take the girls?"

"There's an old trail we used to follow for camping, that takes you over the border. I set them at the foot."

Ancelin's cell phone rang loudly, making her jump.

"Detective." Ancelin's voice cut through the room. "Phone for you. Someone has been trying to reach you."

Carl's hand shot to his belt, and he swore at himself when he realized he had left his phone in the motel room.

He grabbed the phone from Ancelin, checking his watch. It was almost eight a.m. in Idaho. "Detective Hamilton speaking."

"Detective. Chief Miller here. Been trying to call you all morning."

It must be urgent. "So sorry, Chief. I left my—"

"We got a phone call. The girls called home."

Carl froze. "What? When?"

"Last night. Mrs. Rivera called us this morning to tell us. They're heading for Maryland."

Maryland. "Thank you, Chief. I've gotten some leads here in Canada. Let me finish up, and I'll catch a plane back this afternoon. We'll find them."

He handed the phone back to Ancelin, his hands shaking. They were still alive. He allowed a tight smile to cross his face. Now to organize the rescue parties.

Chapter 18

"One state down," declared Jaci.

They stopped at the 'Welcome to New York' sign at the opening of the bridge and savored the distance they had gone. It had taken them three days to find a place to traverse the lake between New York and Vermont.

"How long has it been?" Sara picked up a stick and ran it along the white picket fence in front of a house. The state map they had grabbed at a gas station was tucked under her other arm.

Jaci tried to count all the days they had been gone. "I think it's been about three weeks."

She had never been away from home this long. Her mind flashed back, The Hand's words echoing in her mind. The Carcinero. The Butcher. She shuddered. No one could misinterpret the connotation behind the nickname.

"How long before we're out of food?" Amanda asked.

Hunger gnawed at Jaci's stomach, at her brain, at her eyes. "I don't know. We've rationed it well, but I think we've only got two days left of one slice of bread a day. After that we still have the flour."

"At least there's plenty of water." Sara's now-tangled blond hair fell in her face as she leaned over the bridge.

They followed a southwestern road through a small suburban area. The houses were small and spread out. Even above the fences and rooftops, the tall, clinging branches of forested trees peered over. The one-story houses were built on cinderblock foundations, vinyl siding covering the sides.

Jaci felt open and exposed. She quickened her pace, trying to get through the suburb.

Amanda snorted. "What are we supposed to do with the flour?"

It took Jaci a moment to remember what they'd been talking

about. "You mix it with water and make a gruel."

"Sounds yummy," replied Amanda.

"We're out of luck when the flour's gone. We can probably go a few more days, but then we'll have to stop somewhere and dig through trash or something."

"There won't be trashcans," said Sara. She pointed to a large green blob on the map. "It's a big national forest, one of the largest in the country."

"In the middle of New York?" Amanda scoffed.

"We're not in the middle," Sara said. "We're at the border."

"What's the terrain like?" Jaci peered at the map in Sara's hands.

"Rough. Mountains and valleys."

"And no people?" Amanda asked.

Sara turned the map sideways and squinted. "Some towns, I think. I don't know; it's hard to read the legend."

They had reached the end of the street, and the last house had no fence. The street wrapped around the houses in a circle, going back out to the main road they had left behind. Behind it loomed a dense forest. The tangle of undergrowth and dark towering plant life made the woods in Canada look sparse.

They crossed the yard and stepped into the foliage. Hardly any sunlight peered through the trees.

Jaci shivered and rubbed her arms. "At least we won't run out of water." A tiny stream trickled to her left, and she could hear more water in front of her.

The girls followed Jaci, bending under branches, stepping on thorn bushes, and sliding down small ravines. They were very quiet.

There was no sign of development. "Is it just a forest out here, Sara?" Jaci asked.

"Um…" Sara consulted the map again. "There are some roads that cut through here, besides the towns."

Jaci nodded. "Okay. Let's try and avoid the roads."

As soon as the sun went down, all light in the forest vanished. Amanda pulled out the flashlight, and they walked in a huddled group for a bit.

Mosquitoes buzzed around Jaci's face. She slapped at them. Her shoes suctioned into the mud beneath her, and she lifted her head. A large lake blocked their westward path. Rivulets of water soaked the ground around it and tall water reeds swayed in the breeze.

"Oh, please. Not more water," said Amanda.

"Restroom break." Jaci smashed a mosquito on her arm. "We may as well stop here for the night."

A sudden gasp from Sara made her whirl around. "What?"

Sara's eyes were fixed on a point just in front of them. "I—I thought I saw something."

"Like what?"

Sara tore her gaze away from the trees. "I thought it was a person."

"I'm sure it was just your imagination," Amanda said.

"Everyone calm down, okay?" Jaci said. Her voice trembled and she took a deep breath. She tried to sound confident. "We're safe here. But move away from the water."

Amanda shuddered. "No telling what sort of water animals might be in there."

She picked up a rock and chucked it into the reeds. She held up the compass, pointing the flashlight at the plastic face.

"We can't wade through that water. But if we head south, we're still going in the right direction. Then we can go west again as soon as we get past the lake."

"Sounds good to me," Jaci said. The sooner they were out of the woods, the better.

She lay down in the tall grass and winced as she felt a rock in her back. The grass smelled like freshly turned dirt. "Too bad we don't have any good bedrolls."

"Yeah," joked Amanda. "We need to be more prepared the next time we go to the mall."

The three girls huddled together for warmth. Jaci lay awake, listening for predators, scared to sleep until exhaustion overcame her adrenaline, and she slept.

A fine mist covered the valley in the morning, emphasizing the highs and lows of the hills around them. Jaci mopped at her face with her wet shirt. Her back ached where the rocks had poked her muscles all night long.

They stopped for lunch at noon, still in view of the lake.

Sara put her hands on her stomach, her face gray. "I'm still hungry. I'm so hungry I feel sick."

Jaci was, too. "We'll get used to it."

Amanda took the lead and they followed her around the lake. She held the compass in her hand and checked it constantly.

The shoulder bag weighed Jaci down. She tried to move it, wincing as she did so. She pulled her collar back and glanced at her shoulder. Raw, red skin showed where the bag rubbed her.

Early in the evening the forest began to darken. Amanda pulled out the flashlight. "Should we keep going?"

"No." Jaci shook her head. "Better to travel by daylight, anyway. Save the batteries."

Sara tossed down an empty water bottle. "We're out of water."

Jaci picked it up. "Hold on to these. We'll need to refill them the first chance we get."

"Where, from the lakes we find along the way?" Amanda asked.

Jaci thought of the lake they had left behind. She didn't want to drink any water from it. "No. Later. When we get somewhere. Where's the closest town, Sara?"

"I'm not sure," the younger girl admitted, wrinkling her nose. "I think we're right here." She pointed at the map. "But we could be here." She pointed at another spot.

Her eyes lifted from the map. "Do you hear something?"

Amanda rolled her eyes. "Not again, Sara."

Sara waved a hand at her. "Just listen."

Jaci heard nothing. "What was it?"

"I thought I heard an ambulance, or a fire engine."

"That would mean we're close to a town. Perfect! We need water and food." They had eaten all the bread, the fruit, and the canned goods. The only thing left was the flour.

"Hey," said Amanda. "We're in the middle of a national forest. Surely there's no danger in going to the police?"

Sara frowned, but Jaci spoke up. "You're right. Then we'd get help and they'd protect us—maybe even take us home!"

"I vote we sleep here," Amanda continued, "and tomorrow we make our way into town. All in favor?"

"Aye," said Jaci, raising her hand.

Sara raised hers, too. "Looks like I'm in."

"Okay," Amanda said, throwing herself on the mossy forest floor. "See you tomorrow."

October 3
Pittsfield, Massachusetts

Carl was getting antsy. He had been here for four days now, and other than keep organizing search parties and instructing the police on procedure, he didn't have much else to do.

Even if the girls had traveled twenty miles a day since leaving Vermont, he doubted they had gotten further south than Massachusetts. Just in case, he had men on alert all the way across Maryland's state border.

But as each day passed, the urgency wore off a bit, and he found the men becoming more relaxed, less guarded.

Carl didn't think he could stay here playing watch dog much longer. He couldn't rule out that the girls might come through this way. But what if they didn't?

He stared at the blaring television set in front of him, then picked up the motel phone and called Kristin. It would be cheaper to use his phone, but cell phones were easy to intercept.

Kristin answered, the familiar sounds of an "I Love Lucy" rerun playing in the background. "Hello?"

"Hi Babe." Carl got right to the point. "What do you think? Should I still be here?"

"What are your hunches? Do you think the girls are coming?"

He hesitated. "No, I don't think so."

"Where do you think you should be?"

He pondered the question. He had picked up a jar of Best Maid kosher spears on the way back to the hotel, and he popped the lid off. "I think I need to come home and refocus my efforts. If they find something here, they can call me."

"What about that family who placed the call?"

"They have nothing more to offer."

"Maybe you should go there and refocus. We know the girls were in that town."

Carl sucked on a spear and considered that possibility. "I could go there. I could see if any other people saw them or know which way they went. But there are so many routes they might have taken. I don't know how to narrow it down."

"Sounds like you have too many options."

"There's something bothering me, something nagging at me."

"Hmm."

He could just picture her, phone to one ear, blond hair wrapped around a pencil on top of her head, tapping her jaw.

"Well, you're pretty sure it was The Hand, so you don't have any would-be suspects to question. Do you think there's someone else involved? Someone else who helped The Hand kidnap the girls?"

"I'm still not one hundred percent convinced it was The Hand.

There's no real motive. That's the thing. Why would he go from petty theft to murder?"

"Isn't it just about them being in the wrong place at the wrong time?"

"No." He crunched on a pickle and wiped juice from his forearm. A face formed in Carl's mind, and it took him a moment to recognize it. "Mr. Rivera. That's it. Something about Mr. Rivera."

"I thought he checked out."

"But I didn't do a background check on him. That's what's bugging me."

"Do you have to come home to do your background check?"

Carl shook his head. "I may go to Mexico. Thanks for the help, Babe."

She chuckled. "Anytime. Good luck, Hon."

Carl hung up, mind already jumping to the next task. He pulled out his notes. Gregorio Rivera. Education: University of Pedrita in Zacatecas, business negotiations. Work: International Accounting Alliances.

He pulled out his laptop and accessed the wireless internet. He first Googled 'International Accounting Alliances.'

A website popped up, showing smiling professionals and several pages of services. The central hub was located in Dallas.

He jotted down the phone number and address. Why call if he could just show up?

Next he Googled the University of Pedrita. Interesting. Nothing came up. Next he tried 'universities of Zacatecas.' Still nothing even close to 'Pedrita.'

Certainly Mr. Rivera hadn't made up a university. Quick way to get his cover blown.

Carl pulled his phone back out and dialed the Federal Bureau. "I need a background check ASAP on a Gregorio Rivera."

He leaned back, studying his computer screen. Forget Zacatecas. It was time for a visit to Dallas.

Chapter 19

Early the next morning they crossed a narrow, two-way road. The woods bordered one side of the road with old country homes on the other side. They continued past them, walking on the outskirts of town until the buildings were closer together.

A little before noon they reached the center of town. An old sign posted on the hillside read, "Johnsburg, Population: 2,450."

"Quaint," said Amanda, raising an eyebrow.

Sara looked at the map. "We're in one of the little towns. It's so old. I didn't know places like this still existed."

"Creepy, if you ask me," Amanda said, shaking her auburn waves as they walked past a darkened second-hand store. "There's a reason why they don't exist, except in old horror movies."

"We should be safe going to the police here," Jaci said, casting a glance at Sara.

Sara paused and sat down on a bench in front of a building. It looked like a government building, with big glass windows and tall pillars. "I need to rest a little. Then we can maybe find some food?"

"In the trashcans?" Amanda joked.

"Whatever." Sara put her head in her hands.

Jaci sat down next to her. She studied a long line of cars parked along the curb on both sides of the street.

Amanda shifted her weight from foot to foot. "I'm hungry, and hot."

"I'm tossing this bag." Jaci got up and stepped to a trashcan by the sidewalk. "It's empty and a burden to carry around."

"What if we need it again?" asked Sara.

"Let's put all the water bottles into two bags, and leave the other one behind," Amanda said. "We can take turns carrying them."

"Okay," agreed Jaci. "Put the can opener in the Tupperware and keep that, too. And don't throw away the flashlight or the compass."

Behind them a bell rang, and she looked around in surprise. "Oh, it's a school." That explained the cars.

Kids of all ages began pouring down the steps, oblivious to the girls. Screaming and yelling, the younger children raced past them, dividing between the waiting string of cars and a line of buses. Parents gathered them up; buses herded others away.

The older teenagers formed little clusters, boys shoving each other and acting macho while girls giggled and chattered.

Jaci eyed them enviously. What a nice, carefree life. She didn't think she'd ever be able to giggle and chatter over frivolities again.

Who cared what shirt Poppy was wearing? Who cared if Candice didn't make choir? Who cared if the track team took first at state?

"Let's go," Sara said, standing up and starting down the sidewalk.

"Right." Amanda jumped to her side. "The police department must be somewhere on this street."

"Since it's probably the only street in the town," Jaci laughed, catching up to her friends.

"And about the police thing—" Sara began.

"Look out!" Jaci cried.

Her warning came too late, and Amanda tripped over a boy kneeling on the sidewalk. She stumbled and caught herself.

"Hey," he said, straightening up. He gave a toss of his head as a piece of his straight brown hair fell onto his forehead. "Watch where you're going."

"You were the one kneeling on the sidewalk," said Amanda.

"I was just tying my shoe," he replied. He tugged on his gray sweater, which fit snugly over his broad shoulders.

Amanda ducked her head, her demeanor changing. Grabbing a strand of hair in her hands, she ran her fingers through it, cocking her head to one side. "Oh! Excuse me. I-I'm sorry."

"Hey, that's okay," he said, his voice lightening and giving her a boyish grin, the corners of his deep-set hazel eyes crinkling. "Don't worry about it. I should've put up a warning sign. My name is Neal. What's yours?"

"Oh, I'm...um..." She appeared confused, batting her eyes and staring at him.

Amanda's shirt was dirty, a strand of grass poked out of the top of her head, and a black smudge darkened her cheekbone. Certainly this kid wasn't going to miss that. Such theatrics. "Don't get sidetracked," said Jaci. "The police, remember?"

Sara poked her. "Yeah, Amanda. You're Amanda."

"Amanda. My name is Amanda." She shot Jaci an annoyed look. "I wasn't sure if I was supposed to tell."

"Amanda? What, is it a secret? Are you sure it's your real name?" The boy laughed. "Who are your friends?"

"My friends?"

"Yeah." Neal raised an eyebrow. "Or are these girls just following you around?"

"This is Jaci, and that's Sara."

"Are you new here? Cause I think I know everyone in town. I didn't see you in school."

"No. Just passing through," Jaci answered. "Bye, Neal. Sorry for the inconvenience."

Amanda remained rooted to the spot. "It was nice to meet you, Neal."

He hesitated, and then said, "Well, if you're just passing through, I guess it wouldn't hurt to hang out for a bit. I mean, you look like you could use some lunch...maybe a shower..." He trailed off awkwardly, and Jaci bit her lip to keep from laughing.

So he had noticed their condition. He didn't seem very threatening. Just a boy.

"You know, a shower would be really nice," Jaci admitted. "And lunch. But don't you think your mom would flip?"

"Yeah, so maybe not a shower. But you could freshen up a bit, relax. You've been camping awhile, I guess, huh? My house isn't too far away. Besides, my brother might want to meet you."

Jaci hesitated. They didn't really know this kid, after all.

"Um, no. We need to get going." The thought of food was tempting, but there was no way she would willingly walk into a stranger's house. Sara huddled closer to her.

"Come on," said Amanda, annoyance evident in her voice. "We need to accept help when it's offered."

Jaci ignored her. "So there's you and your brother at your house? Anyone else?"

"Oh, of course," he said. "My grandmother will be there."

Jaci's reluctance faded away. "Oh, well, maybe just a really quick lunch."

They needed food, after all, and this would be better than digging through trash bins. She looked at Sara. "Do you feel okay about that?"

"Do you?"

"Yeah. I think that's fine."

"Great." Amanda swung her arms. "Let's go."

Neal shrugged. "Okay. Follow me."

They stood on the sidewalk, staring at an unkempt, moderate-sized house. The overgrown lawn almost swallowed the front door that didn't fit right, and the paint was peeling off the shutters.

"Who did you say you live with?" asked Sara.

"No one," Neal said. "I mean, we live with someone. With family. We're doing just fine."

Jaci glanced at Sara. "Like, your grandma?"

"Yeah, yeah. We live with our grandma." Neal pushed open the front door and stepped in.

Amanda hesitated in the doorway. He turned halfway and beckoned. "It's okay. Come on in."

The sunlight that filtered in through the bent blinds on the windows revealed a cluttered mess. And it stank of trash and mildew. Neal turned on a light, further illuminating the disorganized house. He poked his head in the kitchen and began calling through the house. "Hello? Anyone home?"

He started down the hall and turned a corner, stepping into another room.

Amanda went down the hall after Neal. Jaci let go of the doorknob and dashed after her, not about to let her out of her sight.

"Ricky, what do you think you're doing?" said Neal, crossing his arms over his chest.

Maroon curtains were pulled shut over the windows, blocking any sunlight from brightening the room. Over in a corner of the dirty red carpet, nearly concealed by the darkness, sat a boy who looked just like Neal, all the way down to his clothes.

He lifted his eyes, rather sheepishly. In his hand was a firecracker, flickering in the dark room. A bucket, a glass plate, and a sleeping bag were the only other objects in the room.

He put the firecracker down on the plate and stood up. "Hey, Collins, what's up?"

"You know you shouldn't be playing with fire. Mom'll have a cow."

Jaci grabbed Amanda's arm and glanced at Neal. *If he'd have said Grandma it would've sounded more natural.* She saw Ricky raise an eyebrow.

Turning to them, Neal said, "Ricky's a pyro. He's not supposed to touch fire or matches. And he knows it, too."

Ricky shrugged. "I like fire. And I'm being careful." He gestured at the bucket full of water. "I've timed it. I'll dunk it before it hits the explosive."

Ricky studied the girls in the doorway. "Who are all of you, anyway?"

"I'm Amanda, this is Jaci, and over there is Sara."

Jaci cleared her throat, crossing her arms over her chest. "We're going now, Neal."

It was clear he was a liar. She didn't feel afraid, just majorly put out. She eyed the boys. "Are you guys twins?"

Ricky grinned, a cocky expression on his face. "Yeah, we're twins. And identical. But I'm Ricky, the cute one who gets all the girls." He raised an eyebrow.

"Quit fooling around. I—" Neal glanced at Jaci. "Mom and Dad said no fire. The consequences are very serious. We've been over this so many times."

"I'm sure you mean your grandma," Jaci cut in dryly. "Since she's the one who lives with you?"

Neal's ears turned pink. "Right, of course, we live with her. But our parents still have a say in things."

Ricky grinned. "You'd think you were the older twin. Nothing to worry about, Collins. Trust me."

Neal stepped over to the firecracker. "Put that thing out."

Ricky picked it up and dunked it into the waiting bucket.

Neal said, "This is my irresponsible brother, Ricky. Are you hungry?"

"Yes—" Ricky began, but Neal shoved him, and he shut up.

"If you don't mind." Jaci's hands shook, and it took all her will power not to let herself into the kitchen.

"Uh, there's not much here," Ricky said, shooting a look at his brother. "We're a little short on groceries."

"We don't mind," she said. "We'll find something."

Neal looked less certain. "I'll show you the kitchen."

The fridge had sour milk and a half-eaten container of yogurt. Sara opened a drawer and a cockroach waddled out.

"Ew," she said, then grabbed a spoon.

Jaci's stomach growled as she yanked open a cupboard. A bag of Doritos. She pulled it down, ripping it open. Ah, the smell of powdery, salted cheese.

"Sorry there's not more," Neal said, his face flushed in the dim kitchen light. "There are lots of places that serve lunch, or there's the deli. We'll take you there. We've got money."

Jaci closed her eyes, feeling the Dorito soften on her tongue. "Anywhere," she said.

She opened her eyes, remembering Neal's original offer of cleaning up. "Um, can I use your restroom first?"

"Peanut butter." Sara climbed off the counter, twisting the lid off a jar, her spoon still in her mouth.

"Oh, sure," said Neal. "Use our parents' though. Cleaner. You can take the peanut butter with you."

The three girls stepped into the master bedroom. Jaci closed the door and locked it. Her eyes fell on an end table near the bed. She stepped to it and tried to pull it across the carpet.

"Amanda, help me," she grunted.

"What are we doing?" Amanda joined her, pushing while Jaci pulled.

"Making sure no one comes in while we're in here." They placed the end table against the door.

Sara turned on the light, illuminating a dusty but well-kept room. Even the queen-sized bed was made. A beautiful hand-woven purple and green afghan dangled over the foot.

"At least it's clean in here. There's your bathroom, Jaci." Amanda pointed.

"We should hurry." Jaci headed for the bathroom. "I don't know if we can trust these boys. They're lying."

"Lots of boys lie." Amanda shrugged. "They won't turn us in, if that's what you think."

It wasn't what she thought, but it made her uneasy. She wanted to hurry and get out of here.

Jaci closed the door behind her and examined the bathroom. It looked like it hadn't been used in weeks.

She turned on the water in the shower. A bottle of shampoo sat neatly on the rim. Either a mom or a grandmother lived here with the boys. They were just normal teenagers, after all.

She filled three water bottles in the sink before stepping into the shower. She showered in under seven minutes, and Sara and Amanda were just as fast.

Half an hour later, Ricky and Neal herded them out of the house. Their clothes were still worn and dirty, but their bodies were clean again.

Jaci tried to remember how long it had been. They had bathed right before leaving the cabin in Canada. And that had been—she tried to count in her head—five or six nights ago.

As they left the gloomy house behind and stepped back into the warm sunshine, Jaci noticed the boys' sweaters were a slightly different color of gray. She turned to the boy next to Amanda. "Which one are you?"

"Neal," he answered, then looked at his brother. "Did you get my wallet?"

"Oops." Ricky hurried back into the house. He returned after what seemed a long time, waving a black wallet in the air.

Neal took it from him and eyed his brother as he opened it. "How much did you take?"

"Like I need your money," Ricky snorted, pulling his brother a few paces in front of the girls.

Jaci studied them. Was it Neal in the light gray, or Ricky? Not that it mattered. They would eat their lunch and be on their way, leaving Neal and Ricky to sort out their own lives.

Chapter 20

"You can order whatever you want. But the total has to be less than four dollars," the twin in the dark gray said once they got to the deli.

"For all three of us?" Jaci hoped the food here was cheap.

His brother held the door open for them. "Just get what you want, and don't worry about the price. He thinks he's being funny."

Jaci looked back and forth between them. "How do we tell you apart?"

Dark Gray smiled. Jaci noticed he had a black shirt under his sweater. "I'm Ricky. And if you look really closely, you'll see that I have gold in my eyes. Neal doesn't."

Amanda squinted and studied Ricky's eyes, then shook her head. "Not seeing it."

Her expression lingered on him, and she cocked her head to the side. "What about me? Do I have golden flecks in my eyes?"

He stepped forward, putting his hands on her shoulders. "No." He shook his head. "Your eyes are green."

He let go of her shoulders and followed Neal into the restaurant. "You girls go sit. We'll order and surprise you."

"So," Amanda said as she slid into her seat, "what do you think of them?" She didn't wait for an answer. "I think they're very nice... and very cute."

"We want to be easily forgotten," Jaci reminded her.

"Hmm." Amanda smiled as if she hadn't heard. "It's hard to say which one's cuter, really."

One of the twins came over with a tray of sandwiches. Jaci noted the black undershirt. Ricky.

"Hi." He handed food out to them. "I'm Ricky, if you didn't realize. Can I sit here?"

"Sure, sure," Amanda said. She gave him a big smile as she made room between her and Sara.

Ricky looked up at Jaci as he handed out sandwiches, his hazel eyes piercing hers before he turned away.

Jaci sat for a moment, surprised at the way her stomach fluttered. She shook her head and took a bite out of the BLT sub, closing her eyes and savoring the tang of the tomato and mayonnaise, mingled with the crunch of bacon and lettuce. Perfect.

Ricky spoke to Sara around a mouthful of food. "What's your name? I can't remember."

She took the sandwich he offered her. "Sara." Her eyes met his and she looked away.

"Hi, Sara." He bumped her shoulder. "Nice to meet you, Sara. So, where are you guys from?" He unwrapped his second burger and took a huge bite.

"We're from Idaho. We walked here." Amanda tapped her fingers on the table.

"You walked? That's posh. So how old are you guys?" He took another bite of his hamburger.

Neal sat down in the booth behind them. In stark contrast to his twin, Neal ignored his food. He stared out the window for a moment, rubbing his chin.

"What's wrong with him?" Jaci asked, nodding at Neal.

Ricky turned and patted Neal on the shoulder. "He carries the world on his shoulders. Heavy burden."

Neal left his booth and came to join them. He sat down by Sara.

"What about you?" She lifted her brows toward Ricky. "Don't you have any responsibility?"

Ricky eyed her and took a long sip of his soda before answering. "Nah. I avoid it like the plague." He nodded at her. "But you never answered my question."

"She's fifteen," Amanda said. "So am I. We're the oldest."

Ricky reached over and fingered her hair. "Your hair is really red."

"It's actually auburn, but if that's a compliment, thanks," she said with a quick grin. "And how old are you?"

"We're seventeen," Ricky answered, sitting back and taking another bite. "Our birthday was in August. So you guys walked here from Idaho? Intense."

"Well, not exactly," Jaci said. "It's a long story."

He shrugged. "You've got time. And you haven't told me your name yet."

He picked up some matches from the center of the table and began fiddling with them. Neal slapped them back down.

Time. Time was not something they had. Her brow furrowed, the urge to get moving again making her fingers twitch. "Jaci. My name's Jaci." She picked up her trash.

Sara ran a hand over the table. "We've been here too long. Trouble follows us."

"Well." Neal stood and reached into his pocket, pulling out his wallet. "If you're really serious about leaving, you're going to need more food, aren't you?"

He nodded at the deli behind them. "Pick out a few things for the road. We'll walk with you until you leave town."

Chapter 21

Back in the street, they heard a siren wail. "That sounds close," Sara said.

A column of smoke ascended from a group of houses on the next street. Neal and Ricky exchanged glances before sprinting toward the fire. The girls ran after them.

The twins stared at the blaze that consumed their house. Two fire trucks were already there, but it was obvious that the fire had had its way with the dusty, dry house.

"The house," Ricky moaned, digging his fingers into his brown hair.

"How did this happen? I saw you put the firecracker in the bucket."

"Neal, I'm sorry. I took it out when I went back in for the wallet. I just wanted to dry it out. I didn't think it would explode!" Then he snapped his fingers. "The power outlet was sparking yesterday. I must've left it too close."

"Idiot."

The two stood there a moment, and then Neal backed away. "Come on." Keeping their eyes on the ground, he and Ricky moved down the sidewalk.

Amanda blinked, frowning. "Aren't you going to stick around? What about when your parents get home?"

"Or your grandma, or whoever," said Jaci, joining in.

"They're not coming home," Ricky said. "It's not even our house."

Jaci gasped, and Amanda said, "What?"

"We lived in that house with our grandmother," Neal said. "The state gave it to her. Then Ricky started having problems. They talked about separating us. Well, our grandmother died two weeks ago. We knew what would happen if the state found out. So we—"

he gestured helplessly. "We had the body cremated and didn't tell a soul."

Jaci frowned. Was it that easy to cremate a body? "Didn't they ask questions?"

Neal shook his head. "Why would they? We had all the right information. Her social security card, date of birth, date of death. We had to sign a waiver saying we didn't want an obituary printed. We were doing a good job of not getting noticed."

He sent Ricky a murderous look. "Especially since the police always have an eye on Ricky."

"Police?" Jaci looked at Ricky. "What have you done?"

"Just problems with school."

"That's it?"

His hazel eyes focused on her, a flash of anger crossing his features. "What are you, a judge?"

She crossed her arms over her chest, refusing to back down. "You lied to us. I want to know what kind of people you are."

"We're good people," Ricky replied, holding her gaze. "We make mistakes, like everyone else." He cracked a smile. "Me more than Neal."

"Well, I think you just broke your probation," Neal said. "We better get out of here before they find you and throw you in jail."

"Do you have money?" Jaci asked.

"We've been using Grandma's stash in the cookie jar," Neal said. "I have a credit card, it's Grandma's card but it has my name on it. She had a savings account, but we can't get into it. The state would probably put it in a trust fund for us, but we'd have to go to foster homes until we're old enough to take it."

"Is your credit card paid off?"

Neal nodded. "The bill's paid in full every month from Grandma's checking account. I don't know how long we can use it. Once the payment bounces, the credit card is no good."

"Why don't you take out a cash advance?" she asked.

Neal shook his head. "I don't have a PIN authorized to do that."

"What about you?" Jaci asked Ricky. "Do you have a credit card?"

He made a face. "I guess that comes with the whole responsibility thing. Never wanted any, so I didn't get a card."

"Do you want to come with us?" Sara asked, directing the question at Neal.

Jaci spun to look at her. *Kind of sudden, wasn't it?*

"Huh? With you?" Ricky said.

"Are we still going?" Amanda asked, looking disheartened. "I thought we'd stop by the police station here, and, you know… go home."

"No police," Ricky said. "Or did you not catch that part of the story?"

"And Ricky's on probation," added Neal.

"We're not going to the police," Sara said.

Jaci pressed a hand to her temple. "Wait, wait, wait. We haven't decided anything yet."

Sara looked at her and repeated, "I'm not going to the police."

"Me neither," echoed Ricky.

Jaci frowned at Sara, then glanced back at Ricky and Neal. "Excuse us a moment. We need to talk."

She grabbed Amanda's forearm and motioned Sara to step back.

Amanda jerked her arm away. "Are we going to the police or not?"

"Not." Sara crossed her arms over her chest. "Go without me if you want."

"Sara," Jaci sighed, exasperated. "Why are you being so stubborn? And why did you invite the boys to go with us?"

"They need a place to go. They can protect us."

Amanda leaned forward. "They have money. We almost double our numbers. We'll be safer."

"Safer." Sara nodded. "It'll be good for us."

Jaci said, "Okay. But at some point—" she looked at Sara—"we *are* going to the police."

She spun back around, lifting her chin and directing her words to Neal. "We're getting out of here, and you should come too."

"Hey, why not?" Ricky shrugged. "We've got nothing to lose. I don't know camping, but I can start a fire. And if we're trying to avoid people—out there's the best place to do it. You can go for days without seeing anyone."

"All right," Neal said. "We leave here now. Everyone knows everyone here, and they'll be looking for us. You know our story; what's yours?"

"Not here," said Jaci. "Wait 'til we're out of town."

He pointed at the plastic bag in Sara's hand. "That's not going to be enough food. We'll have to get more."

"We'll be spotted," Ricky said, eyes flicking around them.

"We have to get food," Neal insisted. "We'll send one of the girls into a store. Buy one of those reusable bags and get as much food as possible."

Jaci wished she hadn't tossed their other shoulder bag. "All right. But let's hurry."

Two hours later the city was behind them and the forest engulfed them once again. The boys didn't say much as Jaci and Amanda told them their story. Of course they didn't mention anything that had happened to Sara. That was Sara's business, if she wanted anyone to know.

And Callie. They had left out Callie.

October 4
Dallas, Texas

International Accounting Alliances.

Carl stared at the one-story, white-washed building in front of him. About the same size as a trailer home, it wasn't what he expected from a firm with an international presence.

A quick glance around the parking lot showed only three other vehicles. An old blue and white pick-up, a green Volkswagen, and a long red Thunderbird.

Carl got out of his rental car and felt suffocated by the humid Dallas air.

The door to the building was locked. Carl worked the knob several times before giving up. He tried to see past the closed blinds on the windows and walked around the building. All the doors and windows were locked. He pulled out his cell phone and dialed the Dallas police.

A moment later a young, alert voice said, "Dallas police department, Sergeant Green speaking."

"Sergeant Green, I'd like an expedited search warrant. Who should I speak to about that?"

While he waited for his search warrant, Carl sat in the shade of a sycamore tree and watched the building. No sign of life. No one came out or went in. Carl had already formed his opinions, and he doubted that anyone worked here.

When the police arrived with the search warrant, he went to work forcing his way into the building. The inside looked like a school cafeteria. Long tables with attached benches lined the room from front to back. A desk in the back had a computer on it.

Carl crossed to it, noting the dust collecting on the surfaces. An old phone sat by the computer. He took it from its cradle and checked the dial tone. Hanging up, he pushed the 'on' button on the computer and the screen lit up. The familiar Windows music blared out of the speakers and a login prompt appeared.

Now what? He knew for a fact that Gregorio Rivera hadn't gone to the University of Pedrita. But that didn't make the man a criminal, only a liar.

He was also very certain that the man didn't work for Accounts whatever. Again, that didn't make him a criminal. But it did make it very suspicious that he had been gone the very weekend his daughter disappeared. Gone on a business trip for a fictitious company.

Carl needed to see that background check. But he knew it could be a few weeks before it came back.

Carl opened the desk drawers. Empty. The only other room was a bathroom.

He scanned the small bathroom and was about to leave when he saw a sliver of paper poking out under the mirror. He touched the glass. A medicine cabinet. Opening it, he found a sheet of paper taped to the inside. Handwritten dates and events covered it, with several of them crossed out by red ink.

It was the fourth line down that caught his eye: "February 17. The Hand and Cisnero. Guadalajara, Mexico. Orange and Purple." A red line marked out the phrase. All the lines were crossed out, except the last four.

Carl stared, trying to make sense of it. His eyes ran down the sheet, stopping at another line. The penmanship was difficult to read, as if written in a hurry: "September 12. Nikolai. Rogaland, Norway. Purple and Teal."

The next one read: "October 7. Maverick and Avenger. Sydney, Australia. Yellow and Purple."

The last four hadn't happened yet. That's why they weren't crossed out. This was huge. This was a key. He just didn't know what it unlocked.

He needed a copy of this paper. He took it down, careful not to tear the tape. He kept a digital camera in his car. He would take a picture, put it back, and get out of here. He had some major deciphering to do.

October 5
Shelley, Idaho

"Mr. Rivera."

Gregorio Rivera lifted his head from the trunk of his car as Carl approached. In spite of the overcast day, the man wore dark sunglasses. His yellow tie added a splash of color to the black suit.

"Detective." Rivera closed the trunk and brushed his hands together. "You have news?"

Carl glanced at the red-brick house. "In a manner of speaking. I have a few questions first, though."

"Do you have any information on my daughter?"

Carl wished he could read the man's thoughts. "Do you?"

Rivera's demeanor became colder. His jaw tightened, shoulders stiffening. "Why would I? I'm not the detective."

Carl shrugged, trying to play it cool. "Maybe you have connections."

Rivera moved to the front of the Honda Civic and stepped into the driver's side. "I have a plane to catch."

"Oh? Business trip?" Carl tried to keep his voice neutral.

Rivera lifted his chin. "Yes. You had questions?" His voice was sharp and impatient.

Carl placed his fingers on the rim of the car door. "I tried to find information about your life as a student at the University of Pedrita. Funny thing is there doesn't appear to be a University of Pedrita. Anywhere."

"Are you investigating me or my daughter's disappearance?"

Carl tightened his jaw. "It's my job to do both. I never know when one investigation might lead to another."

"It was a small, private university. Maybe it went out of business."

"There still should be some indication that it existed."

"You might have to go to Mexico to find it." Rivera placed his hand on the door. "Excuse me. I need to go."

Carl didn't move. "I also went to Dallas. I spoke to your boss at International Accounting Alliances."

Rivera's back went straight, and when he spoke, his voice came out strangled. "And?"

"He says you're doing a good job. Holding up company image. Since there is no company." Carl leaned in closer. "So what do you do on your business trips, Greg? Anything illegal?"

"Do you have any legal grounds to arrest me?"

Carl stood up straighter. "Not yet, Rivera. But I'm not done investigating."

"Then I suggest you step away from my vehicle."

Carl moved backwards, tasting bitter frustration in his mouth. If only he had something to get the guy on. "Have fun in Australia."

Rivera slammed the door and sped away.

Chapter 22

Ricky and Sara came through the trees, Ricky carrying Sara's bag over a shoulder. Her nose was pink and her face splotchy. She looked away from her friends and stopped at the tree line, scanning the forest as if searching for something. Always crying.

"Here." Ricky handed Jaci the bag and sat down on the log next to her and Neal. "The water bottles are inside." He pulled out a rock and ran his fingers over it.

Jaci took one out and dumped it into the flour. It made a thin gruel, and she added more flour.

"Sick. I'm not having any." Amanda stood up and walked away. She motioned to Ricky, but he pointed at the bowl of flour paste.

All their food was gone, except for the flour. Jaci took a hurried gulp of the gruel and handed the bowl to Ricky.

Neal glanced at his twin. "Jaci, Ricky and I want to know your plan."

"Plan? I don't have a plan. We're just trying to get home."

"That's what I thought." Neal leaned forward, his hazel eyes intense. "Here's what we need to figure out. What happens when we leave this forest? We can't just walk to Idaho. How are you going to throw these guys off your trail?"

She fingered the decaying bark under the log. "They're not on our trail right now. I guess we keep a low profile."

"But they know where you're going," Neal pressed. "They know where you live. You think you're just going to walk up to your house, knock on the door, and everything will go back to the way it was?"

Back to the way it was. Jaci took a deep breath, hot tears filling her eyes. Things would never go back. She shook her head, feeling like an idiot. She hadn't thought that far ahead. Get home. Just get home. Those were her driving thoughts.

Neal was right. They had to think about The Hand. The reality of being hunted.

Amanda came back and sat on the ground in front of Ricky. "What's wrong, Jaci?"

"Nothing." She blinked back the tears. "We're just making plans."

"Well then, don't you think you should include all of us?"

"You're the one who walked away." Jaci picked up the bowl of gruel on the ground. She doubted Sara would want any, but she should offer anyway.

Three days later, even the flour was gone.

The rolling hills were taxing to cross, and usually they saved their energy by sticking to the valleys. Jaci walked close to Amanda, feeling guilty for talking about Sara. But she was concerned for her. Every once in awhile she glanced over her shoulder to make sure Sara was out of earshot.

"She's so moody these days," said Amanda. "She used to be easy going."

"Let's be patient," Jaci said. Her eyes roved over the shallow stream next to them. The steep bank descended to a creek only a few inches deep. "We can't even begin to imagine what she's gone through."

"I've tried being patient. I don't think she likes me anymore."

"She's edgy and doesn't seem to want to be around us," agreed Jaci. "Everything I say, she either cries or blows up at me."

"Yeah. She spends all her time with Neal and Ricky."

"Whatever it is, I'm worried. She's not acting like herself at all. And Neal and Ricky are nice guys, but how much can we trust them? I mean, they are guys."

Amanda arched an eyebrow over her green eyes. "What about Sara? These things can change people."

"Well, let's keep an eye on her."

Amanda glanced behind her. "Where are they, anyway? I can't even see them."

"Lagging behind again. Come on, let's go back." She turned around and quickened her pace. "Look at that."

"What is it?"

A structure of slender trees and branches wove together from bank to bank. This explained why the river was so shallow. "It's a beaver's dam. I bet if it were gone, this whole canal would be full."

"Cool," Amanda said, scanning the horizon. "How come we didn't notice it on the way down?"

"Too busy gossiping, I guess." Jaci looked to the shore twelve feet away. "I think there's someone on the other side."

She squinted, making out three figures. Sara and the twins, of course. They sat in the shade of a tree, one of them sprawled out on his back, propped up by his elbows, the other leaning against the trunk. Jaci pushed down an uneasy feeling. She wished Sara didn't hang on them so much.

"Hi," Amanda shouted.

The three looked up and Sara wiped her eyes with the back of her hand. The twin leaning against the tree straightened. "Hi."

Jaci recognized Ricky's voice even before she saw the black peeking from the gray sweater.

"What are you doing over there?" Amanda yelled.

He stood up, flashing another smile, and held up an orange backpack. "Found some food."

The backpack appeared to have been left behind by campers. It had marshmallows, a box of graham crackers, chocolate bars, beef jerky, and raisins. They brushed off the ants and shared the food, too hungry to think about rationing.

Neal and Ricky walked on ahead to clear a trail, leaving the girls following behind.

The terrain next to the stream was flatter than the surrounding hills, so they traveled close to the water. There weren't as many trees to step around, either. Just tree roots.

Jaci stumbled over one, almost pitching into the stream, but Amanda caught her arm. "Be careful."

Jaci paused, noticing what she had almost stepped into. A small fire pit, right next to the river. She crouched down and stuck her finger in the ash.

Sara stopped. "What is it?"

Jaci felt a cold shiver run down her spine. "We haven't been here already, have we?"

"Of course not." Amanda shook her head. "That's just an old pit. Probably belonged to whoever left that orange backpack behind."

"It's still warm." Jaci stood up, rubbing the ash from her finger tips.

Amanda lowered her voice. "I'm sure it's nothing. This is a forest, after all. People camp here."

Jaci let out a careful breath. The last thing she wanted was panic in their small camp. "We need to be careful. Not draw attention to ourselves. It might not be anyone important, or it might be someone looking for us. I'll tell the boys."

Sara hugged herself and rocked on the balls of her feet, staring into the fire pit.

Nobody spoke for the rest of the afternoon. Jaci found herself turning her head at every movement. The familiar feelings of paranoia and fear descended on her. She hoped the camper stayed at least a day's walk ahead of them.

The sun went down and with it, all the heat evaporated from the air. Ricky came over to help them set up their fire circle, pulling out his rock to start a spark.

"Any sign of our visitor?" he asked, crouching over the kindling.

"I'm not sure we should have a fire," Jaci warned.

He put his rock back in his pocket. "You'll freeze without one."

There are worse things, she thought.

"Hey," Amanda said, sidling up next to them. Her shoulder bumped Ricky's knee.

"Hey." Ricky shrugged. "We'll be close by."

Jaci felt a surge of panic when he walked away. She didn't want him to go. What if they needed protection?

"I don't like being away from them," Sara pulled on Jaci's sweater sleeve.

Amanda snorted. "That's because you have a crush on Ricky."

"I do not!" Sara said, her face turning crimson.

"Keep it down," said Jaci. "Start gathering leaves for insulation."

Ignoring her, Amanda growled, "Out with it, Sara. What's going on with you and Ricky?"

Sara's mouth tightened. "More than what's going on between you and him, that's for sure."

"Oh, you think?"

"Shut up, shut up, shut up!" Jaci intervened.

"I'm done with this." Sara sat down by a tree and closed her eyes.

"I'm still talking to you, Sara," said Amanda, but Sara didn't move.

Jaci heard someone whisper her name from the shrubbery. Ricky beckoned and disappeared into the foliage. She hurried after.

"What is it, Ricky?"

He nodded back toward the campsite. "I actually came to talk to Sara. Guess I have bad timing."

"It's all the tension. Lack of food, lack of sleep. And I think Amanda's jealous." She raised an eyebrow. "Is that why we're hiding? You don't want her to see me talking to you?"

He laughed. "I could care less what she thinks. I have some questions for Sara. About something she told Neal."

"What did she tell Neal?"

"Well, it's a secret. Can't tell."

"Fine. But don't hurt her."

"Hurt her?" He put his hands over his heart. "Never. Besides, Neal would kill me."

"Well, if that's everything, I should go back."

Ricky reached out and grabbed her hand. "What are you afraid of? That she's going to be Ricky Collins' next victim? Or that you will be?"

A sliver of heat ran through her wrist at his touch. "I'll never be the victim."

He pulled her up, his hazel eyes roving over her face. "Sorry. Wrong word. I didn't mean a victim—like, a real victim." He took her chin in his hand and leaned closer.

Jaci jerked her face away and backed up, keeping her eyes averted. Emotions—embarrassment, anger, desire, confusion—rushed through her in a split second, vying for her attention. "I need to be with the other girls. To make sure there's no trouble."

Ricky jogged a little to catch up with her. "I still need to talk to Sara."

She felt a flash of anger. "Why don't you watch for intruders? You're here to keep us safe. You can talk to her tomorrow."

Ricky stopped walking. "Okay. Yeah. I'll talk to her tomorrow. See ya."

She ran a hand through her hair and sighed in annoyance. A few strands came out of her ponytail, and she paused to stuff them back in.

It was silent at the campsite. She made out the still forms of Sara and Amanda in the dark, sleeping several feet from each other.

Jaci went back to her leaf pile and shoved them into her clothes, trying to insulate her thin body from the cold. Her stomach growled, and she stuck a leaf in her mouth and chewed. She laid her head down and closed her eyes, a bitter taste in her mouth.

October 9
Johnsburg, New York

Carl leaned over the counter in the North Creek Deli and Market. Outside a cold wind whipped through the Adirondacks and howled at the windows.

"Think really hard." He kept his voice warm and encouraging. "What did the girls look like?"

The young man behind the counter with 'Derek' written on his name tag squinted and scratched at his stubby brown hair.

Carl glanced out the window. The hour drive from Queensbury through the mountain range to Johnsburg had been dizzying and breath-taking. Tall pines and dense vegetation surrounded either side of the highway as it twisted and turned through the hills and valleys.

But that wasn't the point. The point was that two boys here had been reported missing. When the New York state police began the investigation, an interview at the North Creek Deli and Market reported that the boys had last been seen with three girls. The police had been quick to contact the Idaho Falls police department.

Carl shifted his weight, working to stay calm. He wanted to verify that these were the right girls. But even if he couldn't, he would proceed as if they were. It was his best lead in days.

"Well, Derek?"

"It's been a few days. I can't remember for sure. But there were three. They sat over there." He pointed to a booth by the window. "Ricky and Neal ordered for them."

Carl glanced at his notepad. He already had the names 'Ricky and Neal Collins' written down.

"Did Ricky and Neal eat here a lot?"

Derek nodded. "Oh, yeah. Almost every day. Maybe every day."

"Did you overhear them talking?"

"Sure. They argued over what to buy."

"I mean, did you hear them talking about where they were going?"

Derek shook his head. "No, man! I had no idea they were cutting out of town. No clue."

"Thank you, Derek." Carl handed him a business card. "Call me if you remember anything."

"Okay." Derek stuck the card in his pocket.

Carl turned away, grunting inwardly. That card would end up in the wash, never seen again. He hadn't learned anything from Derek, but Carl's gut told him this was the right path.

He stepped outside and sat down on a bench, pulling his windbreaker closed. If the girls were out here in this mountain range, how would they survive this cold? Night time temperatures could get below freezing this time of year. Opening the notepad, Carl read over the information again.

"Ricky and Neal Collins. Seventeen, twins. Joselyn Bennett, grandmother, dead."

It had originally said missing, but then the police called Carl and told him they had a cremation record on file for the woman at the local morgue. Carl had crossed out 'missing' and written 'dead.' It remained to be seen if the boys had killed her or not.

"Seniors at Johnsburg Central High." Apparently after four days of not coming to school, the teachers finally reported Neal as missing. Not Ricky—he skipped a lot. But they were concerned about Neal, a devoted student who had already put down pre-med for his undergraduate studies.

"Born Little Falls, New York. Custody battle."

He stood up. The police had said if they found the boys, they would arrest them. They were wanted for arson, and charges might still be pressed for the grandmother's death. Ricky had broken his probation, first with the fire, and now by hiking out of town. Carl shook his head. What kind of psychos had the girls run into this time?

They were out there in the forest somewhere among the thousands of acres. He needed the park rangers' phone numbers. They needed to be on that trail, alerting hikers to watch out for these kids.

He tried to imagine where they would be, what route they would take. The girls wanted to get back to Idaho. Where did the boys want to go?

He would spend a few days here to see if he could glean anything from the boys' friends and teachers. Or even Ricky's probation officer. He needed to get to Little Falls. He needed to see the court records.

Those records might give him a hint as to where the boys were heading.

Chapter 23

Jaci splashed cold river water over her face, shivering as it fell into her sweater.

"Hi." Sara joined her. "Where's Amanda?"

"She was already up when I got up." Jaci searched around the river bank. Standing, she dried her hands on her jeans. "I'll find her."

Sara shrugged. "She's probably with the boys."

"I'll just make sure that's where she is. You ready to head out?"

"Give me five more minutes."

Jaci found one of the boys using his foot to cover a small circle of ash with dirt. From the serious expression on his face, it had to be Neal. The light gray color of his sweater was dirtier now.

"Hi, Neal."

He looked up and gave her a brief smile. "Jaci."

"We're going to leave soon." She glanced around. "You seen Amanda? She wasn't up at our camp."

Neal shrugged his shoulder toward the path they'd made the day before. "She went that way."

Jaci started down the path, straining her ears to hear voices.

She didn't need to go far. She almost walked into the grove where Amanda and Ricky were kissing.

She tiptoed back, careful not to step on a twig or give any other notice of her presence.

"Let's go, Neal," she said shortly, not bothering to look at him as she hurried back to Sara.

Catching up to Sara, she jerked her shoulder bag from the river bank. "Come on."

Sara jogged to match Jaci's stride. "What about the boys?"

"They're coming."

Sara kept pace with her and didn't ask any more questions. Amanda and Ricky stayed behind, close enough that the murmur of their voices carried.

Neal moved ahead, staying in front of Jaci and Sara, moving thorn bushes and stamping on dry underbrush.

The air grew colder when dusk fell, as if the sun had taken the last rays of warmth with it. Just like the day before. The stream gurgled and bubbled over rocks close to the shore.

Jaci pulled on a thread of her pink sweater, watching it unravel. It ran around and around her sleeve before catching and tearing.

"We should stop," Neal said.

Jaci nodded. She walked over to the creek. Only about eight feet across, the opposite bank looked close enough to jump. She leaned over it and cupped her hand to gather the water for a drink. It smelled clean. The water they had gotten upstream yesterday hadn't upset their systems.

Pulling a water bottle from her bag, she began refilling it. Finishing with that one, she rolled it behind her and started on the next.

"I'll see if I can find my brother," Neal said, touching Sara's shoulder.

Sara picked up the bottle Jaci had rolled back and shook it. She held it close to her face and examined it. "Do you really think this water is safe? I'd hate to get dysentery."

"Looks fine. Is this stream on the map?"

"Hmm." Sara unfolded it and examined it. "How am I supposed to know one stream from another? We haven't been plotting our course."

Amanda waltzed over, twirling her arms and swirling like a ballerina. "Hey, you two."

Sara stood up and walked away. Amanda looked over at Jaci. "What's her problem?"

Jaci shrugged. "I don't know. Maybe she's still mad about last night. She didn't tell me." She stood up, brushing dirt from her jeans, and wandered in the direction Sara had gone.

She found her squatting on the river bank, throwing rocks into it. It was dark now, and Jaci could barely see her outline. A twig snapped under her foot, and Sara spun around, hands leaping to her chest.

"It's me," Jaci called out quickly.

"Jaci," Sara breathed, dropping her hands.

"Yeah."

The younger girl stepped to her side and they walked along the bank for a moment. Jaci stopped and moved over to the edge, staring down into the calm water below. The bank was higher here, a good three feet from the stream. The slender crescent of the moon reflected in the water, slightly distorted by the gentle ripples.

Jaci felt disturbed inside, and wasn't sure why. "So many thoughts. So many worries. I need to sit and think and not talk to anybody. Just for a few minutes."

She looked up at the dark sky. Stars were starting to dot the horizon. "I'm going to cross to the other side."

Sara looked down at the water. "How?"

"I'll wade. It's only a few feet deep."

"But it's freezing."

"I'll only be a few minutes. Save me a spot next to you."

"Okay. I won't sleep till you come back, though, so hurry."

Jaci waved her off. "Sure. I'll be right there." Her head felt heavy with fatigue, her eyelids itchy. She wouldn't be gone long.

Chapter 24

The night sky lit up like a giant firecracker, followed by a crack and rumble that shook the ground.

"What on earth?" Jaci pulled herself to her knees and slipped on the wet river bank. Large drops fell from the sky, making dents in the soft earth.

She dug her fingers into the mud. Where was she? Water began to fall from the sky in torrents, soaking her clothing and dripping into her face. The trees overhead shook and the wind roared around her like a train. A tree branch above snapped and crashed to the ground.

She had fallen asleep on the wrong side of the river. She ran through her options. Cross the river now and try to meet up with her friends, or wait out the storm on this side?

She could barely see, except for when lightning lit the sky. Where was the edge of the bank? She crept forward on her hands and knees, stretching her fingers out in front of her. The water roared close by. Any minute now—she should be almost to the edge—

The ground under her fingers crumbled away, and she screamed as she plummeted forward. Her flailing arms hit a tree root protruding from the eroded bank, and she clutched it.

Her legs swung under her, slipping into the icy water, and it shocked her when she couldn't find the bottom. The shallow stream had turned into a raging river, eating away at the bank until it was a steep ledge.

She kicked her legs, trying to find a footrest. She was up to her waist.

"Help!" she cried. Thunder crashed again and the wind whipped her words away from her.

Digging her knees into the bank, she tried to get enough leverage to use her arm muscles to pull herself up. It was too muddy, and she lost her footing. She cried out as her body twisted around, but she didn't let go of the branch.

Her legs were going numb and the water surged beneath her ribcage. "Someone, help me!"

One hand slipped from the root and the raging current pulled her legs downstream, tugging her clothes around her. Her head submerged underwater for a second, and then she managed to get her other hand up to the root again.

She took a deep breath and choked on water. Panic fueled her, and she kicked her legs.

Her feet found a hold and her head emerged. She gagged and coughed. Her stomach tightened, and she threw up bile.

"Please," she moaned, not daring to move a hand to wipe her face. Part of the bank crumbled under the root and fell into the water. The water pulled on her, urging her to relax and succumb to its force.

Dear God, don't let me fall. I don't want to die this way. She held onto her tree root with all her might, but she was weakening. The cold water bubbled up around her neck, making her teeth chatter.

Jaci leaned her head against the muddy bank, her hand going numb. She felt so tired. She closed her eyes.

"Jaci? Is that you?"

She jerked her head up, forcing the heavy eyelids to open. Jaci let out a sob of relief. "Neal? I'm here!"

"It's Ricky." His fingers grabbed her hand, prying her free of the tree root.

"Ricky?" Jaci said, resting her head against the muddy incline and feeling his cold hand clasp one of hers.

"Are you okay?"

She couldn't answer. She wanted to, but her mouth didn't seem to be responding.

He grabbed her other hand. "Everything is going to be fine now, you can stop crying."

Was she crying? "Hurry, Ricky. The current..." Her voice faded away, too exhausted to continue.

"Okay." Ricky gripped her forearms and started to pull.

The water increased in volume, rising up to her chin even though Ricky was pulling her up.

A roar like a waterfall filled Jaci's ears. She twisted her body, kicking at the bank, trying to get leverage. "Do you hear that?"

He paused, and then swore. "The beaver's dam must've broke."

He grunted and pulled harder.

The beaver dam. If that water swept through, it would take her along with it and maybe Ricky, too. A rush of adrenaline warmed her body, and she jerked an arm out of Ricky's grasp, clawing at the bank. "Hurry, Ricky."

"I am!"

She tried to help, digging her elbows into the mud. He wrapped his arms around her waist and dragged her away from the edge. The roar grew louder, and Jaci scrambled forward as if a mountain lion were at her heels.

A flash of lightning illuminated the wave as it thundered past, overflowing the river bank. She heard the snap of branches, and the tree she had clung to tumbled into the water along with a large section of river bank.

The water lapped at her feet and she tensed, climbing to higher ground, afraid she might be swept away, but Ricky held her tight.

When he finally released her, she sank into the mud, sobbing. "Thank you," she cried. "I was praying... I didn't want to die."

"No," Ricky said, pulling her to her feet, "you're not going to die. Come on, we've got to warm you up."

It was wet everywhere, but the storm was starting to dissipate, leaving as quickly as it had come.

Ricky led her away from the mud and laid her down in the tall, wet weeds, then lay down next to her, wrapping his arms around her and rubbing her back and shoulders. "Gotta get your blood going. You're shaking."

He took her hands and pressed them to his chest, and Jaci bent her palms against the black t-shirt. "Where's your sweater?"

"I left it behind. It would've slowed me down. Doesn't do much good wet, anyway."

"No, I suppose not." Jaci closed her eyes and tried to relax.

Multiple aches and bruises clamored for her attention; her body throbbed. Floating debris in the water had pummeled her.

She tossed and turned through the night. A cool breeze tickled her ear. She opened her eyes, and for a moment the world seemed to swirl in front of her. The sun was up, and a few birds were chirping, as if no thunderous storm had burst through the area a few hours earlier.

She sat up, holding a hand to her head to suppress the vertigo. How much of what she remembered was a dream, and how much was real?

Her hand felt hard and stiff, and when she looked at it, she realized it was caked in dry mud. A glance down at her clothes showed they were in the same condition.

Ricky stood on the bank where he had dragged her up, his back to her as he surveyed the depth of the water.

Jaci looked at the swollen rapids beneath them, staying away from the edge of the bank. The water was high, and she didn't trust the ledge to stay where it was. The river frothed white as it fought its way around broken tree limbs.

A shiver ran through her, and she let her legs bend under her. The soft mud squished beneath her body weight. "What happened last night?"

Ricky shrugged, hands in his jean pockets. "Big storm—common around here, actually. Sara told us you had crossed the river."

He looked at her. "It was pretty dumb to come over here alone."

The chastisement hung in the air, and Jaci bristled. "I didn't know a storm was going to come in and triple the size of the stream, okay? How'd you find me, anyway?"

"We heard you. Neal can't swim. Someone had to come." Ricky hesitated. He glanced up at the morning sun. "We should hurry back."

Something in his voice caught Jaci's attention. "Why?"

He shrugged. "Nothing. I thought they would be across the river this morning, looking for us. But they must be waiting downstream."

He kept his tone even, but Jaci picked up on a nervous air. "Was there danger last night?"

He shook his head. "Neal and I took the girls out of the ravine when it started raining. He stayed on the hill while I came back to get you. He'll keep them safe."

It would be a good answer, except for the way Ricky avoided looking at her.

"I meant danger from other people."

He met her eyes. "I'm not sure. Sara thought she saw someone. A man."

"When?"

"During the storm. Don't worry," he added quickly, "Neal will protect them."

Jaci stared down at the mud, thinking. Sara had been seeing and hearing things for weeks. And with all the noise of the water and wind, it might have been nothing. Then again, they *had* seen the fire pit.

"How are we going to get across?"

"The water's gone down from last night, but the current's still strong. We have to wade across, but not here. We should walk downstream until we find a place."

She frowned and studied the water. "I don't really want to get back in there."

She hesitated, remembering her fitful sleep the night before, and then asked, "Did you hear anything last night?"

"I heard you crying for help."

"No, I mean… after that."

"Nope." He shook his head. "I slept like a rock."

"I must've been dreaming," she said, staring into the swirling, murky water below. She shivered.

"Are you cold?" he asked, stepping to her and wrapping his arms around her.

His touch sent a spark through her veins. She jerked away. "I want to wash the mud off my face."

He indicated the brown water. "It won't help much."

"It's better than nothing." Still, she hesitated, afraid to approach the water.

"Let's walk downstream," Ricky said. "We might find a spot that's easier to cross."

The sun came out, beating down on them warmly. Jaci took off her pink sweater and tied it around her waist. It was wet, anyway, and making her colder. She didn't say much, lost in her own thoughts as she stumbled along behind Ricky.

"Was everyone else okay?" she asked.

"What?" He waited for her to catch up to him.

"Last night. Did the storm hurt anyone?"

"Everyone's okay." He stopped walking. "Uh-oh."

The river roared beneath their feet as it was bottlenecked through the sides of a cliff. They stood two feet above the water, six feet between them and the other side.

"It's getting worse," Ricky said. "Maybe we can cross where the dam used to be, or where Neal and I crossed with Sara."

"But that means…" Jaci swallowed, trying not to cry. "We'll have to go back the way we came." They had walked forward all day. Back for how long?

Ricky pointed downstream, "It splits up ahead into two rivers."

"We could jump it."

He grabbed her forearm, fingers closing as if afraid she might try. "Don't you dare. You fall in there, I won't be able to get you out."

She blinked back tears, feeling childish. "I'm starving. I can't walk all the way back there with no food. I won't make it." Her legs trembled underneath her. She needed to eat.

Ricky broke off a branch and tossed it into the water below. They both watched it disappear in the current, pop up again, and disappear for good.

"We don't have a choice. I'll figure out a way to get some food. Sit and rest, okay?" Ricky turned his back on her and jogged away.

Getting to her feet, she moved to a spot where she could reach the water. She had rinsed the mud from her face and arms earlier that morning, but now she had time to clean more thoroughly. She glanced down at her muddy shirt and hesitated. Casting a quick look over her shoulder, she yanked the shirt off and swished it in the water.

Within an hour Ricky was back, looking like a proud caveman as he plopped two fish down in front of her, still squirming with life.

"How'd you do it?" Jaci said.

Their empty, opaque eyes stared outward while the slimy mouths opened and closed, desperate to breathe. She had to be starving for the sight of them to make her mouth water.

Ricky reached into his pocket and pulled out a rock. Then he gathered up a couple of twigs and a few other rocks.

"It wasn't that hard. I went back to where the bank is lower. I lay down on my stomach and put my hands in the water. It's going so fast, I just had to hold still and wait for something slippery to swim into my hand. Then I closed my hands and caught it."

He gave her a quick grin as he began to strike his rock against another. "I've got fast reflexes."

She had seen this rock before. He always played with it. "What are you doing?"

"Well, we're not going to eat them raw, are we? This is my fire-starting rock. It's called flint."

"I know what flint is."

"That's right, you're smart. So you know if I have this rock and any other rock, I can get a spark. It might take awhile, with everything being damp, but we'll get a fire going soon."

Sparks jumped from the rock, landing on the twigs.

"You know," he said, leaning over to blow on the sparks, "it's probably just gonna be us for awhile. Even if we try to go faster than the others, we're going to have to walk back for at least a day to find a place to cross. And then another day or two before we find everyone. Will you be okay?"

He laid the fish on the rocks next to his little fire.

"I guess."

Ricky didn't say anything for several minutes. He turned his attention back to the fish, cooking them on the rocks in the fire until the skin turned pink and flaked with his stick.

"You're not the first person that had bad things happen to you. You can't let it stop you from living the rest of your life."

She studied him. "Where'd that come from?"

He slapped a hot fish down on the dirt in front of her. "Dinner is served."

"Do I just pick it up and eat it?"

"Here." He crouched beside her, using a stick to pull up on the skin. "It comes right off." He slid it off, exposing the hot flesh and bones.

Jaci's hands trembled, and she picked it up, sucking the meat off the bones.

"Most people don't eat the organs," he said, watching her. "Normally."

Everything tasted wonderful. Jaci stopped at the head and eyes, her hunger finally tamed enough to be picky.

Ricky squinted up above the tree line. "There's a bit more sun left. Are you up to walking until nightfall?"

Jaci looked at the other fish cooling. "If I can have one more fish."

Chapter 25

Ricky led the way upstream the next day. Jaci watched him tear pine needles off a branch before tossing the last piece into the raging water below them. The sun broke through the cloudy sky, sending beams of warmth down to the earth.

Ricky had failed to catch a fish for breakfast. It seemed to have left him in a bad mood. He hadn't made any attempts at conversation.

Jaci picked up one of the pine needles and stuck it in her mouth. She sucked on it, careful not to poke her gums or lip. It helped get rid of the taste the water had left.

"So what do you and Neal like to do for fun?"

"Neal's idea of a good time is studying for a test, or reading a text book."

"I take it you're not the intellectual type?"

He laughed. "Come on, now, you figured that out the first day we met."

"So what do you like to do?"

"Oh, you know. The usual stuff."

"Like?"

"Oh, sports, movies, food. What about you?"

"Well, I'm kind of like Neal. Straight-A student. I also like to run. Sara and I were on the track team at school."

"So you like sports, too."

"What about what Neal said? About you being on probation?"

"I got in trouble."

"No kidding. What did you do?"

"Well, it's just this bad habit of mine, ya know? I caught the bathroom on fire and got suspended."

"That's it?"

"Yeah. Overkill, huh? That's what you get in a small town."

They backtracked a little past where the dam had broken before they found a wider place in the stream. It had stretched to twenty feet across, with eroded bank on either side. It looked to be about three feet deep.

"We'll cross here," Ricky said, stopping.

Jaci shook her head. "It looks dangerous."

"It is. See that fallen tree?" He pointed at the far side.

"Yes."

"It's right at the deepest part. Let me get there, I'm a good swimmer. Then you just have to get to me."

Her heart hammered. "Maybe we should keep looking."

"It's not going to get better, Jaci. We can wait a day and see if it gets lower. Or we can try now."

She took a deep breath. "Okay. Let's try."

Ricky descended the bank. The water crept up to his waist, and she chewed her lip, watching him fight the current. He moved slowly, but reached the log and turned around.

"Come on, Jaci. I'm here." He motioned for her.

Jaci slipped into the water, fighting tears as the cold bit into her skin. She gasped as it reached her navel. She wasn't much taller than five foot. She took a step forward and nearly lost her footing. Her hands flailed, looking for an anchor, finding none.

"Look at me, Jaci. Come this way."

She focused on Ricky. A slight frown creased his features, and he moved his hands as if pulling a rope. She took another wobbly step. The water pushed her, and she froze, planting her feet into the rocky bed. She shot out a desperate prayer.

Please give me courage. She took a deep breath and plunged onward.

Within minutes, Ricky's hand grabbed hers and pulled her to the log. She wrapped an arm around it, clinging to it, shaking.

"You did it." Ricky guided her out of the water.

Jaci collapsed on top of the bank and burst into tears.

Ricky pulled her to him. "You're safe now. You made it."

In the afternoon of the next day, Jaci thought she saw motion ahead of them in the trees. She squinted, hoping it was her friends and not hungry wild animals.

A flash of orange caught her attention. The orange backpack. She grabbed Ricky's hand. "Ricky! I think I see them." She pointed up ahead.

She made out Sara and Amanda as they got closer. She stopped in mid-step, noticing their haggard appearance. They huddled together at the base of a tree, mud and dirt covering almost every inch of their faces and clothing.

"Sara!" Jaci called out.

Sara shot to her feet and raced toward them, leaving Amanda to scramble up after her.

Ricky let go of Jaci's hand and caught Sara in a hug.

She turned on Jaci next, wrapping her arms around her neck and clutching her. Silent sobs shook her body. "We were so worried. Are you hurt?"

"I'm fine, Sara. Are you?"

"Shh." Sara pulled away, her face pale. "There's someone out here."

Jaci's fingers tightened around Sara's arm. "What do you mean?"

"We heard him yesterday," Amanda said. "Talking on a radio or something. Saying he thought he'd found our trail."

"Maybe it's a good guy."

Sara trembled. "And if it's not?"

Ricky looked past the girls. "Where's Neal?" he asked.

Sara put her head in her hands and began to cry.

"Where's Neal?" he repeated, an edge hardening his voice.

"He left us!" Sara cried into her hands. "You didn't come back. He tried to cross the water. The dam broke. It swept him downstream."

Ricky jerked as if he had been stabbed. "Where is he now?"

Amanda shook her head. "We don't know. We followed the river here to this point. It forked into two rivers, and we didn't know which one to take. There's no sign of him. We've been here for two days."

"I'm going back."

"No, Ricky, don't!" Amanda cried, grabbing his arm. "We need you."

"I can't leave my brother," he said, his voice anguished.

"Please don't leave us," Sara sobbed.

"I'm so sorry," Amanda said. "It's my fault, Ricky."

Ricky looked at Sara. "What's she talking about?"

"Amanda tried to pull him from the river. But the current was too strong. It ripped Neal's hand from hers," Sara explained.

He shook his head. "It's my fault. I should've come back, like I said I would."

Jaci moved over to a bare spot of ground by a half-finished fire circle and sat. She picked up a rock, noting how her hand shook.

She was exhausted and wanted to cry. "Sara," she said, "come sit with me."

Sara obliged. Jaci gave her a quick hug, then pulled Sara's hair back and played with the ends. "You look like you haven't eaten in days."

Sara leaned forward, arching her shoulders. "Don't touch my hair. It's gross."

"Oh, who cares," Jaci chided. "You always liked me to braid your hair." It soothed her as well, a touch of normalcy in this insanity.

Ricky joined them, crouching to go through the orange bag. "Sara, tell me where you and Amanda looked for Neal."

"We just followed the river downstream until it split. We didn't go in it. Maybe we can help you. We could follow one stream and you the other. But you'd have to find a way to cross it."

"Crossing it's not a problem. You need supplies. What can I take with me?"

"Whatever you want." Sara pulled her chin up. "We're coming with you. Don't leave us behind."

Ricky picked up the orange bag. "Give me a day to find Neal. Just one day."

"No," Sara pleaded. "Let us come with you. Don't leave us."

Ricky looked at Jaci, his eyes imploring her for help. "I can do this better alone. Just stay hidden. Stay quiet, like you did."

Jaci swallowed back her protests and nodded, rubbing Sara's shoulder. "We'll be okay. We did just fine before we met you."

He gave her a smile. "Yeah. That's right."

Sara helped him load up the orange bag with bottles of water. That was really all they had. No bandages, medicine, stretchers. A box of raisins. He didn't need the matches.

There was a scream. Jaci jumped, recognizing Amanda's voice. "Where's Amanda?"

Ricky dropped the bag. "Stay here. I'll find her."

The shriek came from just down the ravine. Ricky took off in that direction.

Jaci and Sara stood paralyzed, waiting.

"Should we go?" asked Sara.

"Yes." The word came out in a strangled whisper.

A few minutes later Ricky and Amanda stumbled through the ferns and trees, carrying a limp figure between them. Sara let out a small cry and hurried forward. "It's Neal!"

Ricky lowered him to the ground at their feet.

"Is he okay?" said Jaci.

Ricky nodded. "He's breathing."

Sara knelt over him. "Where did you find him?"

Amanda pulled on her hair, looking pleased with herself. "I was chasing a rabbit, and I stumbled across him."

Neal stirred. "Oh," he moaned.

"Get water," ordered Ricky.

"Here." Jaci tossed a water bottle to him.

Neal opened his eyes. He tried to sit up but winced and fell back down.

"Where've you been?" Tears welled up in Sara's eyes. "We've looked for you for days! Why didn't you come back to the camp?"

Neal pushed himself up on one arm, flinching a little. "I fell in. I couldn't get my feet on the ground, and I blacked out. When I came to, I was stuck on a log. On the wrong side of the river."

Ricky brushed his hands on his pants and stood up. "You need to rest."

"When did you become responsible?" Neal closed his eyes and leaned back. "Okay. I'll rest."

October 13
Little Falls, New York

"Here you go." The receptionist at the Little Falls courthouse placed a file on the counter. "These are the court proceedings for the legal adoption of Neal and Richard Collins."

Carl opened up the file and began scanning the first document, wondering what exactly he hoped to find. There were no living relatives. The boys had been living with a grandmother, surviving off the government's mercy.

The first page listed the facts: date of hearing, those present, who presided. It was the second page that began to get interesting.

Carl read the minutes. There had been somewhat of a fight to get the boys. The grandmother begged the court not to separate the four-year-old twins. The minutes even stated she would rather have neither if it meant keeping them together.

The judge awarded her custody of both boys. He granted her a government stipend of ten thousand dollars a year, as well as government housing, provided she continued to work. If she lost her job, she was in danger of losing the boys to the foster care system.

A fairly generous verdict, Carl thought. Judge Acuff had bent over backwards to keep those boys together.

There was no mention of any other relatives. He finished up the final verdict and one sentence leapt out at him: "Custody of Abigail Collins: Not granted."

His mind went on rewind. He flipped back to the first page of the file. Somehow he had skipped over the name of the case.

"Jocelyn Bennett vs. the state of New York. Deciding legal custody for Neal, Richard, and Abigail Collins." Abigail Collins. There had been another child.

"Ma'am? Can you copy all of these court records for me, please?"

She eyed him. "I'll need a photocopy of your badge."

He tossed it on the counter. "There."

She disappeared with the file. Carl would wait until he had those copies before he made his next request.

She came back with his badge and the papers.

"Also, Ma'am, I'd like to see the file on the adoption of Abigail Collins."

She examined the file, resting the folder in the crook of her elbow. "Was this not it?"

He shook his head. "No, Ma'am. Jocelyn Bennett was denied custody of the girl. I need to know where she went."

"Let me see if I can find it."

She left, and Carl tapped his fingernails on the counter.

Finally, she returned. "I'm sorry, but I can't show you that file. It's a closed adoption."

"I'm a detective. I need this for a case."

She shook her head. "I'll need a court order from the judge, or a search warrant. His secretary's office is on the third floor. If he thinks you need the information, he might give you a court order before the end of the week."

"Is it still Judge Acuff?"

"Yes, Sir."

"Thank you very much."

It was Monday. He wasn't leaving Little Falls until he had that file.

Chapter 26

Ricky returned from the water after dark. "I'm sorry. The water's too slow now for me to get anything."

Neal shook his head. "We need to figure out a better plan for food. We can't be dependent on just catching fish."

"Maybe some of these plants are edible," Amanda said.

"What about animals?" said Jaci. "Could we hunt?"

Amanda snapped her fingers. "There was a rabbit yesterday. I was chasing it when I found Neal."

A spark of hope warmed Jaci. "If we can catch it, I think I can prepare it." It couldn't be much harder than skinning fish, could it?

"But how do you catch a rabbit?" said Amanda, kicking the dirt with her toe.

"We have to make a trap," Ricky said. "Anyone know how?"

"I think I can build one," Sara said. "I did it once in Girl Scouts."

They gathered vines and twigs for making a square trap, following Sara's instructions.

"Try to mask your smell," Neal said. "The animal will smell us and stay away." He picked up some dirt, rubbing it on his hands.

"Should we risk a fire?" asked Ricky.

Neal shook his head. "We better keep a low profile. We still don't know who's out there looking for the girls."

Sara and Neal finished wrapping some vine around a few twigs, tying it in places to make it tight.

Neal gave the trap a test, then smiled and held it up. "Done!"

They completed four more before they were too hungry and tired to do anything else. Together they marched into the woods and laid out the traps.

"Now we sleep," Neal said. "And hope that tomorrow, we have rabbits."

Jaci shivered in the light wind, hugging herself. They were starving and freezing. And there was somebody out there, close by, who could be a danger to them. They wouldn't survive much longer.

She felt the knowledge enter her heart like a lead rock. They were going to die out here.

Neal glanced at her. "We're going to get you girls out of this. I promise."

"Thanks," Jaci said. She moved closer to Sara and buried her face in the younger girl's hair.

October 14
Little Falls, New York

Carl stepped down from the Canal Side Inn, a wonderful bed and breakfast in Little Falls. He rubbed his protruding belly. Too many meals like the one he had just finished had increased his girth.

A bicycle bell rang behind him, and Carl moved to the right. He watched the bike turn left, heading toward the Erie Canal. What a historic city. Full of charm and interest.

He pulled out his phone. Judge Acuff had listened to his tale with interest and promised him a court order within two days. Judges were busy, though. Carl wanted to call and remind him, but he didn't want to aggravate the man.

He put his phone away. He itched to do something. Maybe he would take a stroll through the Historic Canal District. It might help clear his mind.

A pleasant autumn breeze blew off the direction of the canal. The phone in Carl's pocket vibrated. He stared at the caller ID for a brief moment before answering.

"Detective Hamilton speaking."

"Detective, this is Ranger Lewis, checking in. I'm with the Adirondack Park Services for Area five, which includes—"

"Yes, yes. Do you have word on the girls? Have they been spotted?" Carl leaned forward on the railing over the canal, watching a large barge drift downriver.

There was a pause on the other end. "No, Sir."

"Thank you. Keep me informed."

Carl stood for a long moment after the call, cradling his phone in both hands. He dialed Idaho.

"Idaho Falls police department, this is Monica. How may I direct your call?"

"Hi, Monica. Detective Hamilton. No dispatch today?"

"Nope. It's Patty's turn."

"Listen, I need to get a search party organized. A huge one. It's going to take some work, but I'd like to get a lot of experienced hikers from the cities within and around the Adirondack park system. Can you pass me through to the chief? I'm going to need his help."

"Sure thing."

Carl waited for the call to transfer. He couldn't expect a lot from a search party. They were most effective when undertaken days after a person went missing. And it had been over a month.

Chapter 27

Jaci woke up shivering. A thin sheen of crystalline frost covered everything—the trees, the bushes, the ground, even her arms and legs. She vigorously rubbed the frost off her jeans.

So quiet. In the morning the birds usually chirped in the trees, or a lizard scurried in the underbrush. But today it seemed so still.

"I'm starving." Sara's hazel eyes were opened just a little, peeking up at her.

Food. She pushed herself to her feet. "The rabbits!"

"Right." Sara was up in an instant.

Neal sat up, running his hands through his frosty brown hair.

"You coming?" Jaci asked.

"Of course."

They made their way to where they had left the traps. Neal picked one up. "Empty."

"Not this one!" Jaci grabbed a trap and held it up.

The rabbit within the twig box scooted away from her, staring out with liquid black eyes. The large ears trembled in fear.

Sara held up another. "Anyone want a mouse?"

Out of the other three traps, two more had rabbits and the third was empty.

Ricky eyed the trappings when they returned. "That's it? Three rabbits and a mouse?"

"All right, Jaci," said Amanda. "You're up."

Jaci stepped forward and took the traps. This would be far worse than skinning a fish.

"I'll help," said Ricky.

Amanda interrupted. "Oh, Ricky, I was hoping you'd try and catch fish again. Neal can help her."

"Sure," Neal said.

Ricky shrugged. "Fine. I'll see if I can get a fish to top off our breakfast of rodents." He started down the path to the water.

"And I'll come along," Amanda said.

"Come on, then. Maybe I'll make a spear this time."

Neal sat next to Jaci. "I'll kill them for you, okay?" he said. "Then we'll skin them together."

"Who, Amanda and Ricky, or the rabbits?"

He laughed. "The rabbits."

He took the small animals out of their traps one at a time. He turned sideways, out of Jaci's sight, but she saw his arms wrench and heard the crack.

It's food, she reminded herself.

Neal did the hard stuff, using the strength of his fingers to break the skin and rip it off. She looked away, not able to watch.

Ricky came back from the river, empty-handed except for his spear. It proved unsuccessful at catching fish, but was perfect for lancing small animals and roasting them over a fire.

"Thanks, Jaci," Sara said as she pulled apart one of the rabbits. "This is great."

"Neal did it. That was an awful job." She picked meat off the bones. "We'll be out of this forest soon, won't we, Sara?"

Sara paused. "Well, I lost the map in the rainstorm. But if I remember right, I don't think the park goes on much farther."

Ricky looked at them. "Then you're going to the police?"

Sara shrugged.

Amanda said, "We have to, and we should call home. Our parents must be going nuts. It's been, what, two months?"

"It's been about five weeks," Sara snapped, her eyes narrowing. "Anyway, if the lines are tapped, they'll know everything. What if they find us first?"

"Then don't go to the police," said Ricky.

"Not an option." Amanda rose to her feet. "Let's get moving."

After about two hours of walking, Sara came to a stop. "Listen."

Jaci drew up beside her, ears straining.

A man was talking, not more than a hundred yards in front of them.

Ricky grabbed both of the girls and pushed them against tree trunks. Then he dropped down to his knees and peered through the bushes.

"I know they're around here. I smelled their fire this morning. The girls picked up two hikers, two boys. Right, I'm trying to keep them out of this. I'm backtracking to the fire now. When I find the fire, I'll follow their trail."

Jaci couldn't hear the response, only static-like words that burst from the radio.

Ricky stood up, pressing against Jaci and whispering in her ear, "I have to warn Neal and Amanda. Don't move."

Jaci panicked, gripping the tree trunk. She watched Ricky slide to the ground and crawl away.

Breathe, she told herself. Her face was hot, sweat beading along her hairline.

"Sure, sure, my GPS is on. Find me at any moment. We have to hurry, though. There's a search party in here looking for them, too."

Jaci closed her eyes, letting those words register. Then this man wasn't part of the search party. He was with the other party.

A branch cracked behind her. She stiffened. Where was Ricky? She scanned the trail in front of them, but he had vanished.

The bushes next to her trembled, and a man stepped between the trees she and Sara were pressed against. His camouflaged vest and green turtleneck helped him blend into the surrounding foliage.

If he turned around, or even glanced over his shoulder, he would see her and Sara.

Jaci sank against the tree, willing him to keep going forward. A hand touched her arm, and she jerked her head. Sara motioned around the tree.

Jaci gave a slow nod. As quietly as she could, she moved to the opposite side of the tree. Sara did the same. They stayed that way, staring, motionless, until Jaci let her legs give out and sank to the ground.

"What do we do?" whispered Sara. "Should we run?"

"Let's stay right here. Get down low, in the bushes. Ricky knows where we are. He'll come back for us."

"Okay." Sara dropped to the ground, nearly disappearing in the leafless brush.

Jaci had no idea how long they sat there, nerves taut, when she heard someone approaching. She peered through the bushes, catching sight of dark green pants. Jaci drew back.

Please don't look down, please don't look down, she prayed.

Sara covered her face with her hands. It was a small movement, but it was enough. The man turned his feet in Sara's direction. Sara tensed.

Jaci knew at any moment the girl would try to run. Jaci's hands dug around the twigs and roots, searching for a weapon. Her fingers closed on a heavy branch.

"Ah-ha," The man said, bending toward Sara's bush. "Looks like I found something."

Jaci stood up and hit him over the neck as hard as she could. He turned to face her, surprise on his face, and she smashed the branch into his nose.

He stumbled backwards, blood streaming. His hand fumbled in his pocket.

She swung again. The man reached a hand up to block her, and she kicked his leg. He tripped over a stump behind him and fell backwards.

She swung the branch down with all her might, again and again and again. Then strong arms gripped her shoulders and jerked her up.

"Oh!" She gave a startled cry.

Her captor spun her around. She stared at the man in front of her, at his snarling, angry face, the camo vest. There were two men.

He gripped her wrist until it went numb, and Jaci felt her fingers open, dropping the branch. It was over. She lowered her head.

Behind him Sara screamed, the high-pitched shriek echoing through the trees.

Neal came crashing around the trees, several rocks in his hands. "Jaci, duck!"

She did. Most of the rocks missed, but one smashed into the man's head. He swore and let go of Jaci.

If he had a gun, he would go for it now. He made no move to grab one, just covered his head and started running.

Ricky burst in, followed by Amanda. "We can't let them get away," she said.

"Amanda," Neal barked. "Move Sara and Jaci away from there."

He took off after the man. Ricky, brandishing his spear, followed.

Chapter 28

Neal and Ricky returned hours later.

"Let's go," Neal said, helping Sara to her feet. "We need to get out of here. Everyone close together." Neal took up the lead, setting a death march pace.

After several hours of walking, the first brief sounds of civilization began to waffle in through the trees. They could hear the rush of cars, though it wasn't frequent. Finally, Neal began to slow their pace.

"Ricky?" he asked.

"Good," Ricky called back.

Jaci's legs burned from their mad dance through the trees. She slowed, grateful for the change.

"We'll be out soon," she said, surprised at how anxious she was to get out of the forest.

"Where do you suppose we'll come out at?" Neal asked. His voice was level, calm, although slightly out of breath.

Ricky shrugged. "The only city I know outside of the park is Little Falls, and I haven't been there since we were kids."

Next to Jaci, Sara stirred. She lifted her head and blinked as if she had just woken up. "I know that name. I think that's where I was born."

She tripped and stumbled forward. Jaci grabbed her arm and steadied her.

Unexpectedly, her own knees gave out. Jaci grabbed at a young cedar, feeling the bark dig into the palms of her hands. "Can we rest? Just for a bit?"

Neal didn't want to stop. She could tell in the way he hesitated.

"We'll stop when it's too dark to see. At sunrise we're out of here. Tomorrow we'll use my credit card and eat somewhere."

"I'll stay with her," Ricky said. "We won't be long."

"Hurry," said Neal. "Don't lose sight of us."

Jaci leaned against the tree and closed her eyes. Her head ached. She swallowed, noting the dryness in her throat. "Ricky? Do you have the water?"

"Yeah."

She opened her eyes and watched him pull a bottle from the orange bag.

"Here." He handed her the water bottle, touching her fingers before pulling back.

"Are you scared?" he asked her, zipping the bag and swinging it over his shoulder.

"Yes. Are you?"

"Yes," he said, looking away from her. "Let's go. We can't lose the others."

October 16
Little Falls, New York

Carl was on edge. No sightings of the teenagers anywhere, and the judge still hadn't given him his court order. He had called twice yesterday. Perhaps today he needed to ask in person.

He slipped into the city courthouse and rode the elevator up to the third floor. He rocked back and forth on his heels, staring at the numbers as they lit up.

He recognized the cute brunette with clips in her hair behind the glass window. He had spoken to her last time. Carl cleared his throat, stepping up to the speaker.

She looked up.

"I'm Detective Hamilton. May I speak with Judge Acuff?"

She stepped to the counter and looked down at a piece of paper. "Oh. Detective Hamilton. I have a court order here for you, would you like it?"

He fought back the urge to push his hand through the hole and snatch the paper from her.

"How long has that been there?"

"Since yesterday afternoon." She picked it up and offered it with a smile. "I tried to call you, but the phone number was disconnected."

Carl glanced at the pink sticky-note on the order. His number was written down in big, bubbly lettering, but the last digit was wrong.

Don't stress it. You got it now. "Thank you."

The elevator took too long. He read through the order as he flew down the stairs.

Bursting into the Vital Records office, he waved the court order at the receptionist. "I have it. My court order."

He slapped it down on the counter and grinned at her. "The file on Abigail Collins, please."

She glanced over the court order. "One moment."

He tried to be patient. In a moment he would know where little Miss Abigail had gone. If the boys knew—if they had any idea— they might be trying to reach her.

She handed him the file. Carl walked over to a chair and sat down.

The first pages were photocopies of the court proceeding where the grandmother was denied custody of Abigail. The next two pages detailed the hearing that gave Elizabeth and Mike Yadle custody of Abigail Collins.

Back up. Carl read the names again. Elizabeth and Mike Yadle. But those were Sara's parents. He stared at the page in his hands, trying to make sense of it.

He glanced at the date. Thirteen years ago. In that moment, all the pieces came together in his head.

Abigail Collins was Sara Yadle. By pure chance, pure coincidence, Ricky and Neal Collins had met up again with their sister, after thirteen years apart.

Unless Sara had known about them and was trying to find *them*. That was a possibility.

He stepped up to the clerk. "Can you copy this?"

She examined the file. "I'm sorry, I can't. It's restricted information."

"That's fine." Carl waved a hand. He didn't need the written paper. "Thanks for your help."

As soon as he was in the hall, he pulled out his cell phone and dialed the Yadle's number. His hands trembled.

"Hello?"

"Mrs. Yadle, Detective Hamilton here."

"Did you find something?"

Her voice went up in pitch, and Carl flinched. He could just picture her, clutching the phone, waiting for news.

"Nothing I can say right now, Mrs. Yadle. But I do have a question for you. When you adopted Sara, were you aware of any living relatives?"

"Um... yes. There was a grandmother. We don't know where she is now, though, and she's had no contact with Sara. We didn't want her to get confused... Sara, I mean."

"That's all?"

"I'm not really sure, Detective. It's been so long. I remember the grandmother wanted custody of Sara but the government wouldn't grant it. My husband and I had been waiting to adopt for years, and we got a call. There was a toddler available. There were siblings, too, but the grandmother wouldn't give them up."

There had been siblings.

"Why all these questions, Detective? Do you think Sara's biological family is somehow involved in this?"

"I can't say anything more, Mrs. Yadle. Just one more question. What was Sara's birth name?"

"Abigail."

"Thank you, Mrs.Yadle. I'll get a message to you if I learn anything vital."

Chapter 29

Jaci slowly opened her eyes. It was too cold to sleep any longer. She sat up. Sara and Amanda were curled up next to her.

"Morning, Jaci." Neal gave her a weary smile from the tree he leaned against. Ricky slept on next to him.

Her body ached, reminding her of yesterday. She shuddered. "Thanks for keeping watch."

Sara stirred and sat up, shivering. "Gotta pee." She pushed herself to her feet.

"Don't let her go alone," Neal said, his lips tightening.

"I won't." Jaci got up. "I need to go, too."

They made their way into the forest, their breath leaving little clouds of vapor.

"I'll be a minute longer," Sara said. "Go back without me."

Jaci paused. "Neal said not to leave you alone."

"I'm fine," Sara snapped. "Just go!"

"Okay."

Amanda was up when she got back. She still had her arms pulled inside the knit sweater. Morning sun filtered through the leaves, but it didn't give any warmth.

"Be back in a moment." Amanda stumbled away from the group.

Jaci stepped closer to Neal. He splashed water from a warped plastic bottle onto his face, then handed it to her. She took a swig of the acrid water and watched him approach Ricky, who still slept against a tree trunk.

"Ricky," he said, tapping him with his foot to wake him. "Wake up, it's morning."

Amanda returned, her green eyes wide. "I think Sara's sick. She's throwing up back there."

Jaci stuffed bark into the orange bag. Their food for the day.

"Does she need help?"

Amanda shook her head. "She said not to worry. She told me to go away. What do you suppose she has? Next thing you know we'll all have it."

"I doubt it," Neal interjected. "She's pregnant."

Jaci spun around. Pregnant? But she was only fourteen. She couldn't be pregnant!

Ricky shook his head. "I don't think that was the best way to spring it on them."

Jaci stared at the twins. "You know this for sure?"

Neal nodded. "Yes. She told us."

"Oh my gosh," Amanda said. "That explains *a lot*. Wow. So she's not—Sara's not a virgin anymore."

"You did not just say that," Jaci said.

Amanda looked at her and shrugged. "What, it's just a fact. She's the first one of us to—"

Something inside Jaci snapped, and she lunged at Amanda. "Amanda! Shut up, just shut up."

Ricky tugged on the orange backpack across her shoulders and pulled her away.

Jaci fought tears and clutched the bag strap. Her hands trembled from the rush of anger. "Poor Sara," she sobbed.

Ricky gave her a hug. "She'll be okay. She's got you."

If Sara noticed that everyone seemed a little quiet around her, she didn't comment.

Jaci chewed her bark in silence, wishing she could approach Sara, but not sure what to say.

They drank the last of the water. They hoped to reach a city by lunch time.

"All right, come on," Neal said. "Just like yesterday." He took the lead, pushing them on at a brisk pace.

After an hour of walking, they hit a road winding its way through the trees.

"Off the road," Neal said when Amanda stepped toward it.

"But we'll be able to go faster."

"Stay off," he repeated.

Amanda made a face at him but obeyed.

The forest sloped down from the road. They stayed out of the ravine, walking sideways to keep the road in sight. There was no traffic.

They followed the road as it went south and then veered west.

Another three hours, and the forest began to thin. Pastures appeared, followed by farm houses and cows.

"There's an old barn," Neal said, pointing.

Jaci turned itchy, tired eyes in the direction he pointed. "How is it staying up?" She laughed at the sight of the building leaning over, half of the roof caved in.

"I don't know," he replied with a smile. "But it will hold for one more night."

Chapter 30

The barn door slammed shut, raining clumps of hay down on Jaci. She bolted up, blinking, trying to see in the semi-dark.

"Brr!" Ricky stood by the door, shafts of sunlight illuminating him as he rubbed his arms. "It snowed last night."

The rest of the group stirred, moving into sitting positions around the dried yellow hay.

Jaci hugged her arms around her knees. The pink knit sweater she wore hung loosely off one shoulder, exposing her thread-bare blue t-shirt beneath.

Ricky sat down next to her. "I think your sweater's a little big for you."

Jaci glanced at the sweater Silvet had given her. The old woman's clothes had been loose even when they stayed in the cabin several weeks ago. Now, Jaci couldn't get the sweater to stay on both shoulders

She reached a hand up and touched her collar bone, feeling the way the skin stretched tight.

"Anything out there?" asked Neal.

"Nope," said Ricky. "Not even a cow."

"How much snow?" Sara asked.

"Not much. Looks like an inch."

"What now?" Jaci didn't want to walk in the snow. She glanced down at her shoes. Her left toe was visible.

Neal shrugged. "It's up to you guys. Head out in the snow or wait here 'til it warms up?"

Neal had only one shoe and a sock. If Neal was willing to walk in the snow, Jaci could do it too.

Ricky rubbed his forehead. "I vote we call a cab."

"Let's wait," Sara said. "It'll warm up by noon."

Neal focused on her. "How are you feeling today?"

She blushed a little, and shot a glance toward Jaci.

Jaci swallowed, telling herself not to cry again. "It's okay, Sara. We know."

Sara blinked, confusion on her face. She looked at Neal.

He nodded. "I told them yesterday."

The brims of Sara's eyes turned red. "Excuse me," she said. She stumbled over her feet in her hurry to get away from them.

"I guess we'll just sit and wait for awhile." Ricky found a spot under a large beam of wood that had partially collapsed, throwing the hay into shadow.

Neal stood up. "I'm going outside."

"I'm sorry," Ricky said. "About Sara, I mean."

Jaci gave a short nod. "We all are."

The sun came out by ten in the morning, shining brightly enough to melt away any lingering frost. They headed out.

Neal tensed every time a car approached, grabbing Sara's arm as if preparing to run.

"Are we running from something?" Amanda asked, lifting an eyebrow.

"Just playing it safe," said Neal. He seemed jumpy.

An hour later they found Stinger's Bar and Grill.

The worker served up orders in small ceramic bowls. Jaci took a moment to breathe in the aroma; hamburger meat, bacon, bread, cheese. She grabbed a tray and followed behind the others.

Neal reached the check-out register first, and glanced behind him as he held out his credit card. "Ah, we're all together."

The girl at the cash register took his card and examined it, smacking loudly on her gum. "You got ID?"

"Um, yeah." He pulled out his driver's license. "Can you tell me how to get to the police department?"

"It's in Rome, about half an hour from here."

"Half an hour," repeated Ricky.

Jaci did the mental calculations. Half an hour by car. About twenty miles, depending on the speed. That meant a whole day on foot.

"How do I get there?" Neal asked.

Jaci tuned out the directions and pushed a strand of hair behind her ears. Her stomach twisted painfully. Hot slices of roast beef, pasta, and garlic bread. So many options!

"What entrée would you like?" the serving woman behind the counter asked.

"Roast beef, please." Jaci watched Sara set her tray down next to Amanda and Neal. "Ricky. Tell me about you and Sara."

"And for you, young man?"

"Huh?" He blinked, tossing his brown hair out of his face and looking at Jaci. "Sara?"

The woman cleared her throat.

"I don't have any cough drops," Ricky snapped, shooting her an annoyed look.

Jaci pointed to the macaroni salad. "That too, please. And a slice of garlic bread." She waited while the woman placed a spoonful in a small bowl. "That's all, thanks."

"Just give me one of those sandwiches." Ricky pointed. "What about Sara?"

"I don't know." Jaci kept her voice low. "You seem so close. Something about the two of you—actually, the three of you, you, Neal, and Sara…" It nagged at her.

"I'm not flirting. It's different. I don't know how to explain it."

"Does Sara know it's different?"

They set their trays down at a table. "Sure. Yeah."

Jaci sat down next to him. "Forget it." She dug her fork into the food.

Then the nagging coalesced into a solid thought, and she stopped. "Your last name is Collins."

"Yes." He grabbed up his sandwich and took a huge bite. "And yours is Rivera."

"But I think—" She shook her head. "No. Let's eat first."

Chapter 31

Jaci tried not to eat too fast. She couldn't wait to talk to Sara. It all made *sense*. Their closeness, the bond between them, even their *eyes*-- that hazel color.

She tapped her fingers on the table, watching Ricky finish his sandwich. She pushed her chair back. "Come on."

Amanda was talking, using her hands for emphasis, when Jaci approached.

"Sara," Jaci interrupted, "what's your last name?"

"Have you forgotten, Jaci?" Sara asked. "Yadle."

"No, not that one. Your biological last name. Before you were adopted."

She paused a moment. "Collins."

Ricky looked at Sara. "Really?"

"Yes," she said, giving Jaci a puzzled look.

"But you know that's our last name too," said Neal.

"Yeah. So?"

"Is it just coincidence?" Ricky asked.

"How should I know?"

Jaci's excitement became certainty. "You're related."

Neal stood up. "Let's head out of here and talk about this."

The sun was straight up in the sky, casting short shadows from the shops across the sidewalk.

"It's weird because all three of us are orphans," said Neal. "Otherwise, I wouldn't think much of it."

"Also remember that Sara was born in New York," Jaci added.

"Yes!" Ricky said, snapping his fingers. "In Little Falls. And we were also born in Little Falls. Shortly after our parents' death we moved to Johnsburg to be with our grandmother."

"The problem is," Amanda said, "Sara doesn't know anything

about her birth family. Not even if she had siblings."

"Yeah. All I know is that my parents died in an accident."

A slight frown darkened Ricky's features. "Certainly the state would've kept us together. Not let her be adopted out."

"The state wouldn't let Grandma take any more kids," said Neal. "Remember? They kept trying to take us away from her?"

Jaci noticed a phone booth at the gas station a few yards away. "Okay. It's time to get to the bottom of this. Let's call."

They marched over to the phone. Sara hesitated.

Jaci picked up the phone and rattled it at her. "Come on. Call home, tell them we're okay. Ask your questions."

Sara took it and dialed, the tip of her nose turning pink. She paused, taking a few deep breaths.

"Sara," she said into the phone. "Operator," she mouthed to her friends. Then her face paled.

"It's ringing! Mom?" She began to cry. "Yes, it's me. No, no, we're okay. Mom, I love you. We're—what? We're going to find help. I think we're going to the police… Um-hum… Uh-huh… Yes."

She wiped her tears with the back of her hand. "I know. Mom, some—some bad things have happened." She sobbed and put a hand over her mouth. "Mom—Mom, listen to me. I have a question for you."

Sara paused, and then snapped, "Mother! I don't have time. This is really important. Do I have any family left alive? From my biological parents?"

There was silence, and Jaci realized she was on her tip-toes, straining to hear what was said on the other end.

Neal leaned back. "If the call's being traced, time is important. She needs to get off now."

Jaci nodded, her heart sinking. "Sara. Let's go."

Sara clutched the phone tighter. "I need to know now. Was I an only child? Wasn't there anyone else?"

Jaci stepped up to the pay phone and put her finger on the hook. "Sara. I'm going to hang up."

Sara didn't look at her but started speaking faster. "I have to go. We'll call you from the police station. Mom, I'm going to go now."

She blinked several times. "Bye, Mom, and tell Daddy I love him too. Bye!" She hung up the phone and dropped her head into her hands.

Neal stared at her. "Well?"

She lifted her head and wiped her face. "Mom—my mom—she

doesn't know for sure. She thinks I had two brothers. Twins. But she's not sure. They've spent my whole life pretending like no one else existed."

"You're our sister."

"Yes, I-I think I am."

October 18
Little Falls, New York

Carl pulled out the fax he had received from Idaho. The chief had called his cell phone and ordered him to the nearest police department to make a secure call. As soon as he got to the Little Falls police department, Carl had called back.

"The girls made contact," Chief Miller said, his low voice punctuated with excitement. "Sara Yadle called home."

Sara. Abigail Collins. "Yes?" Carl leaned into the phone. "Where are they? Are they alright?"

"Elizabeth Yadle took the call. Sara, Jaci, and Amanda are fine. She said they might be going to the police."

A thrill of joy had warmed Carl at those words. The girls were all still alive. *Focus.* "Where are they?"

"Sara didn't say."

"She didn't say?"

"Mrs. Yadle said she was in a hurry to get off the phone."

But they were alive. And going to the police. "What about those missing boys? Were they with them?"

"Mrs. Yadle didn't mention them. You can call and get the details of the phone call, if you want."

"No, it's not important right now. I'll catch the next flight out of here and organize an alert."

"Why would you come home? Chances are they're still back east. You'll be able to reach them quicker if you stay where you are. As soon as they're picked up, however, get them onto a secure charter flight and bring them home."

"No problem." Carl already had that in mind. He wasn't leaving these girls out in the public eye for any longer than he had to. Immediately he put a plan into action. They were out of the forest, so he called off the search parties.

Right after he did so, he got a call from the sheriff of Herkimer county.

"Herkimer county?" Carl echoed. Should he know that name?

"Yes. It's a large county, taking up most of the north and west of the park system."

Ah. Someone from inside the forest. "Yes?" He felt only the slightest interest. The girls were out, and his mind was elsewhere.

"It might not be anything," the sheriff said, his deep voice gravelly, "but we found a body."

"A body?" Quickly he recalled the conversation with his boss. All the girls were found. Was it one of the boys? "A boy?"

"A man. It happens from time to time. A hiker comes in, doesn't register, no one knows where he is. He falls down, gets hurt, dehydrated, and we find him later."

"All right." Carl nodded, his attention fading. "Something about this one is unusual?"

"It looks like he was bludgeoned to death. We ran a check on his ID, and it's fabricated."

Carl pulled out his notepad. "I'm working on something else right now, but I want to get back with you. What number can I reach you on?"

The sheriff gave his number, and Carl tucked the information away. This could be related.

That aside, he called Idaho and asked Monica to make a fax with the girls' pertinent information and send it to all police departments in New York and Pennsylvania. He couldn't imagine the girls being anywhere else, but just in case, a fax was also sent to each state police department.

Now Carl hovered around the Little Falls police department, trying to stay out of the way. They had been very helpful, letting him set up a kind of office. His hard plastic chair sat by a fax machine on top of a cardboard box. They had even pulled over a telephone and plugged it into the landline.

But the phone hadn't rung and no faxes had come in. Carl resisted the urge to call Idaho Falls again. That's where he should be, but it was unlikely the girls were going to make contact with a police department out west.

The fax listed the numbers for the Idaho Falls police, the Little Falls police, and the FBI. Every police department on the list had confirmed receipt. He could do nothing else.

He read over the girls' details again. Sara Yadle. Fourteen. Blond hair, hazel eyes, Caucasian female.

Jacinta Rivera. Fifteen. Brown hair, brown eyes, Hispanic female.

Amanda Murphy. Fifteen. Red hair, green eyes. Caucasian female. Each name had an individual picture attached.

He tried to imagine what they looked like now. More than a month of camping. Thin, emaciated, dirty. Perhaps sick, even physically hurt.

He sat down in his plastic chair and stared at the phone, willing it to ring. If only he knew what city they were in.

Chapter 32

It didn't snow that night.

By noon they had reached Rome. The outward sprawl of houses and the sounds of engines and horns honking indicated a large population.

"Look at all the places to eat," Jaci said as they turned down a street.

"All right, here's the plan," said Neal. "Let's get some food first. Then, I want us to find a clothes store and everyone buy a coat and a sweater. And me a pair of shoes."

They started down the street, and Sara grabbed Jaci's arm. "I don't think we should go to the police."

"It's okay. We're far from Canada now. The police will help us."

Sara shook her head. "We'll have to separate from the boys. We'll be vulnerable."

This wasn't about being afraid of the police. It was about leaving Neal and Ricky. She put an arm around Sara. "It won't be for long."

Sara didn't look convinced, but she let Jaci pull her along.

They found a Subway for lunch, and there they asked for directions to the police station.

"Go left on St. James," the cashier told them. "Just up the street. You'll see it."

After eating they headed up to St. James.

"Look, a clothing store," Jaci said, pointing to a store called Erin's Way. Skirts, boots, shirts, and chunky necklaces dangled from the window mannequin.

Half an hour later, they congregated at a street corner, waiting for the walk signal to turn on. Donning their new jackets, they appeared remarkably normal.

Neal had kind of a beard thing going on. It matched his gray jacket, making him look like the outdoors-y type.

Jaci's navy blue jacket fit snugly, with only a lime-green V over the chest as an accent. The warm fleece sleeves stretched all the way to her palms. She wrapped her bony arms around herself, appreciating the warmth.

"Let's talk about going to the police," said Neal. "Are we sure it's the right thing to do?"

"How can it not be?" Jaci asked. "They must be looking for us."

"Yeah," Amanda chimed in, wearing a pink vest-jacket. "They'll protect us and make sure we get home."

"You know what it means for us," Ricky interjected. "This is where we part ways. They'd ship us to a juvenile detention center for sure."

The light changed to a walk, but nobody moved.

"Let's do this, then," Jaci said. "Don't come in with us. After the police have called our parents, you call Sara's parents. Her parents can ask for custody of you until the courts can decide what to do with you. Like foster parents. Then you come into the police station and join us, once you know that's been done. They should let us stay together."

Ricky nodded thoughtfully. "Might work."

Neal asked, "How will we know if Sara's called her parents?"

Jaci shrugged. "Give it an hour or two. They won't wait longer than that."

"Okay." Ricky nodded. "Yeah, we can do that."

"Good," Amanda said. "That's settled. Can we go now?"

Sara balked. "I'm telling you, I don't want to go. I don't feel right about it."

"Then don't come," Amanda responded. "Stay with the boys. We'll be fine."

The light changed to a walk for the second time. Amanda threw her arms up and started across.

Sara shook her head, biting her lip. "I can't. Something's wrong."

"What do you mean?" Jaci asked. She was starting to get nervous.

"I don't know. I just don't think we should go."

"What if she's right?" asked Ricky.

"Well, I guess we'll find out when we talk to Sara's parents," Neal said.

"And if something's gone wrong?"

"Sara. You girls need someone who can protect you. Ricky and I can't."

Jaci watched Neal's face. He was afraid for them. He knew something he wasn't telling them.

Sara blinked back tears. "You can more than the police."

Ricky squeezed her hand. "It'll be fine."

"And if it's not?" she repeated, pulling her hand away. They reached the other side where Amanda waited, her stance impatient.

"Then we'll find a way to help," Neal assured Sara. "We won't be with you, so we'll be able to help."

"What can you two possibly do against a police force?"

"You might be surprised," Ricky said, giving Neal a sly smile.

"And what is a police force possibly going to do to us?" Amanda shot back. "Let's go."

"All right," Neal said, stopping on the sidewalk in front of the station. "This is where we say goodbye."

"For how long?" Jaci asked.

"Not long," Ricky said. "Either we'll be joining you in there, or we'll all catch up in Idaho. Soon."

Sara turned on Neal, who had the orange backpack strapped to one shoulder. "Don't lose that. It's all we have left."

He nodded. "I won't."

Jaci thought of all the tree bark inside. Not exactly valuable.

"Can you remember my phone number?" Sara asked Ricky.

"Yeah."

"My mom's name is Elizabeth. My dad is Mike. The phone number is two-oh-eight, three-five-six, four-three-one-nine." She looked at Neal. "Help him remember."

"Uh-huh." Neal mouthed the numbers to himself. "Got it."

"Don't wait too long to call."

Ricky nodded. "Right. We'll call."

"Okay." Sara took a deep breath and gave them both a shaky smile. "We'll see you later."

Neal reached over and hugged her. "Take care."

Jaci looked at Ricky. She wanted to say something. But what?

Their eyes met. He licked his lips. "Well. Goodbye, Jaci."

"Bye."

"Come on, let's not make a scene," Amanda said, grabbing Jaci's arm and pulling the girls toward the building.

Jaci clutched at Ricky's hand, grasping his fingers for a moment before they slid away. Her throat ached.

Amanda opened the doors to the building and Jaci turned around, leaving Neal and Ricky behind. She focused on the tiled room in front of her, the silver elevator behind the white reception desk in the middle of the room.

Jaci stepped up to the clerk, the other girls falling in behind her. She tugged on her ponytail and cleared her throat. "Excuse me?"

The clerk looked up, blinking her clumpy black eyelashes. "Yes?"

"We'd like to speak to someone in your police force. We're in trouble, and we need help getting home."

The clerk looked them up and down and then picked up her desk phone.

"Sergeant Gates? I've got three girls down here asking to speak to an officer. Oh, okay. Sure." She hung up.

"Someone will be right down. Why don't you have a seat?" She gestured to a number of chairs against the wall.

"Sure," Jaci said. She moved in the direction of the chairs. She gripped one and lowered herself into it. Sara's nervousness was contagious. She glanced at the elevator behind the clerk's desk, at the security scanners in front of the entrance.

"We've got to get out of here," Sara said. "Before it's too late."

The elevator chimed and a portly man stepped out. He smiled at them and said, "Hi. I'm Lieutenant Hansen. If you'll come with me, please?"

Jaci stood and the others followed her lead. Her head throbbed. If they were going to change their minds, it was now or never.

He escorted them down a hall and came to a stop at a room, which he unlocked and motioned them in. He stepped inside with them and grabbed a metal chair. He straddled it and faced them.

"We know who you are, and you'll be safe here. We've been expecting you since yesterday. You're in police custody now. We won't hurt you. Do you need anything? Water? Food?"

Jaci exhaled, feeling her heart rate slow down. They were safe. "What happens now?"

"We have a task force waiting for you in Pennsylvania. One of our sergeants there has been put on your case. We're keeping it quiet for now, just in case the wrong eyes and ears are looking for you. Once we turn you over to his custody, he'll help you get safely reunited with your families."

Jaci smiled at Sara. *See?* she wanted to say. *Everything's fine.*

Sara didn't look relieved.

"Can we call our families?" Amanda asked, popping her fingers.

Lieutenant Hansen frowned. "No. We can't let it leak yet that you've been found."

He stood. "I'll be back for you in a few hours."

Something tickled Jaci's mind, and she blurted out, "You said you were expecting us. How?"

He shrugged. "The department in Pennsylvania called and said you were coming. I don't know how they knew."

He walked out of the room and closed the door, locking it behind him.

"Wait," Sara called, but the door was shut.

"Sara," Amanda said. "It's okay! Look." She gestured around the room, which was furnished with a sink, a toilet, and two bunk beds. "They're going to take care of us."

"You're a fool, Amanda," Sara snapped. "Why didn't he ask us any questions? What are our names? Where did we come from? How can he help us?"

"The police must be on top of things. Of course everyone's looking for us. He recognized us."

"He's been expecting us?" Jaci echoed. "Someone said we were coming? How? Who would have known?"

She felt a heavy pit in her stomach. "We didn't even tell Sara's mom."

Sara trembled. "The Hand. He found us. He traced our call, and we're going right into a trap."

"The police can't be corrupt," Jaci said, shaking her head.

"Well, someone somewhere is corrupt," Sara said, her voice full of scorn. "And now we're trapped."

"It's not hopeless yet," said Amanda. "Ricky and Neal are still outside."

"A lot of good that does us. We can't even get a message to them," Jaci stated.

A gloomy silence descended. Jaci sat down on the floor, head in her hands. Amanda looked around the room, for once seeming desperate and scared. Sara just stood with a blank expression on her face.

Chapter 33

Lieutenant Hansen returned after a few minutes. He and two other officers guided the girls behind the station, loading them into a mid-size SUV police cruiser.

"Don't worry," Hansen said, his smile warm. He placed one hand on the back door. "We'll have you safely home to your families soon." He slammed the door, and the cruiser roared to life.

None of the girls said anything for the longest time. Sara curled into a ball on the bench, dropping her head and rocking back and forth.

"Do you think they're listening to us?" Amanda said to Jaci. Jaci shook her head.

Sara looked up. "What will Neal and Ricky do? When they can't reach us?"

Jaci said, "Maybe they'll tell your mom."

"Yeah," Amanda said, her eyes widening. "They'll get help. They'll find a good person."

A good person. Jaci doubted she would ever know who was good or bad again. She wasn't even sure she could trust her own family.

They drove for more than an hour, getting farther and farther away from Rome, New York. How would Ricky and Neal ever find them?

An engine revved loudly seconds before the cruiser slammed forward.

Jaci screamed, reaching her hands out as the SUV flipped upside down and came to a stop. Her face rammed into the bench before she crumpled into a heap.

She opened her eyes, tasting blood in her mouth. Everything blurred in front of her, but her fingers felt the ceiling ridges underneath her. Adrenaline surged through her, and she forced herself to her feet.

Someone whimpered next to her. She tried to focus on the huddled form. "Sara." She shook the girl's arm. "Sara, are you hurt?"

Sara got to her feet. "What happened?"

"An accident." Jaci didn't know whether to fear or hope. "This might be our chance to escape."

She looked around for Amanda. She heard the sound of distressed metal behind her. Someone was trying to open the door. She tensed.

"Jaci, I can't wake Amanda."

Jaci hurried to Sara's side, feeling for Amanda's neck. *Please, please don't let her be dead.* She wasn't. There was a pulse, strong and steady.

"How is everybody?" The voice came from outside.

Jaci knew that voice.

"Ricky and Neal," Sara breathed.

"The driver has a nasty gash on his face, but his heart rate is good," said Neal, his voice right by the door. "The man next to him is waking up. I think they'll be okay. They were wearing seatbelts."

The door creaked open, revealing a darkening sky. Jaci pressed her fingers to the opening, trying to help widen the gap.

"We weren't going that fast, after all," Ricky said, his tone defensive. He helped Jaci out. "Are you all right?"

"Amanda's unconscious." He had a bright red gash on his forehead. She touched it.

"Yeah, that." He touched her own head. "You have a matching one."

She pressed a palm to her hairline. It came away red. "I hit my face."

Ricky got his arms under Amanda, the orange backpack strapped across his back. He scooted her across the upside down van. "I need some help with Amanda."

"Hold this for me. I'm going to need both hands."

Neal tucked a gun into Jaci's jeans pocket and joined Ricky, wrapping his arms around Amanda's torso.

Jaci touched the cold metal. "A gun?"

"Is everyone all right?" Neal asked as they pulled Amanda out.

"Yeah," Jaci said, waving it aside. "My vision's blurry. Doesn't matter. We've got to run." They weren't out of trouble yet. "How are we going to get away?"

She squinted, trying to find the getaway car that Neal and Ricky must have brought with them.

"On our feet," Ricky said. "Come on, let's cross that highway."

"On our feet?" she echoed. "What happened to your car?"

He pointed to a crumpled black object. "There."

They were almost across the road when they heard, "You! Stop where you are."

"Go, go, go," Neal said, struggling to move quickly under the load he shared with Ricky.

"He's going to radio for back-up," Jaci gasped, her footsteps faltering.

"No, he won't," Ricky said, "because then he'd have to admit that you girls were in Rome. You're a top-secret case."

"But we're not," Neal reminded him. "They come after us, they get the girls."

A gunshot sounded behind them.

"Stop, or I will shoot again," the man shouted, running after them.

"Jaci," Neal shouted. "Shoot his legs."

She grabbed the gun Neal had stuck in her jeans pocket and jerked to a halt.

"I can't!" She held the cold metal in her hands and pictured in her mind the glint of metal in the sunlight, Claber's hand extending.

"Jaci." Neal's voice was urgent, demanding. "Do it now."

"You can't make her do that," Ricky yelled.

"You have to, Jaci!" Neal snapped. "I can't get to you in time."

Jaci turned around. *You have to do this.* Where was he? "I can't even see him," she wailed.

"Just do it," Sara yelled.

She thought she saw a blurry object coming closer. Jaci pointed the gun, closed her eyes and pulled the trigger once. The gun exploded loudly, knocking her backwards.

"He's still coming! Do it again," Neal hollered.

She pulled the trigger two more times.

"He stopped." said Neal.

"Did I kill him?" Jaci shrieked. Her hands trembled as she kept the gun trained on the spot where he had gone down.

"No," Sara said, running back to grab her arm. "And he made it across the street before he collapsed."

Sobs wracked her body, and Jaci clutched the weapon in her hands.

Callie. Callie was shot. Claber shot Callie. She let Sara drag her along, hardly able to breathe.

They stumbled forward for another ten minutes, Ricky and Neal dragging Amanda between them, before they slowed down.

Neal let go of Amanda and bent over, resting his hands on his knees and panting.

"What did I do?" Jaci cried. "I shot a policeman. What if I killed him?" Her head throbbed. She couldn't focus on anything.

"We need to break into a farm house," Neal said. Perspiration dripped from his brow.

"Maybe we can knock and beg for help, or if we have to, just take it, but we need medical supplies. Amanda's hurt. Jaci's cut. And you," he added, touching the bloody gash on Ricky's face.

Ricky jerked his head away. "What if they call a hospital? Or the police?"

"Don't worry about it," Neal retorted, eyes flashing. "We take one thing at a time."

They approached the first farmhouse they saw. It was evening, and so far no one had come after them. The sky had a pasty gray color to it.

Jaci pressed a hand to her throat, her sobs dying down to tiny gasps. It hurt to breathe. She tightened her grip around the barrel in her hands, trying hard to maintain rational thought.

Ricky glanced back at her. "Sara, take the gun from her."

Sara reached over, grasped the gun and pulled it away. She tipped it upside down and shook it, then knelt and buried it in the grass and leaves.

Chapter 34

Jaci stumbled along, allowing Sara to pull her forward. They stopped in front of an old house. Halos ringed the lights around the windows. She stared at them. So ethereal.

"No dog. That's good," said Neal.

"So what's the plan? We just knock on the door and ask to spend the night?"

Sara's voice was in her ear. She tried to pull away, but Sara's hand was tight on her arm.

"No, I think it's better to hide. It looks like it might snow. We need to get in there somehow without being noticed. They won't turn us in if they don't know we're there."

"There might be a cellar. A lot of the old houses in Idaho have one."

Too loud. Jaci whimpered and put her hands over her ears. Or tried to. Her hands didn't move.

"Good thinking."

Jaci felt herself being pulled along again. There was a black hole in front of her, sucking out all the light. Sara guided her toward it. Jaci dug her heels in and fought against Sara's grip.

She panicked, crying out. Two more hands grabbed her forearms and pulled her in. Silky hairs brushed her face, stuck to her mouth and eyes, tried to suffocate her.

Then she was alone. Someone turned on a light. The orb danced around the stifling darkness around her.

"This thing probably hasn't been used in ages."

"Put Amanda down here—careful, Ricky. Okay, good."

"She doesn't like dirt," said Sara.

Someone groaned, low and pitiful. A moan.

"Amanda?"

"Neal? I must have blacked out. What happened?"

"Ricky and I rescued you from the police."

"How?"

"Not that hard. There's two of us. I created a diversion while Neal snuck into the police station."

"And you found out where they'd taken us?"

"Yeah. I walked past a room and overheard them talking about you."

"But then what? What did you do, hitch a ride?"

"We had to steal a car."

"You guys stole a car?"

"Okay, I stole it. Neal came along for the ride. We rammed it into the police van."

"Ricky's a pro."

"I've never rammed a police car before."

Jaci heard their voices as if from far away.

"I think I hurt my arm somewhere."

"Let me see. Well, I'm not a doctor, but I don't think it's broken. I think you sprained it above the elbow."

"What happened to Jaci?" Jaci turned her head at the sound of her name.

"She's not okay, Neal."

Neal scooted closer to her and grabbed her shoulders. "Jaci? Can you hear me?"

Of course she could hear him. There was nothing wrong with her ears. She blinked.

"What happened to her?"

"She shot someone."

"You're all outlaws now. Just like us." Ricky's voice was closer to her now. Strong arms went around her, bringing with them a scent of smoked pine.

"Is she in shock?"

"I think so. She's not shaking, sweating, or feverish, though, so I think she'll be okay."

She closed her eyes. She would be okay? Like they knew anything.

October 19
Little Falls, New York

The antique phone in Canal Side Inn rang at precisely seven in the morning. Carl's arm flopped off the bed, banging the end table before grasping the phone.

"Hello?" He cleared the morning grog from his throat.

"Detective Hamilton, this is Lieutenant Hodges with the Little Falls police department."

Carl sat up. "Did someone call about the girls?"

"Not exactly. But there was an incident in Rome yesterday. The report from the state trooper said a stolen vehicle rammed into a police transport off of highway 81. Interviews with the toll booths reported two teenage boys behind the wheel. One said they looked alike. You had mentioned the girls might be traveling with the missing twins from Johnsburg."

"Ricky and Neal."

"We think so." There was no mistaking the pride in Lieutenant Hodges' voice. "One of the twins was previously arrested in Johnsburg for automobile theft."

Carl was already changing his clothes. "Do you mind getting me the phone number to a local car rental?" He had no idea how far Rome was. But if he left now, he might make it before lunch.

"No problem. Should I call Rome and let them know you're coming?"

Good question. Carl considered it. "No. I'll surprise them."

Rome, New York

Rome was only an hour from Little Falls. An hour gave Carl plenty of time to think. And he had questions.

Rome was right next to the Adirondack Park, and a logical place for the girls to come out. The girls had phoned Mrs. Yadle. The boys had stolen a car and chased down a police car. None of it made sense.

The only conclusion Carl came up with was that the two boys were chasing something. Something the police had.

The girls. It had to be. And why hadn't the police contacted either Little Falls or Idaho Falls?

He parked his rental car at the police department, slipping on his sunglasses. It was a bright, beautiful October day. He opened the glass door and marched to the clerk desk.

"Detective Hamilton." He flashed his badge. "I'm here to investigate yesterday's incident."

The woman looked at him. "One moment, please."

She picked up the interphone. "Sergeant Gates, there's a man here to speak with you. About what happened yesterday."

She looked up. "Take the elevator upstairs. Second room on your left."

"Thank you." Carl glanced around at what appeared to be a quiet, normal police station.

Sergeant Gates, a large man with sandy blond hair and an easy grin, greeted him at the door and invited him in.

Carl sat in the upholstered chair by the desk. "I'm Detective Carl Hamilton. Can you tell me what happened yesterday when that police cruiser was hit?"

"Where did you say you're from, Detective?"

Carl pulled out his badge and handed it to him. "Idaho."

Gates examined it, lifting a brow. "Idaho." He handed it back. "And you've been put on an investigation in New York?"

Carl shook his head. "No. I have other business here. I'm more interested in the perpetrators of the attack."

"Ah." Gates nodded. "Two of our officers were traveling to another facility. Somewhere along Highway 81, a large truck crashed into it from behind, knocking the vehicle from the road. It ended up upside down in a ditch."

Carl scribbled quickly. "Who did the truck belong to?"

"Anthony Stout. He was unaware that the vehicle was missing, as he was in the library studying. We informed him when we called him."

"Do you know who was driving it?"

"We don't know as of yet. The toll booths along the way saw two teenage boys driving a black Toyota Tundra. Perhaps you have some ideas?"

"None that I can say." Carl could tell this man was playing his cards close to his chest, fishing for information. "What about the officers? They didn't see anything?"

A shadow crossed Gates' face. "One was unconscious at the time. The other was shot, apparently while in the attempt of pursuit. He hasn't woken yet."

Carl looked up, a heaviness gripping his chest. "I'm sorry to hear that. The boys were armed, then?"

"He was shot with one of our guns. They took a gun from one unconscious officer and shot the other."

Carl shook his head. Not good. "Has the weapon been found?"

"Not yet. We're searching the surrounding countryside. And as soon as we know who we're looking for, we'll have alerts out."

"Did you check the car for prints?"

Gates checked his watch. "I believe the results should be in within the hour."

That meant, within the hour the New York police would know Ricky Collins had been in that truck. He would be wanted for grand theft auto, destruction of property, obstruction of justice, and assault of an officer. Big charges.

Somehow, Carl knew, he needed to find that boy before the police did. "Do you have a motive, Sergeant? Do you know why the boys would be after the police?"

Gates shrugged. "It must have been some sort of vendetta. We suspect they've been in criminal mischief before."

"Were there any other passengers?"

Gates' eyes shifted to the upper left corner of the room. It was quick and subtle, but Carl saw it.

Whatever he's about to say, it's a lie.

"Just the officers."

Carl leaned back in his chair, staring at his notepad and biting the tip of his pen. He debated calling the man on his lie.

He glanced up. "Did you see the fax yesterday that went out to all police departments in New York and Pennsylvania?"

A slight widening of the eyes. "Fax?"

Carl opened his file and pulled out the confirmation sheet. "Yes. Looks like your department confirmed receipt at 7:02 PM."

"Oh, yes. That fax. I saw it."

Carl leaned forward. "Have you seen those girls, Sergeant?"

"No, Detective. I haven't. But if they show up here, I'll definitely give you a call." Gates stood and came around his desk. "I'm sorry I couldn't be of more help. Was there anything else?"

"Oh, you've been of plenty help." Carl stood as well. "One more thing. Where was the cruiser going?"

"Buffalo," the man said, a little too quickly.

Carl wrote it down. "Thank you. I'll be in touch."

He left his card on the desk and let himself out. The man was lying. Carl had studied his map, and I-81 would never get someone to Buffalo. Gates had tried to pretend he hadn't seen the fax. And he lied about the girls. They had been here.

He stepped out of the elevator and came around to the clerk's desk. "I didn't catch your name. What is it?"

She looked up from her typing. "Betty."

"Did you work yesterday?"

She nodded and went back to her typing.

He placed his badge on the counter. "I'm about to arrest this entire department for deliberate obstruction of justice. I have a few questions, and if you answer them correctly, I might not have to do that. So, if you'll please stop what you're doing and come with me?"

He had her attention now. She stood stiffly and came around the desk.

Carl smiled and slipped his arm around her forearm, guiding her out of the building. He grabbed his badge before they left.

"It's all right. I won't hurt you. I need to know what you saw yesterday."

Chapter 35

Light slipped into the cellar from the crack where the doors met. A rooster crowed outside. Jaci blinked and sat up, wincing. Her head hurt.

Ricky smiled at her. A line of dried, black blood trailed a gash on his forehead. "You look better. How are you?"

She tried to remember why she wouldn't be fine. Where was she? Why was he hurt?

And then the memory came back to her in a flash. The crash, Ricky, the gun— "Oh," she cried. "I shot him." She covered her face with her hands.

His fingers brushed her shoulder. "You saved us. You didn't really hurt him. Do you remember how we got here?"

She pulled her trembling hands away. "Yes. I remember everything." Strange the way she could picture the night before, not as a participant, but as an observer.

Neal crouched near a crack in the cellar door, watching. "The farmer is out there."

"Besides," Amanda added, lifting a shoulder, "even if you killed him, it's not like he'd be the first we've killed."

Jaci focused on her, blinking. "What?"

Neal and Ricky both looked at her.

Amanda waved a hand, looking flustered. "Well—those men after us—the ones in the woods."

"What about them?" Jaci felt like she should know the answer, but all she felt was confusion.

"Amanda." Neal shook his head.

Jaci turned to Ricky. "What happened to those men, Ricky?"

He swallowed, eyes seeking out Neal. "We had to stop them from following us." Neal closed his eyes.

"What did you think, Jaci?" Amanda sounded puzzled. "That the boys left them there to sleep? So they could come after us again?"

Jaci pressed her hands to her head. "You killed them?"

"Only one." Neal's face was rigid, knuckles white where they gripped the cellar door. "The other one we wounded in the leg. He got away. We tried to follow him, but we think he might have had a car."

"That's why you had us moving so quickly."

"Yes." Neal exhaled.

Jaci shook her head, trying to relieve the buzzing in her mind. "You killed him. And everyone's okay with this?"

"Actually, Jaci—" Amanda began. Ricky stopped her with a sharp look.

"They had no choice," said Sara. "They made the right decision. Those men had to die. I hope the other one slowly bled to death in the forest."

Jaci took several deep breaths, trying to keep a grip on reality. Why had everyone known this except her?

Neal turned back to the opening in the doors. "He's getting on his tractor."

There was a roar as the engine turned on. "Okay, tractor's on and he's heading for the fields. Let's go." He pushed the door open and climbed out.

Ricky put a hand under Jaci's elbow, pulling her up slowly. "Are you okay?"

"I'm fine." She yanked away from him.

"Remember, there might be someone in the house still," Amanda warned. "So we're just gonna grab some food and take off."

"Right," Neal said, his hand lingering on Sara's as he helped her out. "And some pain killers."

Jaci rubbed her arms. New jacket, bought yesterday. Only yesterday?

Ricky led them to the house. The front door opened with a creak. They could hear a shower going and a woman's voice singing tunelessly upstairs.

Jaci watched her friends rummage through the cupboards, grabbing bread and cheese and fruit and anything they could carry. They stuffed the orange backpack, and then their pockets. Ricky grabbed a gallon of milk.

Do something. Jaci opened a drawer. "Neosporin. Well, a generic form of it. And pain killers." She held them up.

Neal joined her, sifting through the drawer. "And a credit card." He glanced at her as if for approval.

She didn't care. *Should she?* She turned away. *What did it really matter?*

The shower stopped running.

"Okay, let's move," said Neal.

"Should we leave a note or something?" Sara asked, fingering a notepad.

"No," Jaci said. "But we'll pay them back someday."

Neal gestured. "Time's up. Come on!" They left the farmhouse, struggling under the weight of the stolen goods.

Within ten minutes the milk was gone and most of the food too. Ricky crumpled up the milk jug and tossed it aside.

"We need a plan," said Amanda. "Are we still trying to walk home?"

"I don't want to walk home," Jaci said. "I want someone to give us a ride in a limo, all the way to Idaho."

"What about when we get home?" Sara asked. "Can't the kidnappers just come get us again?"

"Why do they want you so bad, anyway?" asked Ricky. "I would think you girls are proving to be more trouble than it's worth."

"They'll never stop hunting us," Sara said woodenly. "I knew it the moment we escaped."

"It's because we know them," said Amanda, stating it as if it were obvious. "We've seen their house, we've seen their faces. We can identify them."

No mention of the necklace, although Jaci knew she still had it. "It probably doesn't help that you killed one of his men."

"Maybe we need to find The Hand and kill him," Neal said sardonically.

Amanda sighed. "Easier said than done. Looks like he's paid off half the police force."

"Other people are looking for you," Ricky said. "Good people. Get to the FBI. The FBI will move you and give you different names. You'll be safe."

"Never mind," Neal said. "Let's just think on it and head west."

They entered a small wooded ravine an hour before dusk. The temperature began to drop. It would be a cold night. A cutting wind began to whip the tree branches around them, sending a cascade of red and yellow leaves down to the earth.

It sliced through Jaci's jacket. She stretched her fingers, feeling how they tightened in the cold.

Her mind kept flashing back to the moment that man had found her and Sara. She had leapt out at him and hit him. And then what?

Ricky rubbed his hands together. "You know, maybe we should stop and build a fire. That would at least keep us warm."

"Keep moving," Neal responded. "You'll stay warmer."

"Who died and made you dictator?" Ricky grumbled. But he stumbled on after his brother.

Jaci stepped closer to Neal. She wanted to ask him about that day. He had come upon them. He knew what had happened. "Neal?"

He glanced at her, not slowing his pace. "Yeah?"

The words stuck in her throat. "Nothing."

"You okay?"

She nodded. He watched her a moment but said nothing more.

When Neal finally agreed to stop, they were too tired to make a fire. They crawled under several bushes and slept in a heap.

October 20
Rome, New York

"We got the fax from your supervisor last night," FBI agent Kyle Marlogue said. "As soon as it's approved, we'll organize a raid, hopefully for this afternoon."

Carl stood with the phone to his ear, surveying the open suitcase. He had started to put away his toiletries and then stopped, not sure if he was leaving or staying put.

The FBI office in Syracuse accepted Betty's testimony. She had admitted that the three girls had come in. That was all she knew. She'd been quarantined to a safe house until the FBI could get to the bottom of this.

The FBI agent continued. "Seems to me like there's some back dealing going on. I'm not sure if the Rome police department remembers its loyalties."

"Agreed. With Betty's disappearance, we have to act quickly. If they suspect we might know, they'll destroy whatever evidence remains. We have to catch them off guard."

Carl's cell phone lit up on the bed, vibrating on the dark maroon bedspread. "Hold on a second. My boss is calling me." He picked it up. "Detective Hamilton speaking."

"Carl. I've been calling on the hotel phone for twenty minutes. I need you to call me on the landline. Now."

Carl frowned. "I'm on the phone with the FBI."

"Finish up and call me." The chief hung up.

Carl continued his other conversation. "All right, so where are we now?"

"We meet in an hour to discuss today's schedule. The raid will be a priority. I'll call you before noon to give you the details. You can't come along, but as soon as we have the building and officers in custody, you can join us for questioning."

That answered his question. He had to stay in Rome. "Great. I'll wait to hear from you." He called Idaho.

"Carl," the chief said without preamble. "I need you on the next flight home."

"What? I've got a lot going on here. The FBI are going to raid the police department sometime today. I need to be there for that."

"No, you don't. I sent them the file on the entire case, including all the information you sent to me. They don't need you. But I do."

Carl felt a knot form in his stomach. No amount of paperwork or writing could make up for his gut feelings and instincts on this case. This was his case. Now when they were so close to finding the girls, and getting to the bottom of this conspiracy, his boss wanted him to pull out?

"What's going on?"

"Gregorio Rivera disappeared."

Whoa. Completely unexpected. "What do you mean? He was on a business trip."

"Yes, and supposed to come home two days ago. His wife's freaking out. She didn't call until yesterday. His hotel number doesn't work, his work number is disconnected, and his cell phone goes straight to voicemail. She doesn't know what to think."

"I know what to think," he growled. "The scumbag left her. He realized I was on his trail, so he flew the coop."

"Right. So I need you back here now. I'm getting a search warrant for their property and I want you with the team. Find out where he went. Get phone logs. Find out who he's been talking to. I want to know if there's any connection between him and his daughter's disappearance."

As much as he disliked the guy, Carl couldn't imagine that he had paid The Hand to kidnap his daughter. He hadn't known she would be at the mall that night.

This felt like a tangent. While important, it wasn't going to help bring the girls back.

He decided to try one last time. "I can fly out first thing tomorrow. Let me take care of this here."

"Carl, I know you want to be there. But Rivera's gone somewhere, and something tells me it's important to this case. Get yourself back here. Next flight."

Carl had no choice in the matter. He finished packing and zipped up his suitcase. He would call the FBI and tell them to proceed without him.

Chapter 36

The western road looked like it headed into more suburbs, so they turned south, walking parallel to a paved, two-lane road, lined by woods on both sides.

They had no food. The day was long, empty, and cold.

Finally, the sun began to set.

The next day, they turned at Genesee Road and started heading west again. The sunset glowed a brilliant purple and orange.

In the distance they could hear a train on its track. They followed the sound.

There was a small bridge where the track crossed over a shallow ravine lined with gravel and grass. This was where they decided to stop for the night.

An hour later they sat huddled together under the bridge, staring into the flickering fire.

Early the next morning, the loud horn warned them seconds before the train rolled overhead. Dust piled down on top of them. Coughing and sputtering, they rolled out from under the bridge.

Neal started to kick dust onto the charcoal that remained from their fire.

The day remained overcast and cloudy, with a brisk wind blowing from the east. They came to a T in the road and stopped.

Amanda pulled out her compass. "This way's south," she said, pointing.

"Wait." Neal frowned.

"What's the problem?"

Neal didn't answer.

"We can't avoid a town forever."

"I'm not avoiding a town. I'm looking for a grocery store. It's been three days with no food."

"I can steal us food," said Ricky. "We don't have any money. Your credit card has probably been alerted."

Neal reached into his back pocket and pulled out a plastic card. "I took this from the farmhouse."

"Where's a grocery store, then?" said Sara. "We're starving."

"I think we should follow this road north." Neal chewed on his lower lip, waiting for their response.

Ricky disagreed. "We're trying to get to Idaho, not Maine. Let's go south."

Neal shook his head. "Uh-uh. We're going north."

Jaci stepped toward Neal. "Let's go north."

"We better find a grocery store then," Ricky said, shooting his brother a threatening look as they turned right.

Forty minutes later they arrived at Langford's Superette, a small but suitable market.

Neal bought fresh fruits, vegetables, bread, meat, cheese, and ice-cream. He swiped the card at the single register and the teenage boy didn't even look at the name.

They seated themselves on the wooden picnic benches in front of the store to eat. They relaxed, enjoying the autumn sunshine, in no hurry to get going again.

A van pulled up and Jaci watched with mild interest as a large family tumbled out.

"Vacationers." She nodded at the license plate. Montana.

"Hmm." Neal scooped out the last of the ice-cream with a plastic spoon and licked it clean.

"Montana's close to Idaho." Sara stared at the van with a kind of longing expression.

The mother shouted at a teenage girl to get the baby out of the car seat. The girl struggled to do so, then balanced the screaming child on her hip.

For a moment her eyes glanced over them as she approached the entrance of the store, and she slowed ever so slightly. Her eyes never left their faces before she disappeared inside.

They had been noticed. "We should go," Jaci said, standing up.

"I have to use the bathroom," Sara said.

"Me, too." Amanda went with her.

"Bathroom break," Neal said. "Meet back out here in ten minutes."

There was only one bathroom, behind a pair of swinging orange doors. Sara went first, with the rest of them standing in an impatient line.

Jaci glanced around for that family, and noticed the teenage girl still watching them. She began to speak to her mother, who looked over at the girls.

"We need to hurry," she said to Ricky.

"Sara just finished. You're after Amanda."

"That's not what I meant," she said, and jerked her head in the direction of the women. "Look."

"What? There's no one there."

She turned and saw that Ricky was right. "Oh. I guess they left." Their disappearance didn't make her feel any more comfortable.

When Amanda came out, Jaci hurried inside, rushing through the necessities. She washed her hands, anxiety flooding her. She stared at her dirty face, the red-rimmed brown eyes.

Hurry, hurry! We've stayed too long. Gotta get going.

She unlocked the door and ran out, looking around for her friends. Ricky stepped inside and locked the door. Sara and Amanda were examining the chocolate bars, and Neal waited his turn for the bathroom.

Jaci walked outside, just to check. The minivan was still there. She noticed the family at a picnic table, a red cooler open in front of them. She ducked her head, trying to keep a low profile, and started back for the store.

"Wait!"

Don't turn around. Just keep going. She quickened her pace. A hand grabbed her arm and she gasped, whipping her arm away and whirling around.

The teenage girl stood there. She looked about eighteen, tall with long reddish-brown hair and side-swept bangs. "I'm sorry. I didn't mean to frighten you." The girl hesitated, and then she said, "Are you Jacinta?"

Nothing could have shocked her more. "Do I know you?" Jaci searched her face.

"It is you, then," the girl said, her eyes widening. "You've been in the news for weeks—you've been missing since September—"

Jaci gasped, hands flying to her mouth.

The girl turned around, beckoning at the crowded picnic table. "Mom, it's them. It *is* them."

Her mother stood up and came over, an expression of confusion on her face.

The girl turned back to Jaci. "I'm Megan. Are you in danger? Are you being held captive? How can we help?"

Jaci began to cry. They had been found.

Megan's mother stepped forward and hugged Jaci. "It's okay. We'll help you. Let's call the police."

Jaci shook her head, jerking away. "No. No police. You can't. The police work for him. We just escaped from the police."

Sara and Amanda came out. Amanda looked back and forth between Jaci and the woman.

"What is it?" she asked.

"I'm Megan," said the girl. "We want to help."

Amanda gasped and grabbed Megan's outstretched hands, holding them in a trembling grip. "Please help us!"

Megan's mother said, "Megan, get your father. We're leaving for the hotel right now."

Jaci was unable to stop the flood of tears rolling down her cheeks. She looked at Amanda, afraid to hope. "It might not be safe."

"It doesn't matter. We have to take a chance. We need help!"

"It'll be safe," the woman interjected. "We won't hurt you."

"It's not you we're afraid of."

"No one will know you're with us. You can tell us everything. We have a long drive, our hotel's in Ohio. It's about five hours from here."

Sara looked doubtful. "There's no such thing as safe. They probably know we're here."

"You'll be safe," Megan promised. "My dad works for the FBI."

"What is it?" The man joined them.

"It's the missing girls, Dad," Megan said. "The ones from Idaho."

"Um, hello?" said Neal, joining the party.

Jaci turned to him. "We found help. We're going to Ohio."

Twenty minutes later all five of them were smashed into the van, sitting on suitcases and smothered by pillows.

Jaci was squished next to Ricky and Sara, Amanda sat between the door and the cooler, and Neal huddled behind the driver's seat.

Jaci wiped tears on her jacket sleeve. Dust came away with the water, leaving a brown smudge on the navy blue.

Megan's mother settled into a seat in the middle row. "I'm April Reynolds. You can call me April or whatever you want. My husband is Dave. You've met Megan."

Megan nodded from her place in the back row. "Our oldest son Spencer is in the front, then there's Whitney, and the baby, Becca."

Ricky whistled under his breath. "That's a lot of kids."

For a moment Jaci allowed herself to think of her two brothers. Annoying little César and Seth.

"Who are you?" Megan asked Ricky.

"They're my brothers," Sara said.

"Tell us the whole story," said Mrs. Reynolds.

Jaci hesitated. "Did they—has anything been said—there was a fourth girl."

Ricky and Neal looked at her, their surprise evident.

"Yes," Mrs. Reynolds answered. "They found her body several weeks ago."

Jaci sank back on the cooler and nodded, tears springing to her eyes. Callie.

"Everyone is looking for you," said Megan. "Where've you been hiding, the woods?"

"Pretty much," said Amanda. She blinked quickly, her eyes moist.

"What happened, exactly?" Mrs. Reynolds asked again. "The four of you disappeared in September. The security guard on duty at the mall was found unconscious. Judging from where the body was found, the police thought the kidnappers might have taken you to Canada. But there were no leads."

Sara and Amanda both looked at Jaci.

"It was The Hand. We escaped. He's been determined to get us back ever since."

Mrs. Reynolds nodded. "Of course. You're worth something to him now."

"Well, he lives in Canada. A girl helped us get out, and we've been walking since then. We met the boys in New York, and then found out that they are Sara's brothers."

"Why haven't you gone to the police?" asked Megan.

"We did, once," Sara said. "He had someone working in the police department."

Mrs. Reynolds' eyes darted toward her husband, driving the car.

"Ricky and Neal saved us," Sara continued.

"So we're a little afraid now," Jaci put in. "We don't know who we can trust. We can't call home because the phones are tapped.

We think that's how he's tracked us. We can't go to the police. We weren't sure how to contact the FBI."

"You just did," Mrs. Reynolds said. "We are on our way home from a funeral in Ithaca. It's a miracle we stopped where you were. There was an accident on the interstate, so we decided to take back roads."

"We were about to go south and look for a grocery store in that direction," said Neal. "If we had, we would've missed you."

Mrs. Reynolds leaned back. "My husband will contact his supervisor as soon as he can get a secure line. He won't make such a confidential call from his cell phone. But we'll see that you and your families are safe."

Never had Jaci slept on such a nice bed. She knew it was morning, and she knew she should get up, or at least open her eyes, but she just wanted to lay there. She kept her eyes closed, pretending to be asleep. She hoped no one would disturb her and she could prolong the comfort a little longer.

The door that connected the two hotel rooms opened, and Mrs. Reynolds poked her head in. "Girls, time to get up. We're having breakfast brought up."

"Yes!" Whitney said, an enthusiastic six-year-old. "I love room service."

Megan rolled off the bed. "I get the shower first."

"Shower?" Jaci repeated, sitting up.

Amanda lifted the pillow off her face and reached a hand up to touch her dirty, matted hair. "Oh no," she said. "I'm first!"

"Of course," Megan said, tucking her chin against her chest. "That was selfish of me. You can go first."

"There's another one in Mommy's room," Whitney suggested. She rushed to the door. "Mommy, can we use your shower?"

Spencer poked his head in and grinned at them. "Too late. There's already a line."

Amanda ran for the bathroom, grabbing the hotel soaps as she dove in and closed the door behind her. "See ya!"

Jaci ran after her and banged on the door. "Hurry up!"

Amanda called through the door, "Can you get me a razor?"

Jaci fished through the hotel bucket and found one.

Amanda stuck a bare arm out and grabbed it. "Thanks," she crowed.

Jaci pulled a toothbrush from the bucket and smiled. "Running water!"

The bristles felt sharp and harsh against her gums. She wondered how many cavities she had now. She leaned over the sink and spit. Even the air tasted clean and minty. She pulled her hair back and wandered into the other room, where Megan was talking to her mother.

"Any news?" Jaci asked.

Mrs. Reynolds looked at Megan. "Run across the street to Target and buy some shirts, socks, pants. One for each of them. Oh, and get some underclothes too. Just guess at the sizes."

As Megan turned to go, Mrs. Reynolds smiled at Jaci. "After you've all showered and eaten, we'll sit and talk. There's no rush, so try not to worry right now."

When Amanda exited the shower half an hour later and Jaci got a turn, she felt all of her troubles disappear under the hot water. The pressurized liquid washed away the dirt and grime. She wasn't aware how long she was in there, but then Sara was banging on the door, yelling at her to get out. Reluctantly she turned off the water. She stepped out of the shower and wrapped the towel around her, relishing the softness as she pressed it to her face.

"Here," Megan said, greeting her at the door and handing her a t-shirt and a pair of sweat pants. "Put these on. And here's a pair of underwear. And I didn't know if you needed them, but I got a couple of sports bras, just in case."

Jaci put on the clean clothes, shielding herself behind the white towel. "Those dirty clothes are fit to be burned." She pulled the t-shirt on over her head and sighed. "This feels wonderful."

Megan grinned. "Go eat breakfast."

"What about you?"

"I've eaten. I'll stay and give Sara her clothes."

Jaci smiled. "Thanks." She pushed a hand through her wet hair and crossed between rooms.

Neal and Ricky were watching TV at the small round table. Amanda lounged on the bed, eyes glued to the set.

"Where's everyone?" Jaci asked.

"Mr. Reynolds took them to the pool," Mrs. Reynolds said. "Go ahead, eat."

Jaci helped herself to the bowl of fresh fruit in the middle of the table. "Something's different."

She squinted at Neal and Ricky. "I can't smell you guys. Is this what boys are really like?"

"No," Ricky snorted. "This stage doesn't last long."

His eyes lingered on her, and she felt her face grow warm. "Well, I like it."

Mr. Reynolds and the younger children returned from the pool.

"Spencer," he said, tossing his wet towel over a chair, "take your little sister into the other room and find a good movie to watch. Get Pay Per View if you want."

"No problem," Spencer said enthusiastically. "Let's go, Cowgirl."

Megan stayed with her parents. Mr. Reynolds closed the door and pulled a chair over to the bed. He flipped it around backwards and straddled it.

"Okay, gather round. Let's talk." He ran a hand over his grizzled face. "It's been a busy night and morning for me. First, I called my supervisors and told them what you told me. From there, several things happened at once. Last night they went to your homes and found that all the phones were bugged."

Sara had been right. They had probably bugged the phones as soon as they had realized who they'd kidnapped.

"They debugged them and reassured your families that you're okay. The police department in Rome was already under investigation, due to the foresight of an out-of-state detective. The FBI had one witness saying you three had been in the station, but there were no records of any of you ever having been in New York, and several officers were taken into custody for questioning.

"When you came into our care yesterday, the officers in Rome spilled the beans, naming a contact in Sweden, Pennsylvania. The FBI arrived at the Sweden police department about twenty minutes ago. The guy knew his cover was blown, and he took out two police officers before shooting himself. I was notified five minutes ago."

Mr. Reynolds paused a moment to give that a chance to sink in. "Everything this officer had has been quarantined. His phones are being monitored and his house is being searched as we speak. Given what you've told us, they are looking for anything to link him to The Hand. We should know what they find in the next two hours. We believe the officers in Rome were acting under the direction of their superior in Sweden, not knowing he worked for The Hand. But we haven't ruled them out.

"What it boils down to is that you can't go home yet. The danger isn't over until we have The Hand. And we may need you to help us find him. So tomorrow evening, a helicopter from the FBI is flying to the hotel and you will be put into FBI custody."

"We can't see our families?" Sara asked, her voice tight.

"Not yet. First, you'll see doctors at the FBI safe house. Then we'll make arrangements to get you in touch with your families."

The nightmare wasn't over yet. They wouldn't be going home any time soon.

Jaci wondered if she should mention that The Hand had known her father. That he was the Carcinero. She wondered if that name would mean anything to Mr. Reynolds.

There was just so much she didn't understand. She didn't want to let something slip and put her family in danger.

"Will we be safe?" Sara reached over to clasp Neal's hand.

Mr. Reynolds nodded. "I personally guarantee it. I'll be overseeing your custody arrangements."

"What about what we did in New York?" Ricky asked, an edge of nervousness creeping into his tone. "I mean, we broke the law. I stole a car, and then—we shot a policeman."

Jaci flinched.

"Those crimes have been absolved. In fact, they are being removed from police record. Only the FBI will have them now. We're still trying to ascertain if you boys are in enough danger to place into custody. Our other choice is to turn you back over to the state of New York."

"No!" Sara cried. "They're my brothers. You can't take them away from me. They have to come with us. I need them."

"Yeah," Ricky said. "We want to be with the girls. With our sister."

"I can't promise that. For now you're together. We'll see about later."

"What happens next?" Amanda asked.

"Today you stay here with us. Stay inside, out of sight, and just relax. Tomorrow, you go into hiding. Any other questions?"

When no one said anything, Mr. Reynolds patted his wife's knee and stood up. "Well, that's that." He smiled at them and went into the other room.

"Well," Mrs. Reynolds said, handing the baby to Megan. "I guess there's not much else to do now. Does anyone want anything? A book, a drink, a movie?"

Jaci shook her head. "I'm good for now, thanks. Thank you for everything your family has done for us."

Neal pulled his chair over to the bed and leaned toward the three girls. "Hang in there. You're through the worst of it."

Jaci gave him a grateful smile. Such a protector. Neal was their guardian.

"We're safe now," Ricky grinned, still sitting at the table. "Good job, everybody."

"Tomorrow we start a new adventure," said Jaci, a flicker of optimism growing inside her.

"Jaci, every day you spend with me will be an adventure," Ricky said, giving her a teasing grin. He grabbed the remote control. "But today, we enjoy indoor plumbing and cable television."

She laughed and hit him with a throw pillow.

October 23
Idaho Falls, Idaho

Carl reclined in the above-ground hot-tub at his and Kristin's one-story house. The jar of pickled watermelon rinds that Kristin had surprised him with sat on the plastic table next to the pool. An orange and purple sunset lit up the darkening sky.

Kristin rested drowsily against his shoulder, and he closed his eyes. He forced himself to relax. This was his first day off in weeks. It felt undeserved and wasteful.

Kristin glanced over at him. "What's wrong?"

"Hm? Oh, nothing." He smoothed back her almond-colored hair. "I should've called the FBI. Day off or no, when they didn't get back to me, I should've called them."

"Sweetheart." She pulled away and gave him a small smile. "You've put your heart and soul into this case. You need a break. It's not like the case is resting. Everyone's looking, listening, watching. There's nothing you can do right now. The girls will be found."

He stared out across the manicured yard. The mosquitoes were gone, a chilly wind whipping through the air. "I suppose you're right."

His phone on the patio table buzzed. Carl got out of the tub, wrapping a towel around his waist. He caught the phone right before it buzzed off the table. Office.

Normally, he hated seeing that word on his day off. Today, he felt a stirring of excitement. "Detective Hamilton speaking."

"Carl." It was Chief Miller. Carl glanced at the clock on the wall. Just after seven at night. This was important, or the chief wouldn't be at the station.

"Yes?"

"I need you here now."

"What is it? Is it the girls?"

"Bring yours and Kristin's phones."

Odd request. Carl noted how he didn't answer the question. "Be right there."

He hung up, jittery. "Kristin, something's happened. I have to get to the station. And I have to bring our phones in."

She pulled herself from the pool, shivering, and slipped into a robe. "I'll make us some hot chocolate. It'll be ready when you get back."

Not a word of complaint. Carl felt a surge of appreciation for this woman who supported his mood swings and ambitions. He gathered her into his arms and buried his face in her damp hair.

"I love you."

She giggled and snuggled into his embrace. "I thought you had to go?"

"I do." He stepped back and hurried across the patio. "But I'll be back."

An officer took their phones as soon as he got to the station. Somewhat puzzled, Carl followed the chief into his office.

"Now, just to clarify, I'm not in trouble, am I?" He felt a bit nervous.

"No. We don't think you're phones have been tapped, but we're switching out the ID chip just in case."

"Tapped?"

"Yes. The FBI called about half an hour ago."

Carl leaned forward, gripping the desk. "I almost called them. How did the raid go? What did they find?"

"The raid went as planned. They took the entire station into custody, but only two of the officers appeared to be hiding anything. They still have them in custody."

Carl released a breath. "I guess they don't have any proof, other than Betty's testimony and my suspicions."

"Didn't." The chief gave a tight smile. "They do now."

Carl studied the gray-haired man in front of him. "They found them." That had to be it. Only finding the girls would prove that the police were lying.

Miller's smile widened. "An FBI agent came across them at a grocery store in New York yesterday afternoon. He has them in a hotel with his family. The FBI is arranging an escort."

Carl jumped to his feet. "I'll fly out right away. They're going to need security to get them back here."

"Carl." The chief's voice had a note of warning in it, and he lifted a hand.

"What is it?"

"Based on what the girls have told the FBI, he believes they're not out of danger yet. They're not coming home. In fact, what I've just told you is top secret. Only you and their parents know they've been found. I just thought you ought to know—before I took you off the case."

The words hit Carl like a fist to his head. "What? You're taking me off?"

"Your job is done. They've been found. The FBI can handle it from here. Besides, I've got two new cases for you."

The chief dropped two file folders on the desk. "First: The Hand. Based on the girls' suggestion, their families' landlines and cell phones were checked for bugs. Somehow, The Hand managed to bug every one of the landlines. Which means The Hand has a hornet's nest of associates. I want you to find this man and destroy his hive."

"Ah." Carl nodded and pulled the file on top toward him. "That's why you took my phone."

"Yes. We keep a constant sweep of the landlines in the station but not our cell phones. So far, we've seen no indication that The Hand knew you were on the case. All he has to do is know your cell phone number to tap it. If he finds out you're on his tail, he'll get your number. So keep yourself a secret.

"Second: Mr. Rivera. Find out where that man went. You've got all the search warrants you need to tear this so-called business apart. I want to know what he's doing. Is it drugs? Weapons? Politics?"

Carl took the second folder. "You got it. So the police in Rome. What there?"

Miller waved a hand. "You know how the FBI is. They don't tell if they don't have to. But it appears we had a bad egg in Pennsylvania sending out orders to the Rome department. The FBI found a fax in the trash that had been sent on the heels of our own, instructing the police to bring the girls to Pennsylvania if found."

Carl stood up, the two folders under his arm. "Well. I'm very happy they're safe. Can I tell Kristin?"

"If you're sure she won't tell anyone. We expect The Hand to show himself a little more as he tries to find them."

"Right." Carl patted his assignments. "I'll be here in the morning to start these cases. Now, I'm going home to enjoy the rest of my day off."

***

Acknowledgements

Since this book has been more than...well, a decade in the making, my list of people to thank goes on quite a ways.

But to keep it simple, I would like to thank:

Julie Frauenthal, for asking for each new chapter as soon as I'd gotten it typed up in the 8th grade.

Ada Wax, my junior high English teacher who had more faith in me than I could have paid her to have.

The Fayetteville and Springdale police departments, especially William Turnbow, Paul Shepard, and Jamie Fields, for all the questions they put up with.

Mary Gray and David West, my partners in crime, for pumping me up and giving me fantastic ideas.

My family, but especially my husband and children, for putting up with a mentally absent mom and being excited about her hobby called writing.

CPSIA information can be obtained
at www.ICGtesting.com
Printed in the USA
LVOW03s1426271117
557734LV00001B/41/P